Young Victorian Ladies

Three spirited sisters, all highly individual, find the men who are just right for them

Hazel, Iris and Daisy, the spirited Springfeld sisters, are expected to marry well. But they have other ideas. Hazel, the clever one, wants someone to appreciate her for her intelligence. Iris wants to be loved for something other than her good looks, and sporty Daisy is too busy having fun to think about things as boring as marriage. But each in turn will find the right man to match their highly individual personalities.

Read Hazel's story in
Wagering on the Wallflower

Read Iris's story in
Stranded with the Reclusive Earl

And read Daisy's story in
The Duke's Rebellious Lady

Author Note

The Duke's Rebellious Lady is the third book in the Young Victorian Ladies series and features Daisy, the third of the feisty Springfeld sisters. Daisy is a modern Victorian woman, a member of the Rational Dress Society and a keen cyclist, and writing her story was a joy.

The Rational Dress Society was a radical group who advocated that women cast off their corsets and voluminous dresses and wear more rational clothing, which would provide them with greater freedom and independence. They also advocated equality with men and what was considered a radical concept at the time—votes for women.

Cycling was another way in which women could find freedom in late Victorian England, but obviously bicycles were not designed to be ridden in long skirts. While some women wore divided skirts, Daisy chooses to wear cycling bloomers, knee-length trousers that caused a scandal at the time. But Daisy enjoys shocking people, particularly Guy Parnell, the Duke of Mandivale, her older brother's best friend.

Daisy had a childhood crush on her brother's handsome friend, a crush she is convinced she has grown out of, but a cycling accident and a period of convalescence at Guy's estate put her determination to not fall back under Guy's spell to the test.

EVA SHEPHERD

The Duke's Rebellious Lady

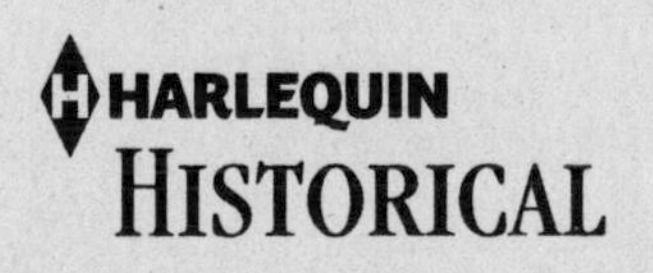

HARLEQUIN®
HISTORICAL™

Recycling programs for this product may not exist in your area.

ISBN-13: 978-1-335-40763-4

The Duke's Rebellious Lady

This edition published by arrangement with Harlequin Books S.A.

For questions and comments about the quality of this book, please contact us at CustomerService@Harlequin.com.

Harlequin Enterprises ULC
22 Adelaide St. West, 41st Floor
Toronto, Ontario M5H 4E3, Canada
www.Harlequin.com

Printed in U.S.A.

After graduating with degrees in history and political science, **Eva Shepherd** worked in journalism and as an advertising copywriter. She began writing historical romances because it combined her love of a happy ending with her passion for history. She lives in Christchurch, New Zealand, but spends her days immersed in the world of late Victorian England. Eva loves hearing from readers and can be reached via her website, evashepherd.com, and her Facebook page, Facebook.com/evashepherdromancewriter.

Books by Eva Shepherd

Harlequin Historical

Young Victorian Ladies

Wagering on the Wallflower
Stranded with the Reclusive Earl
The Duke's Rebellious Lady

Breaking the Marriage Rules

Beguiling the Duke
Awakening the Duchess
Aspirations of a Lady's Maid
How to Avoid the Marriage Mart

Visit the Author Profile page
at Harlequin.com.

To the Canterbury Chapter of the
Romance Writers of New Zealand.
A talented group of writers who have
provided enormous support and invaluable
advice throughout my writing journey.

Chapter One

Kent, England, 1893

Lady Daisy Springfeld knew exactly what love felt like. It was exhilarating, exciting, intoxicating and a little bit scary, but in a nice way. Her sisters Hazel and Iris had described it in such a manner. It was how they had known they were in love with the men they'd married.

Yes, Daisy knew exactly how it felt. Freewheeling on her bicycle down a steep hill in the middle of the Kent countryside, the world flying past her, the wind blowing through her hair—that was exhilarating, exciting, intoxicating and a little bit scary, but in a nice way. And Daisy did not need a man to make her feel like that.

Unfortunately, Daisy Springfeld also knew what heartache felt like. Iris and Hazel had told her about that as well. It was as if your world had turned on its head, as if you no longer knew what was up or down. All you knew was you were consumed with a deep sense of loss.

And, again, it wasn't a man responsible for making Daisy feel that way. A brick left in the middle of the road had caused that unfortunate state. When Daisy's front tyre had hit that obstacle, which had presumably fallen off the back of a cart, she had flown over the handle bars, rolled across the road and landed upside down in a ditch, her abandoned bicycle laying where it fell, its front wheel still spinning.

Thank goodness she was wearing her knee-length riding bloomers. That was the first thought that entered her head when she landed, face down, her legs inelegantly sticking up in the air. If she had been wearing a skirt and had exposed her petticoats and drawers to the world, her humiliation would have been complete.

But fortunately there was no one around to see her fall from grace, or rather her fall from her so-called safety bicycle. All she had to do now was crawl out of this ditch, dust herself down, retrieve her bicycle and no one would be any of the wiser.

Thank goodness for that as well, was her next thought. Ladies who cycled came in for enough criticism. She did not need anyone writing a disapproving letter to the newspapers, reporting her mishap and using it as yet another example of why women should never be allowed anywhere near such devices.

But first, she had to right herself from her inverted position and get out of this ditch. She reached back, grabbed some clumps of grass and attempted to drag herself out backwards. That didn't work. She tried to hoist herself onto her knees and crawl upwards. That didn't work either. Shuffling? No. Instead of freeing her, that manoeuvre caused her to slide further down the side of the ditch.

Daisy looked down at the dank water at the bottom and grimaced. There was nothing for it. The easiest way, perhaps the only way, to extricate herself from this predicament would be to fall fully into the ditch. Then she could swivel round, climb out and be back on the road in no time at all. It wasn't going to be pleasant, but there was nothing for it, and, after all, members of the High-Wheeling Ladies' Cycling Association were made of sterner stuff than most and would not be put off by a little bit of water, no matter how smelly it was, or greenish or stagnant it appeared.

Taking hold of the same clumps of grass that had failed her before, and doing a combination shuffle and crawl, she collapsed in a pile at the bottom and fought to follow her command and ignore the somewhat offensive musty smell of water which was now seeping through her riding bloomers.

Right. Now to climb out, get back on her bicycle and pretend none of this had happened. Bracing herself on the side of the ditch, she hauled herself upright. Pain ripped through her the like of which she had never experienced before, causing her to scream out in agony in a most un-ladylike manner.

Her heart racing, sweat coating her brow, she dropped back down into the rank water and slowly drew in several deep, steadying breaths. The pain had taken her by surprise, that was all. It wasn't that bad, and she wasn't about to be defeated by a little bit of discomfort. Taking a few more steadying breaths, she gripped the sides of the ditch and lifted herself up, this time more slowly. The result was the same. The pain was no less intense.

With a stifled scream, she collapsed back down. Something was definitely wrong with her left foot. It would not take her weight. She looked up at the top of the ditch. It was only just above her head height, yet the sides now seemed like the walls of an impenetrable fortress. Drat it all, she was going to need help. She would be stuck in this embarrassing predicament until the other members of the cycling association caught up with her.

Daisy slumped further, then scowled and hoisted herself out of the smelly water, taking care to protect her left foot. Oh, how the other ladies were going to enjoy her downfall, both literal and figurative. Hadn't she been warned not to rush off ahead, that for safety's sake they should all stay together? But when had Daisy ever listened to a warning?

After what seemed like an interminable amount of time, the chattering lady cyclists rounded the corner and descended the hill at a much more sedate pace than that at which Daisy had chosen to ride. Unlike her, many of these ladies were dressed in the less practical but more feminine divided skirts, in an array of colours. Some had even insisted on wearing fashionably large hats bedecked with ribbons, artificial flowers and feathers, claiming they would feel naked without something substantial on their head. Daisy, on the other hand, preferred a sensible straw boater and secretly scorned the other ladies' fripperies.

'Watch out for the brick in the middle of the road,'

Daisy called out from her ditch, although the warning was unnecessary, as they were all coming to a halt, having spied Daisy's abandoned bicycle.

'Oh, Daisy, what are you doing down there? Are you all right?' asked Lady Prudence Hamilton, gazing down the side of the ditch.

Daisy was tempted to say something sarcastic, such as, *Oh, yes, I'm perfectly fine. I just thought it would be nice to throw myself off my bicycle, plummet into a ditch and wallow around in some filthy water. I find one gets such an interesting view of the countryside from places such as this!*

'I'm afraid I hit that brick,' she said instead, pointing to the offending article. 'And came off my bicycle.'

Lady Prudence picked up the brick and threw it as hard as she could into the nearby hedge, as if in punishment. The other ladies had now dismounted and gathered round, staring down at Daisy, some with smug expressions—as if to say, *this is what happens when you try to go off on your own without the support of your sister cyclists*—others with genuine looks of concern.

Lady Prudence reached out her hand.

Daisy sent her a slightly embarrassed smile. 'I'm afraid I can't stand on my foot. I'm going to need a bit more help to get out of here.'

Lady Clementine Featherstone, the association's matriarch, broke through the colourful ranks of ladies clustered round the top of the ditch, jumped down, put her hands under Daisy's arm pits and hoisted her to her feet. Her matter-of-fact manner suggested that hauling young ladies out of ditches was something she did every day.

But the depth of the ditch and Daisy's inability to take weight on her foot thwarted even Lady Featherstone.

'You two,' she commanded, pointing up at two of the youngest and fittest members of the group, 'get down here and give me a hand. We're going to have to manhandle her up to the road.' Lady Featherstone's husband was a major general in the army, and at times his wife seemed to think that she too was a commanding officer. As much as that usually annoyed Daisy, on this particular occasion it was a rather handy quality.

The two young ladies scowled down at the pungent water at the bottom of the ditch but took no further action.

'Come along!' Lady Featherstone barked out. 'Stop dilly-dallying. Lady Daisy needs our help, and we always help our sister cyclists when they are in need, don't we?

Still frowning, the young ladies carefully descended, trying to keep the mud off the bottom of their divided skirts. Between the three of them they lifted Daisy out, while another cyclist picked up her discarded bicycle.

With her arm around Lady Featherstone, Daisy tried to hobble along, but with each step pain ripped up her leg, making her wince. With determination she did not know she possessed, she suppressed any cries of pain. She would not give further ammunition to the more disapproving members of the group.

'You can't walk, can you?' Lady Featherstone asked, seeing straight through Daisy's subterfuge. 'And you certainly can't ride. We're going to have to find somewhere for you to rest. You're also going to need a doctor to examine that foot.'

As one, the ladies looked up and down the road, as if hoping for a welcoming inn and a man dressed in black carrying a doctor's case to appear magically on the deserted road.

'You, girl.' Lady Featherstone pointed to one of the young ladies who had climbed into the ditch and who was now wiping her leather ankle boots along the grass, attempting to remove the mud and slime. 'You can cycle ahead to find the nearest place where Lady Daisy can stay while she heals. Once you've found somewhere, let the owners know so they can come and pick her up.'

The young woman pointed to herself, as if asking, *Me? Really? Haven't I already done enough?*

'Yes, you, girl. Now, get going.'

'If I may make a suggestion before you go,' Daisy said as the pouting young lady mounted her bicycle. 'The Duke of Mandivale lives near here. He's a friend of the family and I'm sure he'll have no objection to providing me with a place to recover.'

'Capital,' Lady Featherstone barked. 'Off you go, then,' she said to the young lady. 'Find this Mandivale chappie and make him come here and rescue Lady Daisy.'

'I believe the turnoff for Mandivale estate is about a mile past the next village,' Daisy said, pointing her in the right direction. 'I'm sure someone in the village will be able to give you more precise directions.'

Before the young lady had travelled mere yards down the road, a carriage turned the corner. 'Never mind,' Lady Featherstone called out. 'Come back, girl. This carriage can take Lady Daisy to the duke's home.'

The cyclist immediately turned round. After all, it was always expected among the lady cyclists that everyone would fall in with Lady Featherstone's plans. And it seemed she also had the same power over carriage drivers. Obeying Lady Featherstone's hand held up in a stop signal, he immediately slowed down and the carriage came to a stop beside the assembled group.

The door opened and Guy Parnell, the Duke of Mandivale himself, jumped out and smiled at the assembled cyclists. Even though Daisy had seen him many a time since he had grown from a boy to a man, every time she saw him anew it struck her just how manly he had actually become.

Tall, slightly over six feet, broad of shoulder, long of leg and with an upright posture, he would have given the appearance of a soldier if it wasn't for his relaxed manner. The only physical attributes that hadn't changed were his tousled blond hair, his brown eyes and that smile. When he'd been a boy, her mother used to say that Guy's smile could cause the birds to swoon and fall out of the trees—a comment which had always caused her father to look at his daughters, concern etched on his face, and say, 'That one is going to be dangerous when he grows up.'

At the time Daisy had assumed her father was worried about the fate of those poor, tumbling birds. Now she knew different. And the way the ladies were all primping and preening proved her father right. But his good looks had no effect on Daisy. She knew far too much about the sort of man Guy Parnell had become to be so foolish as to fall under his spell.

'What have we got here?' he asked in the easy manner that had been such an endearing part of his character when he'd been a boy. 'Why, Daisy Chain, I didn't recognise you.' His smile grew larger, causing the ladies' preening to intensify, and reluctantly drawing Daisy's eyes to those sparkling brown eyes which were now crinkling at the corners and giving him an annoyingly devil-may-care appearance.

Daisy suppressed a groan. She was familiar with the effect that Guy Parnell had on females. He had once had that effect on her, but she wasn't a child any more, victim of a foolish girlhood obsession. She was a grown woman and could see straight through his seductive charm.

'You've changed your style of dressing,' he said as his gaze slowly raked her up and down, causing the young women in the more conventional divided skirts to titter.

Daisy lifted up her chin. She'd had to endure enough teasing from her brother Nathaniel and other young men about her riding bloomers. It was something she would not stand for from anyone, and particularly not from Guy Parnell.

'My bloomers are designed specifically for cycling and are eminently practical,' Daisy stated.

'Very attractive indeed,' he said, still slowly scanning her appearance.

Daisy fought not to react to his teasing words, to the deep voice that caused a shiver to run up her spine, or the way he was looking at her. It *almost* appeared to be an appreciative gaze, but she was either mistaken—after all, he had never seen her in *that* way—or looking at women in such a manner was second nature to Guy and he couldn't help himself, even with her.

'So, you seem to have been in the wars and need some assistance,' he observed, his gaze moving to the abandoned bicycle.

'Indeed she does,' Lady Featherstone said. 'Lady Daisy has injured her left foot. I've been informed you are a friend of the Springfeld family. So, if you'll be so kind, you can take her to your home and send for a doctor.'

Without answering, Guy strode over to Daisy, lent down and swept her up into his arms, to the accompaniment of a chorus of soft sighs from the ladies.

'Of course I will,' he said to Lady Featherstone. 'It wouldn't be the first time I've rescued Daisy Chain from a scrape.' The laughter in his voice was such a familiar sound. His happy disposition had always impressed her when she'd been a child, and it had never ceased to amaze her how apparently carefree he could be, despite his family life.

'You'll also need to take her bicycle. We can hardly leave it lying here in the middle of the road,' Lady Featherstone commanded as Guy gently lifted Daisy up the carriage steps.

When they were in the carriage, Daisy discovered he was not travelling alone. Why didn't that surprise her?

'There we are,' he said as he lowered her onto the seat and gently lifted her foot to place it up on the bench. 'And may I introduce you to my friend, Miss Ruby Lovelace. Ruby, say hello to Lady Daisy Springfeld.'

'Honoured, I'm sure,' the young lady said.

'How do you do?' Daisy replied, trying her hardest not to be judgemental. The heavy make-up on the woman's face and her overly ornate clothing clearly marked out what sort of woman was his *friend*.

'Well, you two get acquainted while I see to the bicycle.' He sent Ruby a quick wink. 'I'm sure you'll have a lot in common.'

Ruby looked Daisy up and down, taking in her riding clothes, and frowned slightly, either at her attire or the unfortunate odour of stagnant water she'd brought with her into the carriage.

'A lady in trousers...blimmin' heck. That's a right unusual outfit you've got on there, Lady Daisy,' Ruby said, her voice holding a hint of disapproval. It seemed Daisy wasn't the only one being judgemental.

'It's my riding costume. I'm a member of the Rational Dress Society. We aim to reform the way women dress so we're not encumbered by the weight of so many layers and the restriction of corsets and petticoats. If women dressed in a more rational manner, they would be so much freer and could achieve so much more.'

Daisy heard the pride in her voice as she gave the now familiar lecture, and she *was* proud to be a member of such a progressive organisation. She just wished the rest of the world wasn't so disapproving.

Ruby nodded slowly. 'Seems right sensible to me. I sometimes don men's clobber when I'm on the stage and it does make you feel different—stronger somehow and, like you say, freer—but I don't think my public would like it if I wore trousers when I wasn't on stage. But good on you, I say.'

'Oh, you're an actress,' Daisy said, smiling in relief.

Ruby tilted her head and raised her eyebrows, causing Daisy to stop smiling. The unspoken question hung in the air: *so what did you think I was?*

The carriage shook slightly, providing a much-needed distraction from Daisy's embarrassment. She twisted on the bench and poked her head out of the window to see what was going on. Under constant instructions from Lady Featherstone, Guy and his driver were attaching her bicycle to the back of the carriage.

'Right, well done,' Lady Featherstone said once they had finished, dusting her hands together as if she had done all the hard work and not merely given commands. 'Now, you'll need to put my bicycle on the back as well so I can accompany Lady Daisy as her chaperon.'

'I'm afraid there's no room, my lady,' the driver said.

Lady Featherstone humphed her disagreement and examined the back of the carriage, shaking the attached bicycle and luggage, then scowling in disapproval.

'Lady Daisy will be quite safe,' Guy said when Lady Featherstone finally conceded that the driver was correct. 'I have a female companion with me who I'm taking to the railway station. Once we get to town, I can fetch my female cousin to come back with us. While I'm at the station I can also send a telegram to her family so they can send their own chaperon while Lady Daisy recovers.'

Ruby laughed lightly. 'I ain't never been a chaperon before.' She patted Daisy on the arm, as if they were both in on the joke. 'But your virtue should be safe. Believe me, I did my best to exhaust the duke this weekend. Hopefully, he won't need no other ladies for a while.'

Daisy sat back on the bench, her back rigid, her lips clamped tightly together. She tried to block out that comment, and all it implied, but it was impossible when the thought of how Ruby had tried to exhaust Guy was causing even greater discomfort than her throbbing foot.

A wistful expression overtook Ruby's made-up face. 'Although, I hope he recovers quickly and invites me back soon. I've had ever so much fun this weekend. Knows how to treat a lady, that one.'

She leaned forward, as if to confide in Daisy. Daisy held her breath, sure that this was a confidence she would rather Ruby kept to herself.

'In the theatre, all us performers are always vying to be top of the bill. Well, that one's performance—' she pointed her thumb towards the back of the carriage '—is most definitely top of the bill, if you get my meaning.'

Unfortunately, Daisy did get her meaning, but she made no comment, merely swallowed down the lump in her throat, stared straight ahead and hoped Ruby would change the subject.

Lady Featherstone stuck her head into the carriage. She gave Ruby a dubious look then turned to Daisy, her eyebrows raised in question.

'I'll be perfectly all right,' Daisy reassured her. 'It's only a short ride to the station and I wouldn't want to interrupt your cycling tour any more than I already have.'

Despite the presence of Ruby, despite her somewhat inappropriate comments, and despite Daisy's disapproval of the way Guy lived his life, she did trust him implicitly. He might be a notorious womaniser, but he was almost part of the family and had always treated her like his little sister, even if at times she wished he wouldn't.

With one more concerned look at Ruby, Lady Featherstone's head withdrew, and Daisy heard her saying a few quiet yet terse words to Guy before a loud chorus of goodbyes rang out from the assembled ladies.

Daisy leant out and waved to the departing cyclists. With much ringing of bells and backward waves, the colourful band rode off down the road, their feathered hats fluttering in the light breeze.

Guy climbed into the carriage and sat next to Ruby, who placed her hand proprietarily on his knee and her head on his shoulder and smiled contentedly. He tapped his hand on the roof of the carriage. The horses gave a whinny and the carriage moved off slowly down the country road, the sedate pace presumably intended to make the journey as comfortable as possible for Daisy.

But she wasn't comfortable. How could she be, when she was sitting so close to Guy and his latest lover? She turned and watched the passing countryside, fighting to stop her disapproval from showing on her face, and fighting even harder not to think of anything Ruby had said. She neither wanted nor needed to speculate about what Ruby had done to try and exhaust Guy Parnell, or what he had done to her to warrant being rated top of the bill but, damn it all, that was the only thing she *could* think about.

Chapter Two

'So, you've now become a lady cyclist, have you, Daisy?' Guy said, causing her to turn back to the enamoured couple.

'Obviously,' she replied, and braced herself for the inevitable teasing about her clothes, her bicycle, her unfortunate smell or her accident. Teasing was what she had come to expect from him, ever since they'd been children. Guy had been a school friend of her brother Nathaniel and had spent most school holidays with the Springfeld family. The two boys had always made fun of the little sister who wouldn't leave them alone. Although what he had said to Lady Featherstone was right—he had rescued her from more scrapes and accidents than she cared to remember.

In fact, all her memories of her childhood summers seemed to contain Guy Parnell. At the time she had never questioned why he spent so much time at both their London home and their Dorset estate—had just accepted Guy as part of the boisterous gang of Springfeld children. It wasn't until she'd got older that she realised her parents had extended the invitation to him each holiday because they'd known of Guy's family situation and wanted to provide him with the family life he hadn't had at his own home.

'I might have known you'd be riding one of those contraptions. You always were an adventurous child, weren't you, Daisy Chain? Or should I call you Lady Daisy now that you're all grown up?'

'Yes, I ride one of *those* contraptions,' Daisy said, hoping that would be the extent of his teasing. 'And Daisy will be fine, but I suppose I should call you Your Grace?'

He made a mock frown. 'I'd be offended if you did. I don't think I'll ever get used to being the Duke of Mandivale, and whenever anyone calls me Your Grace, or uses my title, I still keep thinking they're talking about my father.'

He was joking, but the joke seemed forced, as if hiding a wealth of pain. That was to be expected. After all, who would not feel pain with a father like the late Duke of Mandivale?

'And I do find your outfit very…interesting,' he said, his gaze flicking to her bloomers and exposed calves encased in blue- and red-striped stockings.

Daisy fought not to squirm as he scrutinised her clothing again.

'And rather flattering,' he added. Daisy wasn't sure if he was jesting or serious. Few people outside the Rational Dress Society approved of a woman wearing trousers, and most men either mocked them or became irrationally angry, as if a lady in trousers was against the rules of nature. But had she heard a note of approval in Guy's voice, even appreciation? She dismissed the possibility. Guy Parnell had always seen her as Nathaniel's young sister, and he was unlikely to change now. And, despite her unsettling reaction to his gaze, or maybe because of it, she most certainly would not want him to see her in any other way.

The country road turned into a village street and they soon arrived outside the railway station.

'Goodbye, then,' Ruby said to Daisy as Guy opened the carriage door and lowered the steps. 'Nice to meet you, I'm sure, and I hope you get better quickly and are back on your bicycle in no time.'

'Thank you,' Daisy replied. 'It was nice to meet you as well, and have a safe journey.' In that, she was being honest. Ruby did seem like rather a pleasant young woman and, as she'd already thought, it wasn't Daisy's place to judge her.

Ruby took Guy's hand and she descended the carriage steps, her head held high, and Daisy had to admire her nonchalant dignity.

'I'll just be a moment,' Guy said, poking his head back into the carriage. 'Once I've seen Ruby safely on the train, I'll send that telegram to your family assuring them you're all right.'

Daisy nodded her agreement and his head withdrew. She peeked out the edge of the window and watched them walking down the platform holding hands, followed by the driver carrying Ruby's luggage. Daisy shouldn't really be looking—after all, none of this was her business—but she couldn't help herself. They moved further along the platform, so she angled herself on the carriage bench, the better to watch them laughing and talking together.

The train pulled into the station and they momentarily disappeared behind a cloud of hissing white steam. The steam cleared and they were revealed, their arms around each other in a none-too-subtle embrace. Once again, Daisy tried not to judge, reminding herself yet again that it had nothing to do with her. But when Ruby took hold of Guy's buttocks and gave them a squeeze, a gasp escaped her lips at such scandalous behaviour in a public place.

She lowered her hands from her mouth and reminded herself that she was a modern woman. Didn't her clothing prove that? She must not be shocked by such displays of...of what? It was too brazen to be called a display of affection. Maybe playfulness. But, whatever it was, Ruby's behaviour made it clear to anyone who was watching that she and Guy were on intimate terms with each other, very intimate terms, and that they didn't care who knew.

She turned back and watched Ruby enter a first-class compartment presumably paid for by Guy, pull down the window, lean out and blow many extravagant kisses in his direction. The train departed and, still smiling to himself, Guy walked back along the platform then went into the station office.

It's none of your business, Daisy repeated to herself, sitting up straight and pretending she had witnessed nothing.

'Right, we'll pick up my cousin on the way home and

I'll notify the doctor,' he said as he climbed back into the carriage. 'Are you all right, Daisy?' he added as he sat down on the opposite bench. 'Your face is pinched. Are you in pain?'

'I'm perfectly all right,' Daisy said, embarrassed that her expression had nothing to do with her foot and everything to do with what she had just seen. Although it should be nothing less than what she'd expect from Guy Parnell. She knew all about his reputation, and if half the rumours she had heard were true then Ruby was not the only woman in his life, but one of a never-ending parade that covered women from all backgrounds, including many from their own class.

A slow smile wiped away his frown of concern. 'Or is that a look of disapproval I see on your face?'

'Of course not,' Daisy shot back.

To her intense annoyance his smile grew wider, as if to say he did not believe her one little bit. 'So, what is it you disapprove of? The way I live my life, or the way Ruby does?'

Daisy sniffed, then mentally castigated herself for making a noise that sounded so prim and proper. 'Well, you have a choice in how you live your life. But what of Ruby? Is she happy with this casual arrangement?' If the sniff had been prim and proper, that was nothing compared to how her clipped words sounded.

He raised his eyebrows and looked up at the carriage roof, appearing to be giving her statement some consideration. 'More than happy, I'd say,' he replied with an easy laugh, causing heat to rush to Daisy's cheeks as she remembered that top of the bill comment.

'Is that the truth or just something you tell yourself to ease your conscience?'

He continued to smile at her, the disturbing smile that used to turn her to mush when she was young. It seemed to say, *I know exactly what you think of me and I find it funny rather than insulting.* 'Ruby is an independent young woman who lives life on her own terms. I would have thought that was something you would approve of.'

Daisy rolled her eyes, as if to say, *well, you would tell yourself that, wouldn't you?*

'Ruby and I have known each other for a year or two now. We see each other intermittently, and that is how Ruby likes it. She's busy with her acting career but contacts me when she feels like spending some time in the country.'

Daisy felt her eyes grow wide and she had to close her mouth, which had dropped open in amazement at how gullible he thought she was.

'It's true,' he said with a laugh. 'I'll admit that taking the country air is not all she does while she's at my estate, but she is always the one to ask me if it would be convenient to visit when she wants a break from the noise and smoke of London.'

'And I assume it is *always* convenient for you as well.'

'You could say that,' he said with a carefree shrug.

'And I also assume she has to pay for her accommodation,' she retorted, causing his smile to disappear.

'Nothing is expected of Ruby and she knows that.' He shrugged then that slow, devilish smile returned.

'It's hardly my fault if, while she's here, she wants to do more than just enjoy the country air.'

Daisy glared back at him, painfully aware that her cheeks were burning.

'You did ask,' he pointed out. 'If you don't want to hear the answer then it's best not to ask the question.'

Daisy turned and watched the passing cottages, wishing she had indeed not asked the question.

'So, now that Ruby has ceased to be your chaperon, as I said I'll fetch my cousin so she can protect your virtue from my licentious ways.' He said this with another easy laugh. Daisy continued to stare straight ahead and wished she had kept her opinions to herself. After all, Guy was merely a friend of her brother. She would not like him to get the wrong impression and think that she actually cared about how he lived and what women he did or did not entertain. And he was right about Ruby Lovelace. She'd given every appearance that she was happy with their casual arrangement, more than happy. No, she had no right to be offended by what she had just witnessed...but, damn it all, she was.

He shouldn't tease, but it was all too tempting to treat her just as he had when they'd been children, even if it was obvious that Daisy Springfeld was no longer that funny little freckle-faced, pig-tailed girl who had relentlessly followed Nathaniel and him around, desperate to join in with their boyhood games.

He tried and failed not to look her up and down one more time. No, she most definitely was not that little freckle-faced girl. He did a quick calculation. He was thirty-two. She was eight years younger than him, which made her twenty-four. Yes, she was most certainly a woman now, and a rather beautiful one at that. Even in that somewhat bizarre costume of baggy knee-length trousers, striped stockings and flared jacket, she was all woman.

It was also obvious that little Daisy Chain had blossomed enticingly. With long chestnut hair piled up under that slightly askew straw hat, soft creamy skin, full red lips and big blue eyes, she was now most definitely the sort of woman who would catch a discerning man's attention.

He coughed to clear his throat. Not that he would ever be such a man. To him she would always be his childhood friend's younger sister, cheeky little Daisy Chain, that pesky imp they could never get rid of.

'I'm surprised your mother lets you roam the countryside. Shouldn't you be dressed up in silk and satin, attending a ball somewhere and finding yourself a husband?' he asked, immediately forgetting his admonition to stop teasing her.

As expected, those disapproving blue eyes narrowed and her nostrils flared. Yes, teasing Daisy Chain was much safer than thinking about her lips, soft skin or that curvy womanly body encased in those ridiculous clothes.

'I'll have you know that I'm a member of the Rational Dress Society, and we do not go in for wearing restricting clothing, such as ball gowns, that impede a woman's freedom.'

Guy bit back a smile. She really was a spirited little minx. That was something that hadn't changed. 'And what about finding a husband, or will that impede on your freedom as well?'

'Of course it will,' she shot back.

Guy was tempted to point out that neither of her sisters appeared to have given up their freedom when they'd married, and no one in their right mind would ever suggest that her mother had lost her independence when she'd married Daisy's father. But in general, he did agree with her. Marriage and freedom did not go hand in hand, and it was one of the many reasons why he had avoided being trapped himself.

'Good for you,' he said. 'I'm sure you're better off with a bicycle than you are with a man.'

Instead of the expected glaring response or even a sharp retort, colour exploded on her face, turning her cheeks a deeper shade of pink. Perhaps he had gone too far—touched on a sore point, or somehow said something wrong. Little Daisy Chain had never blushed. If you offended her, you were more likely to get boxed ears or an angry outburst than shy blushes. Apparently, the grown-up Daisy *had* changed in more ways than just her appearance.

'So, what of your family?' he asked. 'I haven't seen them since Iris's wedding. How are your parents? And I believe Hazel has had another child.'

That had the desired effect. The fire on her cheeks settled down and she recounted tales of what each member of the household had been up to. Guy had mainly wanted to change the subject to save her blushes, but he also wanted to hear about every one of the Springfeld family and was pleased that they were all happy and prosperous. The Springfelds had rescued him from an otherwise bleak childhood and he owed them an enormous debt of gratitude, one he doubted he could ever repay. Caring for an injured Daisy Chain was the least he could do.

'Since the wedding, Iris has been living at her husband's estate in Cornwall,' she continued. 'That's the next destination for the High-Wheeling Ladies' Cycling Association. We plan to base ourselves at their estate and do a tour of the county in the autumn.'

'Yes, I met Iris's husband at the wedding. The two of them seem perfectly suited and extremely happy.' It was tempting to add that seeing such happiness at a society wedding was a rarity, and only found in families like the Springfelds. Instead, he continued teasing. 'And I noticed at the wedding you didn't dress in a particularly rational manner. A lacy pink gown, if I remember correctly, and a ring of daisies in your hair.'

Her eyebrows drew together and she looked at him sideways. Guy hoped she wasn't wondering how he remembered exactly what she'd been wearing at a wedding that had happened three years ago. It was something he was also wondering himself. He rarely noticed women's clothing and certainly never remembered colours or hair adornments. But he *had* noticed Daisy on that day. He had noticed how she was no longer a child, even though he had treated her that way. As if to remind himself that she was Nathaniel's little sister, he had teased her relentlessly at the wedding, just as he was doing now.

'And if *I* remember correctly, you and Lady Penrose were getting rather friendly at that wedding. How is her husband these days?'

Guy shrugged. Perhaps the rebuke was justified, but Lady Charlotte Penrose had made her interest in him perfectly clear at the wedding, and who was he to turn down such an attractive offer? That relationship had run its course and Charlotte was presumably finding solace with some other man now. As for the husband, he was no doubt still spending time with his mistress and their children. The Penroses had an arranged marriage, one made solely because it had been advantageous for both parties. Now that Charlotte had provided the requisite heir, both husband and wife felt free to take lovers whenever they chose. He had not come between a happy couple, but that was not something he could explain to an innocent young woman like Daisy.

'I believe he is happy and content with the woman he loves and the children he adores,' he said instead, something which was the truth, although the woman he loved was not his wife and the children he adored were not his legitimate heirs.

He swallowed to quench the fire burning in his throat. He too knew what it was like to be the unloved legitimate heir.

'So, Daisy Chain, despite your objections to matrimony, I imagine your mother is still trying to find you a suitable husband,' he said, squashing down all thoughts of his father and his childhood.

'Well, she still lives in hope, but I'm sure eventually even Mother will come to realise that no man would make a suitable husband for me.'

Guy doubted that. She was a beautiful, delightful young woman, albeit one who was somewhat feistier than most men of his acquaintance would want in a wife. He also suspected that, deep down, Daisy Chain also wanted the same loving relationship with a man that her sisters and mother had. And he wished her good luck with that. She should be with a man who could love and respect her. He just hoped she was wrong, and such a suitable husband did exist. Although, he struggled to think of any man he knew who would be worthy of her, himself included.

The carriage came to a halt outside his cousins' cottage. He looked up at its stone façade and suppressed a sigh. Hopefully, Florence would be home alone and he would not have to deal with her boorish brother. Horace reminded Guy too much of his father and that was one of the many reasons he chose to have as little to do with him as possible.

'Excuse me for a moment,' he said. 'I'll go and fetch Florence. I'm sure she'll have no objections to acting as your chaperon.' And would have even fewer objections to getting away from her bully of a brother.

He jumped out of the carriage and rushed up the flagstone pathway, suddenly eager for Florence's company. A chaperon was just what he needed. It seemed Daisy's low opinion of him was correct because, the longer he spent alone in her company, the more danger there was in him forgetting that she was not only a beautiful young woman but his best friend's little sister, and the youngest daughter of a family to whom he was eternally indebted.

Chapter Three

Guy disappeared inside the house, giving Daisy time to compose herself. If she was to avoid making herself look foolish again and blushing like a ninny, she would have to remember that she was now a mature adult. She had once followed Guy around like some love-sick little puppy, but she was not that little girl any more. And he was no longer that funny, charming boy she had all but worshipped. He was a man now, one best described as a rake. Ruby Lovelace was proof of that, as was Lady Penrose.

If Ruby's words and her behaviour at the railway station hadn't vanquished any illusions Daisy might have about the adult Guy, then remembering Iris's wedding would do it. The other guests might not have noticed, but she had seen him disappear with Lady Penrose, and they had not returned for quite some time. And, when they had finally re-joined the party, Lady Penrose had looked so much like the contented cat who had got the cream that she'd almost been purring. Her face flushed, her eyes sparkling, she had stayed close to Guy for the rest of the evening, her gaze never leaving him and that satisfied smile remaining fixed to her lips.

Such obvious behaviour could not have been lost on her husband. That was, if her husband had been paying any attention to what his wife was doing.

Daisy shuffled uncomfortably in her seat. That was the sort of man Guy was now—a disreputable womaniser, a seducer of married women and a man best avoided. Not that he had ever tried to seduce her. He wouldn't dare but, if he did, he would quickly learn that she was impervious to his charms.

She looked up at the two-storey brick cottage, her cheeks unaccountably burning once again, and attempted to clear her mind of all thoughts of Guy Parnell and the women in his life. He emerged from the house alone, opened the carriage door and sent Daisy a rueful grimace.

'I'm afraid Florence is unable to join us until later today,' he said. 'Her brother...' He scowled, raised his hands and then let them drop as if this gesture explained everything she needed to know about Florence's brother. 'But don't worry. I'll send for the doctor the moment we get home, and I sent a telegram to your family from the railway station, so I'm sure they'll send someone immediately. In the meantime, one of the maids can act as chaperon.' The man sounded almost panicked.

'It will be all right,' Daisy reassured him, wondering why he would actually need reassurance. 'No one will know we've been alone together, and even if they did, why, you're almost family, aren't you?' Fortunately, she knew that to be true. Other women might not be safe with Guy Parnell, but she would be. Or was that *un*fortunately? No, of course it was fortunately. It was definitely fortunate that Guy did not see her the way he saw other women.

He continued to frown at her, the carriage door still open. 'Are you sure?'

'Yes, I am sure.'

He didn't stop frowning, nor did he get into the carriage.

'It's all right, Guy,' she repeated. What on earth was wrong with the man? Anyone would think it was *his* reputation he was worried about.

Finally, he got into the carriage, tapped the roof and they moved off through the small village. Daisy tried to think of something to talk about, some innocuous small talk, but nothing would come to mind. Guy also seemed incapable of thinking of anything to say, and every time they made eye contact all he could do was give her a small, seemingly uncomfortable smile.

Thankfully, they soon arrived at his estate. When they stopped, she turned in her seat and lowered her legs, but Guy was too quick. Before she had a chance to rise, he'd scooped her up in his arms, and for the second time that day she found herself hard up against his chest, his arms encasing her, and it was no less disturbing an experience than it had been then.

No, that wasn't correct. This time it was more disturbing. The last time, she had been thinking about her foot, her bicycle, the inconvenience she was causing to the other cycling ladies. This time, she was only aware of Guy, of him being so close it would be easy to reach up and touch his cheek and run her finger along the stubble on his chin if she had a mind to. So close, the warmth of his body and his masculine scent surrounded her. She breathed in deeply, inhaling his manly scent and the crisp citrus smell of his soap. It would be so easy to lose herself in the sensation of being held by him, so best she not let it happen.

Keeping her breathing as shallow as possible, she tried to distract her mind by looking up at the house. She had never seen Guy's home before. Nathaniel had been the only member of the family to visit the estate when the late Duke of Mandivale had been alive. Daisy and her sisters had questioned him relentlessly on his return, but out of loyalty to his friend he had refused to answer. All they had got out of him was that it had all been somewhat grim.

Daisy could see nothing grim about it whatsoever. In fact, the expansive three-storey cream stone house was magnificent and fitting for a duke reputed to be rather wealthy. A divided staircase led up to a terrace that ran the length of the front of the house. At the top of the steps was the grand entrance with two large, iron-wrapped wooden doors topped with an enormous arched stained-glass window. Guy carried her up the steps, and Daisy hoped and prayed she wasn't too heavy, as the steps did seem to go on for quite some time.

She flicked a quick look up at his face, relieved to see that carrying her did not appear to be causing him any strain.

'You can probably put me down now,' she said when they reached the top. 'I'm sure I can walk.'

'Nonsense,' he retorted, still holding her close as if her weight meant nothing to him.

A footman opened the door and bowed his head, his impassive gaze suggesting there was nothing untoward about his master carrying a woman into his house. Daisy hoped his lack of expression was because he was a well-trained servant and not because he was used to seeing Guy do such things.

'Lady Daisy has injured her foot,' he told the footman. 'Please send for the doctor and ask him to come as soon as possible.'

'Yes, Your Grace,' the footman said, and departed.

The entrance hall was just as impressive as the house, with its abundance of white marble mottled with grey, black and white-tiled flooring, and pillars standing tall and impressive before pristine cream walls. The hall ended with a grand curved staircase, and Daisy hoped he would not have to heave her up those seemingly never-ending stairs.

Guy carried her down the hall then turned into a richly carpeted corridor, passing several rooms until he found the one he wanted. When he entered, it was obvious why he had chosen this room in the corner of the house. Although a large room, it was comfortably furnished and overlooked two sides of the house, giving a panoramic view of the estate. A perfect room in which to convalesce.

Outside the floor-to-ceiling windows, the gardens provided a glorious view with an assortment of colourful flowers in full bloom. Tall silver birch, oak and yew trees graced the woodland areas, and in the acres of pasture sheep were gently grazing, and there were even a few deer in the distance.

French doors opened onto the terrace, which had a wrought-iron balustrade, and through them she had sight of the tree-lined driveway. She would be able to see everyone who was coming and going, and in the very distance she could see the steeple of a church in the local village. If she was going to have to spend a few days staring out of this window while she convalesced, she couldn't have asked for a better view. Guy really was rather thoughtful.

He carried her to a sofa beside the window and lowered her down gently, then lifted her foot and placed it on an embroidered footstool.

'Hopefully, the doctor will be here soon,' he said, still kneeling at her feet and staring at her ankle. 'But I'd better remove your boot to take away some of the pressure and make you a bit more comfortable.'

Daisy had expected him to call for a maid but instead he gently took hold of her foot and slowly unlaced her boot. If it had been any other man, Daisy would have seen this as rather an intimate act. But it was Guy Parnell, she reminded herself, a man who still saw her as his best friend's annoying little sister. All he was doing was tending to her injury, something he had often done when they'd been children.

Daisy remained frozen. All she was aware of was the gentle touch of his hand on her calf muscle, the warmth flooding through her body, the tingling of her skin and a disturbing throbbing that had erupted deep within her.

These unfamiliar reactions must be the effect of her injury. They had nothing to do with Guy touching her, she told herself as she swallowed, closed her eyes and gasped in a few quick breaths.

'Nasty,' he said.

She opened her eyes to see him still cradling her ankle. Once again, she tried not to read anything more into this than what it actually was. Guy was not observing an intimate part of a woman's body, nor was he admiring a well-turned ankle, but frowning down at one that was swollen and bulging out of her torn stocking.

He looked up at her. 'Do you mind if I have a look to see how bad it is?'

Daisy shrugged and shook her head, not sure how she wanted to answer that question, not entirely sure if she was still capable of thinking.

He removed the garter holding up her stocking and discarded it on the floor, then slowly folded down her striped stocking, revealing the skin of her calves.

He's only doing it to see how bad your injury is, Daisy repeated to herself as the throbbing deep within her intensified and shivers radiated upwards, starting at the spot where his fingers were holding her leg and engulfing her entire body.

With gentle care he exposed her ugly, swollen ankle to his scrutiny.

'Oh, you poor thing,' he said, looking up at her from his kneeling position, still gently cradling her foot.

She looked down at him into his deep brown eyes. His eyes could not have changed since he'd been a child, but she had never before noticed that they contained such a depth of colour, like rich, dark chocolate, or strong black coffee. Her gaze moved to his lips. Had they always been so full, so sensual?

Daisy swallowed, trying to relieve her dry throat. Suddenly aware that she had stopped breathing, she pulled in a quick breath.

He looked down at her purple ankle and his lips curled down into something that looked like disgust. The heat on Daisy's cheeks intensified.

What on earth was she doing, staring at his lips and eyes and getting all quivery and girlish? The removal of her stocking was not some sort of seductive act. He was merely tending to her wound, one that was causing him to scowl.

She blinked rapidly and sat up straighter in her chair. The only reason he felt comfortable removing her stocking was because he thought of her almost as his sister, hardly a woman at all. He had bandaged up innumerable cuts when she'd been a child. This was no different and thank goodness for that.

'You really like to get into scrapes, don't you, Daisy Chain?' he said, staring at her unattractive ankle. 'I remember when you were eight and you nearly drowned in that pond. I still don't know what you were doing there or why you went out so far when you couldn't swim.'

'I didn't realise how deep it was,' Daisy recalled, deciding she would not inform him that she had been following Nathaniel and him. They had told her to go back to the house as they'd wanted to swim. She had thought that once she joined them in the water they would have no choice but to let her stay. Instead, she had literally got in over her head and the boys had had to rescue her.

'Then there was that time you shot yourself in the foot with an arrow.' He shook his head, as if he couldn't believe how unlucky she was.

Again, she had been following Nathaniel and Guy, wanting to join in with their game. They had abandoned their bows and arrows and moved on to some other sport. She had picked up the bow, determined to show them that she was just as proficient as them. But the string had been too hard to pull back, and by the time she'd got the arrow in place it had been mere seconds before it released. She hadn't had time to lift up the bow so had shot her own foot. Fortunately, it had merely gone through the edge of her shoe and not into the foot itself. Once again, it had been Guy and Nathaniel who had rescued her.

'And there were all those trees you got stuck up,' he said, smiling up at her from his kneeling position on the floor. 'You seem to have made a lifetime of having accidents. Perhaps you should give up on this adventurous life and take up a more leisurely pursuit, like painting in water colours or doing a bit of embroidery.' The teasing note in his voice suggested he knew that would never happen.

'It's not as if I'm the only one in the family who's had injuries,' Daisy retorted, her voice defiant. 'If I remember correctly, and I'm sure I do, you and Nathaniel regularly had cut knees and grazed hands and elbows from all your adventures.'

'Yes, but we're...'

She glared at him, causing him to stop mid-sentence. Lucky for him that he did stop. If he had said, 'But we were boys,' he most certainly would have been on the receiving end of one of her lectures.

'You really are one of a kind, aren't you, Daisy?' he said instead, patting her leg with familial affection and standing up. Daisy was unsure whether she was being complimented or insulted but decided she would go with complimented. She did not want to be like other women, she wanted to be just herself, and if Guy Parnell didn't like that, if he preferred women to be more like Ruby Lovelace or Lady Penrose, then so be it.

So what if the only reason Guy Parnell would touch her, carry her in his arms or remove an item of clothing was because she'd had an accident? She most certainly did not want to be like Ruby Lovelace or Lady Penrose and actually know what it was like to be seduced by Guy, to actually have him remove her stockings for some other reason than to examine an injured ankle.

He pressed the button beside the fireplace to summon a footman, and when he arrived asked Daisy if she wanted tea, which she declined. 'Can you organise a bed to be set up in the adjoining room for Lady Daisy's use?' he said to the footman. 'And try and find that old wheelchair of Aunt Myrtle's so she can be a bit more mobile.'

The footman bowed and retreated out of the door.

'And you're going to need some books to read while you convalesce. I'll see what I have in the library that's suitable.'

He left the room and Daisy yet again reminded herself to stop acting like a fool. Guy was being very considerate, treating her like a cherished younger sister who needed to be taken care of, and she was reacting by having some less than charitable thoughts about him and behaving like an awkward child. That had to stop.

He returned with an armful of books and placed them on the table beside her.

'This really is awfully kind of you, and I'm sorry to be such an inconvenience.'

He waved his hand dismissively. 'I'm more than happy to have you here,' he assured her, sitting down in the chair opposite. 'It is the very least I can do. After all those times I stayed with your family, I feel I owe every last one of you a great debt of gratitude.'

'Nonsense. We all enjoyed having you to stay, and it was as if you were a part of the family.'

That easy smile returned, and Daisy fought not to let it have any effect on her, reminding herself of the stern talk she had just given herself.

'And for that I am also eternally grateful,' he continued. 'It was as if you were all my little sisters, although sometimes I suspect you would rather have been a little brother. You were such a tomboy.' He looked down at her bloomers. 'And I suspect you still are.'

That's not an insult, Daisy told herself. She *had* been a tomboy. Guy *had* seen her as a little sister, still did, but she rather wished he did not see her that way now. 'I never actually wanted to be a boy. I just didn't want to have to act like a girl.' Daisy was unsure if that made things any clearer. 'I mean, I couldn't see why a girl couldn't climb trees, swim in rivers and have adventures. The only thing stopping me was the stupid dresses I had to wear.'

'So now you dress like a boy and all your problems are solved,' he said.

'I don't look like a boy,' she muttered under her breath. 'I look like a woman dressed in rational clothing.'

He nodded slowly, still smiling. 'You're right. No matter what you wore, you would never look like a boy,' he said, slowly looking her up and down.

Daisy fought to maintain her huffy expression, which was not easy to do when the blush on her cheeks had moved to her entire body in response to his assessing gaze. She knew he was merely scrutinising her clothing, not the woman wearing them, and instead of blushing she should be pleased that he was no longer making fun of her outfit. But despite these rational thoughts her body refused to act rationally.

She turned to the pile of books and picked one up, quickly flicking through the pages. Then she stopped, looked up at Guy and back down at the book. It was Conan Doyle's latest Sherlock Holmes adventure. She raised her eyebrows in surprise and picked up the next one, then the next. Books by Robert Louis Stevenson… Mark Twain… These were all recently published. Did that mean that Guy actually read?

She looked up at him in question.

'What? Is there nothing to suit your taste?'

'It's not that,' she said looking down at the pile and picking up another book. Thomas Hardy's *Tess of the d'Urbervilles*. 'Did you actually buy these books?'

'Yes. Why? Did you think me incapable of reading?'

Daisy tried to compose her face into a less judgemental expression. 'Of course not. It's just...' She paused and picked up the next book on the pile.

'It's just that you didn't think a man like me would read a novel,' he finished, his voice amused rather than critical or offended.

Daisy shrugged. 'I just thought, what with the way you lived, you'd be too exhausted to read.' Fire burst onto her cheeks. Why had she had to use the word 'exhausted'? It immediately brought back Ruby's words about how she had spent the weekend.

As expected, her blushing cheeks made him laugh. 'Perhaps when my lifestyle has worn me out there's nothing I like better than to curl up in bed with a good book.'

His jest did not help and the heat on her cheeks intensified at the thought of him curled up in bed. That was an image she did not need in her head. She wondered what he wore to bed then, gulping, wondered if he wore *anything* to bed.

She flicked open the next book in the pile, lifted it up to cover her face and stared at the page, even though the words were a blur.

'Anyway, I'm going to enjoy reading this,' she said, her eyes starting to focus on the title page of *The Principles of Evolutionary Biology*.

Damn it all.

Slowly, she lowered the book, her cheeks still burning. 'But perhaps I'll save that one for later and read the Sherlock Holmes first,' she said, putting the book down.

'Good idea,' he agreed, still with that knowing smile.

Daisy flicked open the Sherlock Holmes novel and pretended she was reading, while trying to get that annoying fire on her cheeks to cool down and her foolish imaginings to do the same. If she was to survive her convalescence, she had to avoid using words like 'exhausted', must not picture Guy either in bed or with any other woman and most certainly had to forget what it was like to have him holding her in his arms or touching her naked leg.

Chapter Four

'A good book, is it?' he asked, and she could hear a note of amusement in his voice.

She quickly scanned the page to make sure she was holding the book the correct way and not further embarrassing herself by revealing just how agitated she had become.

'Mmm, yes, very good.' She closed the book and placed it on the side table. This was not the way to behave. She should be making polite conversation, not ignoring her host and burying her blushing face in a book.

'Lovely weather for the time of year,' she said, then cringed.

'I think I prefer it when you're casting aspersions on my morality or suggesting that I'm illiterate than trying to make small talk.'

She frowned at his criticism, but saw he was smiling, that seductive smile, the one her father had warned them about, and she forgot what she was going to say to him. She was sure she was going to chastise him for something, but what it was she was now unsure of.

A light knock distracted her before she could remember. They both looked towards the door as the footman entered.

'The doctor has arrived. Shall I show him in, Your Grace?'

'Yes, indeed. Straight away,' Guy said.

The servant departed with a bow, and a middle-aged man wearing a black suit and carrying the black leather bag that marked him as a medical man rushed in.

After exchanging pleasantries, which might have gone on for some time if an impatient Guy had not cut him short, he turned to Daisy.

'So, you're the patient, are you?' he asked, as if talking to a child.

Daisy would have thought that was patently obvious. After all she was the only other person in the room, and she was the one sitting with her swollen ankle resting on a footstool.

'Right. I'll call for you, Your Grace, when I've finished my examination.'

'Oh, yes, right,' Guy said, surprised that he was expected to leave the room. Daisy was tempted to tell the doctor that as Guy had just removed her stockings it was a bit late to start worrying about decorum.

When the door closed, the doctor took hold of her foot, and with a disapproving look on his face examined her ankle. While having Guy kneeling at her feet and touching her skin had been an unexpectedly intimate and disturbing experience, not so with the doctor. He was all business and looked at her ankle without tenderness, as if examining a piece of machinery.

After a few ums and ahs, he stood up, went to the door and told Guy he could now re-enter.

'Not much you can do for it,' he said to Guy. 'It's not broken, just twisted. Continue doing what you're doing. Get her to rest up and keep her weight off it until she can walk again. Might be a few days, might be a few weeks. Impossible to tell for sure.'

Daisy mumbled under her breath that she was the one with the injury, not Guy, so the doctor should be talking to her.

'So how did this happen?' the doctor continued, still not looking at Daisy.

'I came off my bicycle,' she said before Guy could answer for her.

The doctor turned to face her, his eyes enormous, his mouth open, as if she had said she'd twisted her ankle while dancing naked through the streets of London.

'Then you got no more than was coming to you,' he spluttered out. 'Those machines are an abomination and should never be ridden by members of the fairer sex. Young ladies are not made for such exertions. They're far too delicate.'

Daisy sighed and wondered whether she had the energy for yet another argument with yet another old fool who thought all women were capable of was sitting still, talking quietly while taking tea and maybe indulging in a bit of gentle embroidery.

He leaned down towards Daisy and lowered his voice. 'Let me tell you, those infernal machines do terrible things to a woman's insides, my dear. I strongly advise you to be sensible and never ride a bicycle again, or when you marry you'll be unlikely to be able to bear children.'

'Oh, well, there's no problem then, is there?' Daisy said, unable to contain her annoyance a moment longer and, unlike the doctor, not keeping her voice down. 'I have no intention of marrying or having children.'

She heard a stifled male laugh from behind the doctor, but the man was not the slightest bit amused by Daisy's comment. He stared down at her, his brow furrowed in consternation. 'I implore you not to be so foolish. And, even if you care nothing for your own health, you are setting a very bad example for other young ladies.'

Daisy crossed her arms and looked away.

'My dear, I beseech you,' the doctor continued. 'See this twisted ankle as a sign that you should not ride a bicycle. Women are simply not made for such things.'

Daisy tilted up her chin, her body tensing for an argument. 'And I beseech you to keep your outmoded—'

'Thank you for coming, Dr Howard,' Guy cut in. 'We shall follow your advice to the letter, and I'm sure Lady Daisy will be up and about in no time.'

The doctor nodded to Guy, then gave Daisy one more stern look. 'Keep off that foot—and keep off that bicycle,' he commanded and departed before Daisy had a chance to give him a piece of her mind.

'What a fool,' she said as soon as the door clicked shut behind him. 'Bicycles do not stop women from having children. Why just last summer...' Daisy stopped, suddenly feeling uncomfortable about informing Guy that three members of the High-Wheeling Ladies' Cycling Association had become pregnant.

'What rot,' she stated instead.

'Yes, I'm afraid old Dr Howard is stuck in a previous age,' Guy said. 'He objected strenuously to the railway being extended to the village, thought it would cause all sorts of social problems. You should have heard what he had to say about the potential effects on young people's morals and what they would get up to if they could gallivant all over the countryside.'

On that, Daisy was almost tempted to agree with the doctor. If it wasn't for the steam train's quick access to London, Ruby Lovelace and her cohorts would not easily be able to visit places like the Mandivale estate, but that was unfair, not to mention rather snobbish, and was coming from a somewhat peevish place that Daisy did not like. It was none of her business whom Guy entertained, and she was sure it wasn't the steam train that had caused his morals to be unduly relaxed.

'When he heard that some of the farm hands had taken the train to the seaside and gone bathing, he was beside himself,' Guy continued. 'He was certain they would come down with any number of life-threatening illnesses, so I'm not surprised he thinks bicycles can stop a woman from having children.'

'Ridiculous,' Daisy stated.

He paused, staring over at her with a questioning look. 'So, is it true what you said to the doctor—that you have no intention of marrying or having children—or were you merely trying to shock him?'

Daisy was unsure what the correct answer was to that question, so she shrugged.

'I can't imagine your mother being happy about her

little girl not marrying, and I'm sure she wants as many grandchildren as possible.'

Daisy shrugged again. 'I think Mother knows that I'm not like other young women.'

'Really?' he said. 'You surprise me,' he added, looking at her cycling bloomers.

'All right, yes, Mother would prefer that I was attending balls, parties and picnics rather than cycling round the countryside, but you know Mother.'

Guy gave a small nod, as if to say, yes, he knew her mother well. Knew that even if she didn't entirely approve of what her daughter was up to, as long as Daisy was happy, her mother would tolerate it.

'She's reluctantly accepted that…' Daisy halted. She was going to say her mother had reluctantly accepted the fact that at twenty-four Daisy was all but officially now a spinster. Instead, she said, 'Mother knows that I hate dressing up in all that frippery, standing around and making small talk at balls and parties. I'd much rather be riding my bicycle or playing tennis or croquet.' She looked down at her ankle and frowned. She wouldn't be doing any of those activities for some time. 'Although, Mother has warned me about being too competitive.' Daisy laughed. 'Mother seems to think it's more ladylike to lose.'

'And losing is not something you particularly enjoy, if I remember correctly,' Guy said.

'Of course not. I can't see the point of not trying to win if you're playing a competitive sport.'

'For some women, finding a husband *is* a competitive sport, and if losing at one small game means they win a much more substantial one, then in their eyes they will have achieved a decisive victory.'

'But isn't that cheating? Pretending to be something you're not?'

Guy laughed. 'Well, you know what they say, all's fair in love and war.'

'I don't know if love comes into it very often.'

'On that, we are in total agreement. Which is why I also avoid society events during the season. The warfare waged by the mothers and debutantes is a bit too ferocious for my delicate sensibilities.'

Daisy nodded. She had not seen Guy at any of the balls she had been forced to attend but knew exactly what would have happened if he had graced such events with his presence. A duke, wealthy with extensive estates, not to mention handsome and charming. The mothers would have behaved in an oh-so-polite manner, while fighting tooth and nail to get him interested in their unmarried daughters.

'And what of you, Daisy Chain?' he continued in his teasing manner. 'You must have had a few offers. I'm sure lots of men would be delighted to marry the beautiful youngest daughter of an earl.'

'Yes, I've had offers,' she said, annoyed her voice sounded defensive. 'But I have no intention of marrying anyone, ever. I enjoy my freedom too much.'

'Once again, it seems we have something in common. I too enjoy a life of freedom.'

'Yes, so I saw earlier today.' The moment the words were out, Daisy regretted them. She did not want Guy to think she cared a jot that his freedom involved entertaining women like Ruby Lovelace.

Guy tipped back his head and laughed, obviously not the slightest bit insulted by Daisy's tart statement. 'There you go again, disapproving of the way I live my life.'

'Not at all,' she shot back. 'How you live is entirely up to you.'

'Next you're going to say that it's all the steam train's fault and that it's causing a decline in morality.'

Daisy cringed. Had he read her mind? Did he know that was exactly what she had been thinking? She would hate Guy to see her as just as moralistic as the doctor.

'Of course I don't think that at all,' she stated. 'It's thanks to the steam train that I and my fellow cyclists are able to explore the countryside.'

He raised his eyebrows, still smiling. 'It seems in some people's opinion both of us are using the steam train for socially unacceptable practices.'

Daisy wished he would change the subject, even though it was she who raised it. While she thought of something else to say, anything that would not bring them back to discussing Guy and Ruby Lovelace, she stared out at the view.

'Oh, the doctor seems to be returning,' she said as a carriage turned into the driveway and made its way to the house. Even that old fool of a doctor would make a welcome distraction. 'Perhaps he remembered some other reason why women should not ride bicycles. He probably wants to tell me that it will cause the breakdown of the family or the destruction of society, as some other buffoons have maintained.'

'No, that's Horace's carriage,' Guy said, standing up and moving towards the window. 'It looks like your chaperon has finally arrived.'

The carriage drove round the fountain at the front of the house and came to a stop, its wheels crunching on the gravel.

Guy's relaxed manner changed. His shoulders tensed, his face hardened and his hands clenched themselves into fists at his sides.

She turned back to the window. It was a surprising reaction to the arrival of the chaperon, especially as he had requested her presence. Two people alighted from the carriage, a pleasant-looking young woman, and a corpulent man with a florid complexion.

'Has the chaperon brought her own chaperon?' Daisy asked.

'That's her damn brother, Horace,' Guy said, not tempering his language or his wrath. 'What on earth does that b...' He paused. 'What does that man want now?'

Whatever it was, there was no doubting from Guy's sudden change in demeanour that Horace was not a welcome visitor.

A visit from cousin Horace only ever meant one thing. Trouble. Trouble for Guy, that was. The man was a menace, and Guy could only hope that his visit would be a short one. He walked across the room and sank back down into his chair, preparing himself for the headache the man would inevitably inflict.

The footman knocked and entered. Before he could announce the new arrivals, Guy waved his hand. 'Yes, show them in, James.'

Florence entered almost immediately, her strained smile reflecting Guy's own tension. He stood up and introduced her to Daisy. Florence bobbed a curtsy, while Daisy nodded her head in greeting.

'It's lovely to see you again, Florence. And thank you for agreeing to chaperon Daisy,' he said, signalling towards a chair.

'Oh, I'm happy to do it,' she assured him, looking anxiously at the door. 'It's nice to get away from the house for a while.'

Guy sent her a sympathetic smile. 'The doctor said it might be a few weeks.'

'Oh, good.' She turned to Daisy. 'Oh, I'm sorry. All I meant was it will be nice for me to spend a few weeks here at the estate, and it's always so lovely at this time of year.' She bit her top lip and looked over at Guy. 'I couldn't come earlier because Horace had some household tasks he wanted me to complete.'

Guy tried not to huff his annoyance at the way that man treated his younger sister and took advantage of her gentle nature. Florence was far too kind for her own good. At twenty-two she was quite within her rights to leave the home her brother had inherited when their parents had died, and Guy had offered more than once to provide her with sufficient funds to live independently, but Florence was not like Daisy. She was a traditional young lady who would not leave her family home until she was married.

Unfortunately, there was not much chance of that, not while she continued to live secluded in the country with an overbearing brother who enjoyed discouraging potential suitors.

'And he said I should wait until he visited you himself,' Florence continued. 'He said he had something he needed to tell you. He wouldn't tell me what it was but I'm afraid he has been rather pleased with himself lately.'

They stared at each other with matching expressions of concern.

'I'm sure it will be nothing,' Florence said, biting her lip once more. 'At least I hope—'

'Those steps are a darn nuisance,' Horace said, bursting into the room, his face doing an excellent impersonation of a beetroot. He pulled a large linen handkerchief out of his pocket and wiped the sweat from his forehead.

'They're far too steep,' he said, his unnecessarily loud voice filling the room. 'You should do something about them.'

'I'll take that under advisement,' Guy said, wondering whether it would be possible to increase the height of the steps, perhaps erect a few ramparts in front of the entrance or maybe dig a moat. Anything to deter visits from Horace.

'May I present Lady Daisy Springfeld,' he said. 'Daisy, this is my cousin, Horace Parnell.' Horace sent her a quick look, mumbled a greeting then turned back to Guy.

'Need to speak to you. Urgently.'

Guy swallowed a sigh. Of course he needed to talk

to him, and of course it was urgent. Was it ever anything else?

'Perhaps we can leave the ladies to get to know each other while the two of us take a walk in the gardens,' Guy suggested, enjoying Horace's look of horror at the thought of walking up and down those steps yet again, or actually strolling round the garden.

'The terrace will do,' he said, pointing at the French doors.

'As you wish,' Guy said, the sigh of annoyance he had been suppressing finally escaping. 'If you will excuse us for a moment, ladies.'

'Would you mind opening the windows before you go?' Florence asked. 'This room is a bit stuffy.'

Guy crossed the room and pushed open the large sash windows beside the French doors, then escorted his annoying cousin outside, bracing himself for whatever problem Horace was about to inflict on him.

'I'm so sorry, but I fell in a ditch,' Daisy explained the moment the two men had left the room.

Florence merely nodded and crossed the room towards the open windows, increasing Daisy's discomfort. It was mortifying that she was causing such an unpleasant smell that a guest actually had to ask for the windows to be opened, and even worse that she had to stand beside them to get some fresh air.

'That's the reason for the unfortunate smell. I really am very sorry. There was some rather dirty water at the bottom of the ditch and I'm afraid I fell into it. As soon as my trunk arrives, I'll be able to change my clothes, but in the meantime...'

Florence held her finger to her lips, signalling for Daisy to be quiet, and angled her head towards the window so she could listen to the two men talking outside.

It was somewhat unusual behaviour but, if Florence wanted to eavesdrop, who was Daisy to judge? And if she was being completely honest, she too was curious to know what this Horace fellow was up to, and why his presence was having such an unsettling effect on Guy.

'I know I look like I'm being frightfully rude,' Florence whispered, turning back to Daisy. 'But I want to hear what Horace has to say, as it's bound to be bad news, and it's best to be prepared.'

'Good idea,' she whispered back.

Daisy knew as well as anyone that a woman's fate could be changed irrevocably and often detrimentally by a man's decision. The sooner women were able to decide their own fates, control their own finances and live their own lives the way they wanted to, the better. But now was perhaps not the best time to make that particular speech. Instead, she remained quiet, leaned forward and gave all her attention to the conversation taking place on the terrace.

Chapter Five

Guy stared out at the estate while his cousin attempted to catch his breath. Horace had been a greedy, overbearing and cruel child. Now that he was an adult, nothing had changed. Or perhaps it had. He had got worse. Whatever plan he had in mind, Guy knew it would benefit Horace and be to the detriment of someone else.

Perspiration still dotting his brow, Horace clasped his waist. 'Need to sit down for a while,' he huffed, moving over to the stone bench.

'What brings you here, Horace?' *What devious scheme do you have up your sleeve?*

Horace took in a few more panting breaths and held up his hand to inform Guy he had to wait. Then he reached into his jacket and removed a letter from the inside pocket.

'This has recently come into my possession. Think you'll find it interesting.' He smirked, alerting Guy that its contents would be of interest to no one but Horace.

Guy extended his hand to take the letter but Horace

pulled it away, that smirk still on his face. 'If you want to read it, and I strongly recommend that you do, you're going to have to do so while I'm holding it. Wouldn't want you to tear it up.'

The man really was insufferable. Guy was tempted to walk back into the drawing room and leave his cousin sitting alone on the terrace. That would hopefully wipe away that look of self-satisfaction. But if Horace was up to something devious, and it was certain that he would be, it was always best to know what it was so his plans could be outwitted before they caused any damage. So Guy sat down beside him and skimmed the letter Horace held out to him. It appeared to be a love letter from a woman, one who was excited about expecting a child.

'Very nice,' Guy said when he had finished.

'You must recognise the writing and the signature.' He pushed the letter closer to Guy.

Guy scanned the letter again and looked at the signature, a quickly scrawled *AP*. He shrugged and shoved Horace's arm away from his face.

'Annabella Parnell,' Horace said with satisfaction. 'This is a letter from your mother to your father.'

Guy said nothing, knowing this could not be the end of it. Horace looked far too pleased with himself for that to be the case.

'A man called Boysie.'

The self-satisfied grin grew wider, while Guy fought to keep his own face impassive, determined to reveal nothing to his irritating cousin.

'Your father, or should I say the late Duke of Mandivale, was called Hubert, not Boysie. Your mother wrote a letter to a man called Boysie when she was pregnant, discussing the birth of their child. You.'

Guy continued to stare straight ahead.

'You know what that means?' Horace folded up the letter, placed it back in his pocket, patted his jacket, as if making sure the letter was still there, and smirked again at Guy. 'It's as I always suspected. You should never have inherited the title from your father—or I should say, the man you thought was your father. And you know what else this means, don't you?'

Guy did not give him the satisfaction of answering but stood up and walked towards the edge of the terrace, gripped the balustrade tightly and swallowed down his anger. He would not give his cousin the pleasure of seeing him agitated.

Horace hauled himself to his feet and followed. 'It means I'm the rightful duke.' He waved his hand in a wide arc. 'And all this is mine.'

'That letter proves nothing,' Guy said through clenched teeth, the iron of the balustrade digging into his hands.

'I've already contacted my lawyers. They have assured me I have an excellent case and am sure to win. You had better make the most of your last days here at Mandivale and start thinking about where you're going to live and what you're going to live on now that you're a commoner.' He smirked again.

'How did this come into your possession?' Guy asked, fighting to keep his voice level.

'You don't need to know that. All you need to know is that it is genuine.'

Guy continued to stare out over the grounds.

'So, shall we join the ladies?' Horace said.

Not waiting for Guy's answer, he turned and walked back through the French doors. Guy waited a few moments to absorb the implications of Horace's latest scheme. As a child, nothing would have given Guy more pleasure than to know that the cold, remote Duke of Mandivale was not his father. He had often fantasised that someone would discover that he was actually a Springfeld, and he would be officially taken into that loving family, but he most certainly did not want that now. If he lost the dukedom to his cousin, it would be a disaster.

The man had often said Guy should evict many of his tenants, particularly the ones who were now elderly and no longer able to work their land. If those tenants were evicted, they would have nowhere to go. They would be separated from the people they knew and loved and would have no means of supporting themselves. After years of loyal service, they were entitled to spend their old age in their own homes, in comfort, surrounded by family and friends.

But Horace cared nothing for that. He was a selfish man who thought only of maximising profit and nothing of whether people were hurt by his actions. He would be a disaster as duke. But he was right. If Guy had not been his father's legitimate heir, then Horace would have been next in line, and the letter did suggest that. Somehow, Guy was going to have to prove that the letter was a fake and the late duke really was his father. But how, he had not the slightest idea.

He re-entered the drawing room in time to hear Horace make his cheerful goodbyes to Daisy and Florence. With one last look in Guy's direction, he headed out of the room. Guy turned to the windows and watched him descend the steps towards his carriage. Despite his girth, the man almost had a spring in his step. He stopped. His hands on his hips, his feet planted wide, he looked around, as if surveying his new property, then turned to face the house. Seeing Guy at the window, he sent his cousin a salute, his stance reminding Guy of a victorious general looking in triumph over a body-strewn battlefield.

If Daisy could have walked she'd have excused herself and left the two cousins alone to share this family disaster without the unwanted intrusion of an outsider. But she was stuck. She couldn't even go to Florence and try to comfort her. And her pale face and trembling hands made it obvious she was greatly in need of comfort.

'Florence, please, sit down. You look like you're about to faint,' Daisy said, indicating the chair next to her and wishing she could lead her to it and help her sit.

'This is terrible, terrible…' Florence gasped as she staggered forward and dropped into the nearest chair. 'My brother cannot become the duke. Only yesterday he was saying that a village as small as ours should not have two haberdasheries, and you should refuse to renew the tenancy on one of them. He doesn't care if he destroys a family's livelihood. And he's always saying you don't charge nearly enough rent on all the village businesses. Oh, he can't become the duke…he just can't. Too many people would suffer.'

'I'm sure it won't come to that,' Daisy said in reassurance, not actually sure of anything.

She looked up at Guy, hoping against hope that he could make everything all right for himself and for his cousin. He turned from the window, his face dark with rage, his jaw granite-hard, making his face barely recognisable. He looked over at Florence then rushed across the room, pulled the young woman to her feet, took her in his arms and gently rubbed his hand along her back.

'Don't worry, Florence,' he soothed. 'He's come up with outlandish schemes in the past and they've always failed. That letter is bound to be a fake and I'm sure my lawyers will prove that it is.'

It was the second time today Daisy had seen a woman in Guy's arms. With Ruby, he had embraced her like a lover. Now he was embracing Florence to comfort her. Once again Daisy had to fight off the ridiculous awareness that she would never be embraced by Guy Parnell, would never feel his strong arms around her—not in comfort, and certainly not in passion.

Florence rested her head on Guy's shoulder. She couldn't see his expression, but Daisy could. It was an expression she had never seen on Guy's face before and it looked suspiciously like worry.

He looked up, his eyes meeting Daisy's, and that charming smile returned, even though it did not reach his eyes. His gentle words and soothing touch might be fooling Florence, but not Daisy. Guy thought Horace might be right—that he was indeed the rightful Duke of Mandivale.

'Let's just forget all about the boorish Horace and his irritating schemes, shall we? We don't want him to ruin all our fun, do we?' he cajoled, placing his hands on Florence's shoulders and lowering her back to her chair. 'Perhaps you should divert yourself with your embroidery.' Guy indicated the abandoned basket that Florence had brought with her.

Listlessly, she pulled out some linen and thread and clasped it in her hands.

'And you, Daisy, perhaps you can entertain us with some tales of your cycling adventures. I'm sure falling into a ditch is not the only interesting thing that has happened to you.'

His attempt at bonhomie was not fooling Daisy, and had done little to assuage Florence's fearful expression, but she did her best to oblige. She regaled them with a tale of how the High-Wheeling Ladies' Cycling Association had invaded a male-only cycling race, demanding that it be open to female riders, to the horror of most of the men but to the delight of some. It had caused quite a stir at the time and had even made the local newspaper. They both laughed politely and asked questions, but the worry etched on their faces made it obvious they were giving only half their attention to her story.

She was running out of anecdotes when another carriage rolled up the driveway. She hoped it was not another visitor bringing bad news, but when the carriage door opened Nathaniel jumped out.

'Nate's here!' Daisy cried out, forgetting that she had a twisted ankle and attempting to rise.

Both Florence and Guy turned towards the window, Guy's smile becoming genuine for the first time since Cousin Horace's arrival. He jumped up and quickly left the room. Through the still open window, Daisy saw him race down the steps and greet her brother with much back-slapping and feigned boxing. Then the two all but ran up the steps and erupted into the room.

'Daisy, how are you? How bad is it? What did the doctor say? How long before you're better?' Nathaniel demanded in a rush, taking her hands and kneeling beside her chair.

'I'm all right,' she assured her brother as he kissed her on both cheeks. 'The doctor said it was just a twisted ankle, nothing to worry about. I should be up and about in no time at all.'

'Thank goodness. Guy's telegram said you weren't badly hurt, but Mother was so worried. I'll send her another telegram to reassure her that you're quite well.'

'In the meantime,' Guy said. 'May I present my cousin, Florence Parnell? Florence, this is Nathaniel Springfeld, Viscount Wentworth.'

Florence stood, her hands held lightly together in front of her, her eyes lowered, and gave a small curtsy. Nathaniel stood and turned towards her. Then the most peculiar thing happened. His lips parted slightly and his eyes softened. In fact, his entire face appeared to soften, and his cheeks turned an unexpected shade of pink.

'Delighted,' he finally said, his voice slightly choked.

Daisy and Guy exchanged a curious look. Guy was

no doubt thinking the same as she. When had Nathaniel ever reacted in that manner when being introduced to a young lady?

'What are you embroidering?' Nathaniel asked, slowly approaching Florence.

Florence looked down at the material in her hand, as if surprised to find it there. 'Oh, this? It's nothing, just a linen napkin to add to my...my trousseau.' Florence turned the same shade of pink as Nathaniel, causing Guy and Daisy to exchange another look.

'May I see?' Nathaniel asked, signalling towards the sofa where they could sit together.

'It looks like I might have to send that telegram on your brother's behalf. He appears to have become somewhat distracted,' Guy said quietly to Daisy. 'And it seems your chaperons have forgotten you even exist.'

'Well, at least it's stopped Florence from worrying about her brother, which is more than my cycling tales could do.'

They both looked over at Florence and Nathaniel, who were using an examination of the embroidery for their hands to get rather close to each other.

'He's got three sisters and he's never once taken any interest in our embroidery,' Daisy continued in a whisper although, given that all three of Nathaniel's sisters showed a decided lack of expertise in the feminine arts, that wasn't a surprise. 'Perhaps we need to reverse roles and become their chaperons,' she added, causing Guy to smile.

'Let's put them to the test, shall we?' he said, and actually winked at Daisy. 'Florence, would you like to show Nate round the grounds? It's been a long time since he's visited Mandivale and there have been a lot of changes since I became Duke.'

Nathaniel was instantly on his feet, offering his hand to Florence. 'That would be delightful, and I do need to stretch my legs after that trip from London.'

Florence coyly placed her hand in his and sent him a shy smile. Without a backward glance, they left the room. Guy and Daisy turned towards the window and watched them walk down the drive, their heads leaning in towards each other.

'So are you going to tell me what's happening?' Daisy asked, once her brother and Florence had turned a corner and disappeared behind the garden wall.

'I think that's obvious. Your brother has just fallen in love with my cousin.'

'I'm not talking about...' She turned back to the window. 'Do you think so?'

'Undeniably. I've never seen Nate so instantly smitten. In fact, I've never seen him smitten before, instantly or otherwise.' He turned to Daisy. 'I believe, Daisy Chain, what we just witnessed was love at first sight.'

So that was what love looked like, Daisy mused to herself, still staring at the drive even though Florence and Nathaniel were no longer visible. All soft and mushy, like chocolate that had been left in the sun. Then she remembered what she had meant to say and turned back to Guy. 'But do you really think Horace's letter could be a fake?'

Guy shrugged. 'I don't know. It looked genuine enough.' His attempt at nonchalance was not fooling

Daisy. That tension had returned to his jaw. She knew she shouldn't ask, but she wanted to help, and couldn't do so unless she knew all the facts.

'Did it look like your mother's writing, her signature?' she asked quietly.

He shrugged again. 'I've no idea. Obviously I received no letters from my mother.'

Daisy sighed sadly. His mother had died in childbirth, so of course he would not have received letters from her.

'Are there any letters in the house that she wrote to anyone else?'

His eyebrows drew together and he slowly nodded. 'Yes, I believe there are. In my father's study, I believe there are some letters she wrote to my father before they married.'

'Perhaps we should look at them and see if the signature and writing is the same. If it's not, then Horace's letter will definitely be a fake.'

He continued nodding and a smile crept across his face, this time a genuine one. 'Good thinking, Daisy. You wait here. I'll go and fetch them.'

He went quickly from the room before Daisy had a chance to remind him that she had a twisted ankle and was incapable of doing anything except wait for him.

Chapter Six

Guy paused at the door of his father's study. It was Guy's study now, as was everything in the Mandivale estate, but in his mind this room would always belong to his father, and would always be a place of foreboding.

Unclenching his fists, he turned the handle and entered before he had time to change his mind. Once inside, with the door shut behind him, he closed his eyes, fighting off that familiar childhood fear that had possessed him every time he'd stood on the oriental carpet in front of his father's desk.

He forced his eyes open and looked around. The room was much the same as it had been when he'd been a child. It even smelt the same, musty and oppressive, and Guy was sure his father's cigar smoke still lingered in the air, even though the former duke had been dead for five years.

The mahogany desk and bookshelves full of old account books and ledgers had remained untouched since his father's time, although now layers of dust covered them. Spiders had even had the audacity to spin their webs on the top shelves.

Guy never used this room, had never intended to do so. The last time he'd entered the study was just after his father had died when he'd retrieved the estate's latest account books. He had done so with as much haste as possible, then told the servants to leave it as it was. The unkempt state of the room would have horrified his father, and that gave Guy some satisfaction. Horrifying his father had almost become a mission for Guy when the old man had been alive and, even now, every time he did something he knew his father would have disapproved of, he took pleasure in the thought of the old man spinning uncomfortably in his grave.

He moved his shoulders to loosen the gripping tension. The only time his father had paid him any attention was in this room. He would be summoned to the study so his father could, as he phrased it, 'beat some sense into his disappointment of a son'. No doubt the leather strap was still hanging in the cupboard, waiting to be raised once again in anger, but Guy would not bother to find out.

Those disciplinary sessions might not have changed his behaviour, but they had taught him one valuable lesson. He had eventually learnt how to be impervious to the neglect, to the beatings and the constant reminders that he, a useless, good-for-nothing son, had taken the life of his mother.

He shook his head to drive out any memories of his father. As a child, he had fought hard to learn that lesson. It would be foolish to let that cold-hearted man's behaviour affect him now.

Instead, he strode across the room and ripped open the desk drawers, tipped the contents onto the floor and rifled through his father's possessions. His satisfaction grew with the mounting mess. He was proving to his father that none of those beatings had worked. He was still an ill-disciplined wastrel and always would be.

When he reached the bottom drawer, he found what he was looking for. Piles of letters, some tied together with ribbons, others opened and strewn haphazardly around the drawer. He picked up the beribboned piles, one pile neatly addressed in what was clearly his father's firm handwriting, the other written in a more feminine style that must be his mother's.

He looked down at the disorderly pile of half-open letters. That was not like his meticulous father, whose insistence that everything be kept in a pristine, orderly fashion bordered on the fanatic.

The disorder did, however, answer one question. Where Horace had found his mother's letter. In future Guy would be keeping a close eye on his cousin when he visited the Mandivale estate.

He traced his fingers slowly over the faded blue ink on his mother's letters. Horace's theft didn't answer the second question. Was the letter genuine? The one he had shown Guy could have been real, or he could have stolen a letter to get an example of her handwriting so he could make a forgery.

There was only one way to find out. He bundled them all up and strode out of the room, slamming the door behind him. As he walked away from the study, the pain in his chest diminished with each step until by the time he returned to the drawing room he had all but forgotten about his bully of a father.

Daisy looked up when he entered, a neglected book lying in her lap. 'So, what did you find?' she asked, looking at the pile of papers in his hands.

He placed them on the table beside her. 'Letters. Lots of letters.'

'So, does the handwriting look like the one in the letter Horace showed you?'

He picked up the pile of letters with feminine handwriting, untied the purple ribbon and opened the top letter. His heart sank. 'Yes, exactly the same. And the signature is the same as well, although this one has "AG" not "AP". My mother's maiden name was Giles. She entwined the initials in exactly the same way.' He angled the letter towards Daisy so she could see for herself.

'Oh, Guy, I am so, so sorry.'

He looked back down at the letter, which was addressed to his father, and read the first words.

My dear lord, the Duke of Mandivale

His throat constricted, his eyes itching, Guy could bring himself to read no more.

'I suppose that's it,' he said with forced indifference, placing the letter back on the table. 'When the lawyers see these letters, it will all be over, and Horace will take possession of everything.'

She lightly touched his arm. 'I am so sorry, Guy.'

'But there is one good thing to come out of this.' He forced out a laugh. 'It means that man was not my father. It also might explain why he treated me with such disdain. Perhaps he always suspected I was not his.'

'The way your father treated you was so unfair. And this is also unfair.' She waved her hand over the pile of letters.

He shrugged, as if dismissing the unfairness of his father and the unfairness of the Mandivale estate once again becoming the property of a bully. 'It matters not,' he said as much to convince himself as Daisy.

They sat in silence for a minute, both looking out at the bright summer's day. His gaze moved back to the abandoned pile of letters. He picked up the top one, stared at his mother's writing and traced a finger along her elegant penmanship. 'But perhaps I should read these,' he said, as if to himself.

He sat up straighter, aware that his mother's letters should command a more respectful posture. 'Maybe I'll learn more about my mother, and somewhere in this pile I might learn how my father…' He breathed in deeply and exhaled slowly. 'How the late Duke of Mandivale drove my mother into the arms of another man.'

He looked at Daisy, who was nodding slowly, her eyes still sad. 'Are you sure you want to know what happened? Why she…? How your father…?'

Guy looked down at the letters. 'No, I'm not sure, but I do want to read her letters.'

She smiled a sad, gentle smile and he knew, whatever he discovered, there was no one he'd rather share it with.

'I never knew my mother and have always thought of her as some sort of saint-like person.' He looked at the letter cradled in his hands. 'I suppose I'd always imagined that, if she had lived, my life would have been different. So, yes, it's a bit hard to have those childhood illusions shattered and to know that she was an adulteress.'

'Oh, Guy,' Daisy murmured.

'But I do want to know what she was like, and saints don't really exist, do they?' he said with a shrug. 'She was a real woman, one who perhaps took comfort with another man because she was so unhappy being married to my father. Or maybe she was like many people of our class, and had been forced into a loveless marriage, and this Boysie...my father...was the man she really loved.'

He looked back at Daisy and smiled to reassure her that there was no need to feel sad for him. 'There's only one way to find out what my mother was really like,' he said with more briskness than he felt. 'And, if nothing else, it will pass the time while you convalesce. So, are you up for some letter-reading, Daisy Chain?'

Still biting her lower lip, she slowly nodded.

He handed her the pile of letters written by the former Duke of Mandivale. While he wanted to know more about his mother, he had no interest in reading that man's words. Just looking at his handwriting sent a shiver through him, reminding him of all those missives he'd received at boarding school, demanding that he must change his ways if he was ever to be worthy of the title of Duke. Well, he hadn't changed his ways, and it looked as though his father had been right—he wasn't worthy of the title.

Instead, he reopened the letter written by his mother and skimmed the contents.

'What does it say?' Daisy asked, leaning forward.

'She's just discussing a ball they both attended and informing him she would be pleased to ride out with him on Sunday.'

'Oh, well, that doesn't tell us much. Read the next one.'

He took another letter from the pile. It was in a similar vein. Unlike the letter Horace had shown him, it was all very matter-of-fact and contained none of the passionate prose she had addressed to Boysie.

'She's saying how much she had enjoyed their time together and is looking forward to seeing him at the next ball.' He handed the letter to Daisy.

She read it and replaced it in the envelope. 'You said the writing looks the same, but perhaps Horace's is a forgery. Someone might have copied the way she wrote, but what of her way of expressing herself? Is that the same? Because that won't be so easy to fake.'

Guy wondered how much he should tell Daisy. She was no longer a child, and her curiosity was obvious. She already knew that his mother was an adulteress and had shown no shock at that revelation. Her reaction had been one of concern, for him and Florence. Perhaps little Daisy Chain could be told the whole truth. 'The letter Horace showed me was a love letter, full of affection and, dare I say it, passionate longing. These are all rather formal and rather dull, so it's hard to tell.'

'Oh, well, keep on reading.' She bit her lip, and he knew what she was thinking. Maybe they'd find some letters that alluded to this Boysie person. Then they'd know for certain that Horace's letter was genuine.

He read another letter. It too was perfectly polite and revealed nothing. 'This might be a waste of time,' he said as he handed the letter to Daisy.

'Oh, no, surely not?' she said. 'We've only just begun. I'm sure if we continued we'll...' She looked up at him with those big blue eyes. 'But of course, it is up to you. If it is too painful, we should stop.'

Guy considered her words. Yes, it was painful. It was painful to discover that you were illegitimate. It was painful to know your mother was an adulteress. And painful to know that Horace was the rightful heir. But he had experienced pain before and was well-schooled in how to ignore it. And he did want to know more about his mother's life.

'All right. You read some of my father's letters. Let's see what that old...what the late duke has to say for himself. Maybe he'll mention Boysie and we'll find out who he was, be it a friend, a servant...' he gave a humourless laugh '...or a passing scoundrel who seduced my mother. It would make more sense that a man like that was my father than the late Duke.'

She frowned in disapproval, then looked at the letters. 'Are you sure?'

He didn't want to read the old man's words himself, but he was curious as to what his letters might reveal, so he nodded. Daisy opened the first letter in the pile and he braced himself, waiting to hear what the former

Duke had to say, and reminding himself that words could not hurt you.

Her eyes grew wide as she scanned the letter. 'Oh, he's a bit more enamoured with your mother than she was with him.' She looked up at him then her gaze dropped back to the letter. 'Right from their first meeting, he was infatuated. Listen to this. *"My dearest Miss Giles, If you would do me the greatest honour of allowing me to escort you as we ride in Hyde Park next Sunday it would fill me with a great deal of happiness. Yours, Hubert Parnell, Duke of Mandivale, your most devoted servant".*'

'That doesn't sound particularly enamoured to me,' Guy said, waving away Daisy's offer to let him read it for himself.

'It is. They've only just met and he's already gushing over her. Most first letters are very formal and merely invitations.'

'Oh, you've had a few of them, have you?'

'Yes, I have, actually,' she shot back and scowled at him.

'And how many have you accepted?'

To that, she merely shrugged and picked up the next letter in the pile. 'Oh, it looks like they had rather a good time in Hyde Park. Your father certainly enjoyed himself. *"My dearest Annabella..."*' She looked at Guy. 'Your father is already using her first name, and it's only his second letter to her, and they've only met twice.' She waited for him to acknowledge that he understood the significance of this.

He nodded and signalled for her to continue.

She looked back down at the letter. '"*I'll always remember our time beside the Serpentine and all the fun we had together...*" I wonder what happened beside the Serpentine?'

'My father probably drowned a duck.'

She laughed. 'I don't think so. What does your mother say in response?'

He picked up the next letter. '"*My dearest Mandivale, I too enjoyed our time together at the Serpentine, but you were a very naughty boy.*"' He looked up at Daisy. 'I was right. He did drown a duck after all.'

She swatted him with her hand. 'Carry on—what else does she say?'

He looked back down at the letter. '"*And naughty boys should be punished.*"'

They stared at each other, both wide-eyed, then Daisy's hand moved to her mouth to stifle a giggle. 'I think your mother is getting a bit saucy.'

Guy suspected she was right and such letters were not suitable for a young lady's innocent eyes and ears. 'Perhaps we should stop reading these,' he said, folding up the letter.

'We can't!' Daisy cried out, picking up the next one. 'The only way we'll know the truth is if we keep reading.'

Before he could stop her, she opened the next letter and quickly read its contents. 'Oh, he rather likes that saucy side of her nature. Listen to this. "*My dearest, darling Annabella...*"' She looked up, her eyes wide, making sure the affection in the opening was not lost on him. '"*I look forward to my punishment and please do not hold back. The harder, the better, I always say."* Oh, this is starting to get good!' she said as she pulled open another letter, her eyes moving rapidly over the written words. She put it down and looked at him, her teeth nibbling on her bottom lip. 'I'm not sure you're going to want to hear this.'

Guy cringed. How much worse could it get than knowing that his father liked to be punished, the harder, the better? 'Go ahead.'

She drew in a breath and placed her hand on her stomach. '"*My darling, my Bella, my sweetheart. Kissing your lovely lips has left me so discomposed I can hardly think, can hardly sleep. I must taste your sweet honey again, soon and often. Please tell me you were not just taunting me, and that one day you will let me feast myself fully on all your sweetness.*"' Once again biting her lip, she looked over at him, blushing. 'Well, I never. It's only the second or third time they've met and they're already kissing.'

Guy was unsure what that meant. Did it mean they were consumed with passion for each other, or did it mean his mother had given out her kisses freely, including to men who were not her husband?

'This is not a good sign,' he said, reaching for the next letter in his mother's pile.

'What does she say about him wanting to be punished? How does she feel about the kiss?'

Guy looked down at the letter, then back up at Daisy, and suppressed a smile. 'You're getting rather excited by this, aren't you?'

She crossed her arms and scowled at him. 'I am not. I'm just curious to know what happened.'

'And I'm not sure if this is suitable reading material for someone as young as you,' he teased.

'Don't be ridiculous. I'm not a child. Now, read it out loud.'

He stifled a smile. 'Well, if you insist.'

'I do, I do. What did she say?' She shuffled forward in her seat and tried to look over the top of the letter to read it upside down. 'But, I mean, only if you want to,' she said, sitting up, her eyes moving between him and the paper he held.

He gave a small laugh at her attempt to cover her eagerness.

'"My darling Hubert, my darling Duke, my darling Mandivale..."' He shook his head. How anyone could call that man 'darling' he would never understand. *'"I am so hungry for your kisses..."'*

He stopped reading, folded up the letter and replaced it in the envelope. He wanted to know more about his mother, but there were some things a son did not need to know.

'Gosh!' Daisy gasped. 'She was hungry for him.' She bit her bottom lip again and her teeth ran slowly across the soft, full flesh, as if imagining what it was like to hunger for a man's kisses. Unable to look away, Guy watched her lovely lips part slightly. Was that an invitation?

He forced his gaze to move from her lips up to her eyes. She held his gaze, her lips still parted, her cheeks still flushed, her eyes sparkling.

This was Daisy Chain, he fought to remind himself as he looked into those enticing big blue eyes. He should not be thinking of kissing her, tasting her, savouring her sweet honey.

'I wonder what he had to reply to that,' she continued, picking up the next letter in the pile before he could stop her. Clasping the neck of her blouse, she scanned the letter. 'Goodness, listen to this,' she said.

Guy was about to tell her he had no interest in listening to the man's response when she grasped his arm.

'Stop!' she cried out. He looked round to see what he was supposed to stop doing.

'Florence and Nathaniel are coming. Quick, hide the letters.'

Guy turned to the window and saw the couple strolling up the gravel pathway, arm in arm, chatting and laughing together.

'Quickly, quickly!' Daisy cried, her hands still clamped to his arm. 'Hide them before they get here.'

Guy did as she ordered. He pushed the letters together into an untidy pile, rushed over to the sideboard and shoved them in a drawer while Daisy anxiously watched the couple's arrival. He wasn't sure why he was doing so. After all, they were merely trying to find out whether or not Horace's letter was genuine. But as he slammed shut the drawer, he sighed with relief, as if they had avoided being caught doing something they shouldn't.

Florence and Nathaniel entered the room, bringing with them carefree laughter and joy. Guy returned to his chair and tried not to look guilty. And why should he?

He had done nothing wrong. Perhaps they should not have been reading his parents' private correspondence, but they were doing it for a perfectly innocent reason. No, he had absolutely nothing to feel guilty about.

He looked over at Daisy. She was staring straight ahead, her body rigid, her cheeks still flushed and looking the very epitome of guilt, although she had even less about which to feel ashamed than did he.

He glanced at Nathaniel and Florence, hoping they could detect nothing amiss, but they were paying no attention to Daisy or Guy, too absorbed in each other's company.

He shot a quick look over to the sideboard to make sure he had fully closed the drawer, then back at Daisy. Her gaze was now flicking between the sideboard, Guy and the other couple.

It was so easy to read her thoughts. She wanted them to be alone together again so they could continue reading the letters. Their content had obviously excited her. Was that the reason he felt so guilty? Or did it have nothing to do with the letters? Was it because he had just done the unforgivable and actually imagined kissing his best friend's little sister?

Chapter Seven

The words ‘lips’, ‘honey’ and ‘hunger’ circled round and round in Daisy’s mind, making her already warm cheeks hotter and further inflaming that unfamiliar reaction deep inside her body, the one that was both disturbing and somewhat delicious.

Florence and Nathaniel were recounting a story, something about walking down to the river and seeing a turtle dove’s nest. Daisy could hardly hear a word they were saying, but she nodded anyway, as if fully engaged in the conversation.

As pleased as she was to have her brother’s company, she wished he and Florence would decide to go on another walk so she and Guy could get back to reading the letters. She sent a quick glance towards the sideboard and told herself they were doing nothing wrong. They wanted to get to the bottom of the mystery, that was all. They had no choice but to read his parents’ private correspondence.

Daisy hadn’t known what to expect, but what she hadn’t expected was how the letters would affect her in such a physical way. Reading them sent such a delicious thrill through her entire body. It was as if she too was caught up in the throes of passion. She ran her tongue along her bottom lip. It was as if she could actually feel what it must be like to have a man devour her with kisses, to be caught up in an intensity of desire so strong you hungered for it.

Was that how Lady Penrose and Ruby Lovelace had felt when they'd been in Guy's arms? The expression on Lady Penrose's face had certainly suggested it, and Ruby Lovelace had not minced her words when she'd described the pleasure Guy had given her. Those women knew what it was like to be kissed and caressed by Guy, and more—much more.

She flicked a quick look in his direction, then lowered her eyes and swallowed. Would she ever know such passion? Would she ever look at a man the way Lady Penrose had looked at Guy, with complete contentment and happiness? Would she ever feel the ecstasy that Ruby Lovelace had experienced in Guy's bed? Would she ever know the passion for a man that had been expressed in the letters?

She wanted her freedom, never wanted to be tied down by marriage, but was she sacrificing too much? Her gaze moved to the drawer hiding those letters.

The couple in the letters had not yet been married. Neither Lady Penrose nor Ruby Lovelace were married to Guy, but that hadn't stopped them from taking pleasure in his bed, so why should she deny herself?

She cast another quick look in his direction and was once again struck by what a physically attractive man he had grown into. Could she too take pleasure in Guy's bed, experience what those women had experienced? To do so would ruin her reputation, but what did that actually matter? She bit her bottom lip, outraged at the direction in which her thoughts were taking her. No young lady should think such things. And yet, after reading those letters, it was all she could think of.

Guy caught her eye. She quickly looked away, the heat on her cheeks intensifying, and hoped he could not read her mind or that her blushes had revealed the effect the letters had on her.

She sat up straighter in her chair and told herself that when they recommenced reading the letters she would focus solely on their task. They were trying to ascertain whether Horace's letter was real or a forgery and, if it *was* real, if the letters contained any hints as to who Guy's father really was. Anything else the letters revealed was of no consequence.

Her cheeks cooling, that peculiar throbbing sensation that had erupted deep in her body dying down, she turned to her brother and smiled as if she had heard every word he had said.

'A turtle dove's nest, how fascinating,' she said, causing all three to look in her direction and pause. Damn, the conversation had obviously moved on. Guy sent her a curious look, but Florence smiled back at her.

'Yes, we'll have to show it to you when you're able to walk again,' Florence said.

Daisy had no real interest in birds, but she nodded. 'Yes, that will be wonderful. I just love birds, turtle doves in particular,' she said enthusiastically, causing both Guy and Nathaniel to send her perplexed frowns. Daisy liked birds as much as the next person, but could not tell a turtle dove from a turkey—something Guy and Nathaniel were sure to know.

All right, all right, she wanted to shout at them. *You have both known me long enough to know I'm just being polite. But talking about birds won't make me blush the way thinking about hungry kisses did.*

As the chatter continued, Daisy forced herself to focus on the conversation and not to look at the sideboard.

Fortunately, Nathaniel and Florence did most of the talking and Daisy was merely required to give the occasional nod of agreement, to laugh when expected or to add the odd word or two of encouragement.

A light knock on the door interrupted them and a footman entered to ask Guy where he would like dinner to be served. Everyone in the room looked over at Daisy, including the footman.

'It would be easiest if you set up the dining table in this room,' Guy said, then looked out of the window. 'Although, as it is a pleasant evening, perhaps we could dine on the terrace.' He turned to the others. 'And, as Daisy's luggage is yet to arrive, perhaps we should forgo changing for dinner this evening.'

This suggestion was greeted with enthusiasm by Nathaniel and Florence, a reaction which Daisy suspected was more about them not wanting to be parted rather than a lack of objection to changing into formal evening clothing.

The footman bowed and departed, then a few minutes later several servants entered carrying a white, wrought-iron table and four chairs, followed by the footman wheeling a high-backed cane chair with rolled arms, large wheels on the side and a smaller wheel at the front.

'Well done, you've found Aunt Myrtle's wheelchair!' Guy exclaimed, standing up and examining the unusual piece of furniture.

The servant rolled the wheelchair over to Daisy, and both she and the footman stared at it as if unsure what it did.

'I believe you sit in it, my lady,' the footman said. 'Then you either use the wheels to push yourself along…' he pushed on one wheel to demonstrate '…or someone pushes you from behind.'

'I see,' Daisy said as she levered herself up.

Before she had reached a standing position, Guy was at her side. He lifted her up into his arms and placed her on the chair, picking up each foot and placing it on the raised footrest.

'Are you comfortable?' he asked as he tucked a cushion behind her back.

'Um, yes, very.'

'Right, you're ready for anything now, Daisy Chain,' he said, pushing her through the French doors and out onto the terrace. He parked her by the table then bent down to whisper in her ear. 'It doesn't go as fast as a bicycle, but I doubt if it will stop you from having children,' he said with a laugh.

Do not blush again, Daisy commanded herself. If he could joke about such things, then so could she. To that end, she laughed in what she hoped was a sophisticated fashion, causing Guy to frown at her in confusion.

Florence and Nathaniel moved through to the terrace at a somewhat slower pace. When they finally arrived, Nathaniel pulled out a chair for Florence and she sat down, also at a slower speed than usual. It seemed those two now did everything as if in a dream-like state. Once again Daisy and Guy exchanged looks and Guy mouthed the words, 'Smitten, completely smitten,' causing Daisy to giggle in a genuine, if less sophisticated, way.

The four dined happily together and, if it hadn't been for the pain in her foot, it would have been an idyllic evening. The garden was bathed in the soothing yellow glow of the early evening and birds fluttered between the trees, their chirping providing a musical backdrop to the conversation. Despite the worry that Horace's letter must be causing Florence and Guy, they both talked and laughed as if they had not a care in the world. But then, Daisy thought, Guy was a master at ignoring his problems and focusing only on the pleasure he was taking in the moment.

She knew from what her parents and Nathaniel had let slip that as a child he'd had a tumultuous home life. And yet, when he'd stayed with Daisy's family, he was always full of laughter and fun, as if that other world had not existed. She looked over at him as he recalled a funny anecdote for the group. Was that why he lived the way he did? Was that why he had so many women in his life? Was he trying to devote every minute of his time to immediate pleasure so he wouldn't have to think about any pain he might feel?

He turned to look at her and she realised she was staring at him and, unlike the others, she was not laughing at his story. She smiled quickly to cover up what she had been thinking. He didn't smile back, merely giving her a quizzical look.

'A penny for your thoughts, Daisy Chain,' he said, drawing everyone's attention.

'Oh, I don't think they'd even be worth that,' Daisy replied, and laughed, trying to give herself time to come up with something to say rather than tell Guy what she had really been thinking.

He raised his eyebrows and waited.

'I was wondering where the High-Wheeling Ladies' Cycling Association members were tonight and hoping my accident hadn't delayed them too much.'

'I see. It's a shame your accident meant you couldn't be with them,' Guy said.

Daisy nodded, unsure if that was true. As much as she loved cycling and spending time with the other ladies, she hadn't actually given them, or their trip around the Kent countryside, a second thought since she'd entered Guy's carriage. What on earth was wrong with her? Was she starting to fall under the spell of Guy Parnell, like so many other women had done before her? It seemed she was.

'Yes, it is a shame,' she said.

A shame that I'm allowing myself to forget what sort of man you have become. A shame that I'm forgetting what sort of young woman I am, one who does not fall for rakes.

The dinner over, Guy wheeled her back into the dining room, where the four entertained themselves by playing cards, chatting and laughing.

Guy and Nathaniel had quickly reverted back to their easy childhood friendship, and were even using their boyhood nicknames, Knife and Fork.

'You have to tell me,' Florence said, placing her hand on Nathaniel's, causing Guy to send Daisy another knowing look. 'Why do you call each other Knife and Fork?'

Nathaniel laughed and placed his other hand on top of Florence's. 'We've been calling each other that since we were children. It started when I called Guy "Fawkes", after Guy Fawkes. Daisy thought I was calling him "Forks", and Mother said that, as we were such inseparable friends, we should be called Knife and Fork, and the names just stuck.'

Florence laughed. 'Well, I'm going to have to think of a better name for you, one that suits you better than Knife. You're not at all sharp or cutting. You need a soft and cuddly nickname.'

While Nathaniel smiled in a soft and cuddly manner, Guy and Daisy rolled their eyes simultaneously.

'And Daisy, you're going to have to think of a better name for Guy.' Florence smiled briefly at Daisy, then turned back to gaze at Nathaniel in adoration. Daisy looked from Nathaniel to Guy, who raised his eyebrows in a comical fashion, as if they were sharing a joke. But it was no joke.

Was Florence actually thinking that they were now two couples? Well, they weren't. Florence might have set her heart on Nathaniel, and good luck to her if she had.

She seemed a nice enough young lady, and Nathaniel obviously thought so. But Daisy was most certainly not the perfect partner for Guy, nor was he the perfect partner for her. A rake and a modern, rational woman—that would never work, and Daisy did not want it to work. She had no intention of giving up her freedom for any man but, if she did—and it was a big if—it would be for a modern, rational man. One who treated women with respect and saw them as equals, not treated as disposable commodities to be used for the physical gratification they provided, the way Guy Parnell did.

Daisy squirmed slightly in her wheelchair, those annoying words 'lips', 'honey' and 'hunger' once again invading her mind and causing a not unpleasant but certainly unsettling tightness to grip her deep in her body.

'Are you all right, Daisy?' Guy asked, standing up. 'Is your foot paining you again?'

Daisy waved her hand in dismissal. 'No, it's all right, just a small twinge,' she lied to cover up her embarrassment.

'Would you like a cushion for your foot? Perhaps it should be elevated further,' he suggested, still standing, his brow furrowed.

'No, honestly. It's fine now. Please, sit down. It's your deal, I believe.'

Still frowning at her, he sat down and picked up the cards.

'You will tell me, won't you, if you are in any pain?' he asked.

'Yes, of course. Now, deal the cards,' she said with more impatience than she intended.

They continued to play, with Florence and Nathaniel's flirting becoming ever more obvious, but thankfully Florence made no more allusions to Guy and Daisy being a couple. Eventually, Florence announced that she was tired and would retire for the night, and the others agreed that they too thought it was getting rather late.

Guy called for a maid to help Daisy undress, and when she arrived everyone said their goodnights and departed.

The maid looked at the wheelchair as if unsure what it was and what she was supposed to do with it, so Daisy took hold of the wheels and, to the accompaniment of some rather disturbing squeaks, pushed herself through to the adjoining room. Thankfully, her trunk had arrived, so she'd finally be able to change out of her somewhat battered clothing.

A large bed had been set up in what was obviously another drawing room. The Queen Anne chairs, side tables and occasional tables had been pushed aside to accommodate the large bed, bedside table, dressing table and wash stand. They all looked rather incongruous in a room designed for entertaining, but it was eminently sensible. She would have been unable to make it up the stairs to the bedrooms unaided, and the last thing she wanted was for Guy Parnell to carry her once again.

The maid took her nightgown from the trunk, and with much wriggling managed to help Daisy out of her bloomers, jacket and blouse and into her white linen nightdress. She wheeled Daisy over to the bed, then placed an arm under her legs and one around her back in an attempt to hoist her onto the bed. The maid quickly discovered she was not up to the task.

'I'm sorry, m'lady, I think I'm going to have to get some help from one of the other maids.'

'No, it's all right, Molly. I'm sure I can do it myself,' Daisy said, hauling herself forward so she could get round the high sides of the cane wheelchair. 'Can I just use your shoulder for support?'

The maid crouched down so Daisy could rest on her shoulder and push herself up. She got into a standing position, hopped across the room, then supported herself with the side of the bed. Now all she had to do was climb up and swing her legs onto the bed.

Daisy looked at the bed, which presented almost as much challenge as the ditch had earlier in the day. It was too high for her easily to climb into, so she was going to have to be innovative. She tried grasping the bedclothes and pulling herself up, but even with Molly pushing from behind that got her nowhere. If only she could put a bit of weight on her left foot she'd be all right, but every time she tried to do so the pain reminded her of what a bad idea that was. After several more attempts, she admitted defeat.

'Drat it. I think you're going to have to get my brother to help, as I doubt if even another maid will be sufficient.'

'Yes, m'lady,' the maid said with a quick curtsey, before rushing out, leaving Daisy propped up against the bed like an abandoned and useless piece of furniture.

Daisy sighed. Feeling annoyed that she was so helpless, she made a few more attempts to scale the side of the bed before once again admitting defeat.

The maid soon re-entered, but instead of Nathaniel she was accompanied by Guy.

Daisy stared at him. Her breath caught in her throat and she gripped the bedclothes tightly, not sure if she was about to bury herself in them or was using them to hold her up, as her one good leg had turned to jelly.

'Nathaniel has retired for the night,' he explained. 'When Molly told me of your predicament, I said I'd help. We can't have you sleeping standing up, can we?'

Daisy stared at him, unable to speak, only aware that her heart was pounding so loudly in her chest she was sure he must be able to hear it, even from across the room. Guy Parnell was seeing her in her nightdress. Could there be a more uncomfortable situation in which to be? Not that it should matter, not really. The voluminous white gown covered her even more than her bloomers and stockings had. But, still, it was what she wore to bed and she wasn't wearing any undergarments. Underneath her nightdress she was completely naked.

Without waiting for her to comment or object, Guy crossed the room in a few strides, threw back the covers and in one quick movement picked her up, placed her in the middle of the bed then pulled up the bedclothes, covering her up to her neck.

It had all happened so quickly no one could say there had been any real impropriety, but that hadn't stopped Daisy's mortification from setting her entire body aflame.

'Goodnight, Daisy Chain,' he said with a bow, before leaving the room immediately. He had been present for but a few seconds. Nothing had happened. He had simply helped her out of a difficult predicament and the maid had been present the entire time.

While Daisy had foolishly reacted as if it were an intimate act between a man and a woman that should not have happened, it was obvious that seeing her in her nightgown and placing her in the bed meant nothing to Guy. It was an action performed by an older brother for a little sister in need of help, that was all. And that was how Daisy should be seeing it as well.

But her pounding heart, her gasping breath and the continued tingling where his arms and chest had touched her were making a lie of that assertion. No matter what she told herself, no matter how sophisticated she tried to be, no matter how nonchalant she tried to act, her treacherous body would not play along. She could only hope that her physical reaction, which she could not ignore, had not been noticed by Guy.

Chapter Eight

Guy always enjoyed spending time with his childhood friend, but now there was an added reason to be pleased to have his company. Nathaniel provided a constant reminder of who Daisy Springfeld was and why she was off-limits.

And he needed that reminder.

Lifting her into bed last night had severely tested him. He'd had plenty of women in his arms before—had carried many young ladies to his bed. He knew what desire felt like, was familiar with all the signs of lust, but last night had been different.

When he'd seen her standing beside her bed wearing only her nightgown, her long chestnut-brown hair cascading around her shoulders in gentle curls, raw intensity had hit him hard, leaving him breathless and reeling. As if holding temptation itself, he had looked down at her beautiful face, at those luscious, enticing red lips, and had felt her soft feminine curves under her nightdress calling to him like a siren's song. He had almost lost all sense of reason. Almost. Thank God he'd had enough decency to fight off the baser side of his nature.

The only thing that had stopped him from revealing the true extent of his dissolute character was placing her in the bed as fast as he could and making as hasty a departure as possible, hoping that in her innocence she had not noticed the obvious effect she'd had on him.

Why Daisy was so tempting, he could not fathom. She had grown into a desirable woman, of that there could be no denial, but a lot of women were desirable and he had never felt like a drowning man before, fighting against his lust as if it were a raging torrent. Was it simply because she was off-limits? Was it because she was forbidden fruit and that made the thought of picking her all the more desirable? If that was the case, then he *was* a complete scoundrel, and his reaction to her beauty was further proof that Daisy Springfeld should be kept safe from men like him—or, rather, men like him needed to learn to rein in their degenerate natures and learn to behave.

He stood at the drawing-room door, clasping the door handle, and remonstrated with himself one more time. From this moment forward, he would do nothing to make Daisy feel uncomfortable. He would suppress any lustful thoughts and remember at all times just who she was: his best friend's little sister, the youngest member of a family that had shown him nothing but kindness.

With that in mind, he opened the door and three faces turned towards him. Daisy, Nathaniel and Florence smiled up at him from the dining table and sent their cheerful greetings.

Guy released his held breath. Good. Daisy was not angry with him, nor was Nathaniel. His appalling behaviour had gone unnoticed and had not been reported to his best friend.

He served himself breakfast from the tureens set up on the sideboard, joined the others and tried not to pay any undue attention to Daisy.

This morning she was dressed in a more conventional manner. Gone were the rather amusing bloomers and striped stockings, which were replaced with a pale blue skirt and cream blouse. The blouse even had a few feminine ruffles on it, and some lace around her neck.

Should he tease her about her new clothes, make a jibe about whether lace and ruffles could be classed as rational? Teasing Daisy was what he always did. If he didn't, would the others think he was behaving in a peculiar manner? But, if he did tease her, would she think he was flirting with her? For the first time in his life, Guy was unsure of himself in a young lady's company.

And with Daisy that was not what he wanted. He would hate to lose that easy relationship they had, as if they were siblings. He should start teasing her again, act in exactly the same manner he always did. Or would it be better to avoid speaking to her at all to avoid revealing his inner turmoil?

He stabbed his fork into his bacon and eggs. *For God's sake, man, just be yourself.*

Fighting to think of something, anything to add to the conversation, he looked around the table. Nathaniel and Florence chatted happily but Daisy also seemed uncharacteristically quiet. He could only hope it wasn't because she had seen his unforgivable reaction last night and now felt awkward in his presence.

The moment the servants cleared away the breakfast dishes, Florence and Nathaniel stood up as one, as if they could read each other's thoughts.

'Florence has kindly offered to show me the glass houses,' Nathaniel announced. 'I believe you have an excellent selection of orchids that I'm just dying to see. Then we thought we'd go for a walk in the woodlands so we could visit those turtle doves we saw yesterday.'

Without waiting for a reply, they left the room, leaving Daisy and Guy staring at the closed door.

'Those two really are becoming rather keen walkers all of a sudden,' Guy said.

'And when has Nathaniel ever been interested in orchids? I'm surprised he even knows what an orchid is.'

They turned from the door, looked at each other, smiled and then sank back into silence, Daisy playing with the napkin on her lap.

'Did you sleep well last night?' Guy asked, then wished he had made no allusion to anything that involved her being in bed.

'Yes, thank you,' she said politely, causing Guy to cringe. She was obviously uncomfortable with him. Why else would she be talking in such a stilted, polite manner? It was as if they were now all but strangers.

'And I see your trunk has arrived,' he continued with forced politeness. 'You look lovely today, Daisy.' He cringed again. What on earth was he doing? He never complimented Daisy. Teased, yes. Flattered, never.

'So, you prefer this more conventional clothing to my riding bloomers, do you?'

The tension in his shoulders released. Thank goodness. There was the challenging voice he was used to.

'I think you look a delight, no matter what you wear,' he said, pleased that he had finally remembered how to tease. 'Bloomers, frills and lace or...' He coughed to cover his discomfort. He had almost said 'white nightdresses', but that would have been taking the teasing further than propriety or his own comfort level would allow.

'Or whatever you choose to wear,' he said instead. 'Anyway,' he rushed on. 'While Florence and Nate are indulging in their newfound love of all things horticultural, shall we take that wheelchair for a spin round the garden?'

She nodded and looked over at the sideboard, now cleared of breakfast tureens. 'And perhaps we could take the letters with us.'

Guy also looked over at the sideboard. He too was anxious to find the answer to his parentage, but would reading about his parents' courtship be entirely suitable? But he did need to know for certain whether Horace's letter was real. That was more important than his foolish and inappropriate thoughts about little Daisy Springfeld. That was what he should be focusing on, after all—his future and the future of his tenants depended on it.

He rose from his chair and crossed the room. 'Good idea, Daisy Chain,' he said, opening the drawer and retrieving the letters. He pulled her wheelchair out from the table and dropped the bundle in her lap.

'Right, let's see how fast this thing can go, shall we?' With that he wheeled her through the house and out the back door to avoid the front steps, then down the path towards the river, determined to keep his manner light and to recapture the playfulness that had always existed between them.

Nothing had changed. At least not for Guy. If Daisy needed any reminder of just how he thought of her, his nonchalant behaviour this morning would provide it. Last night, inappropriate thoughts and reactions had racked her mind and body. Being in her nightdress, in her bedroom, being lifted into her bed by Guy Parnell, had sent sizzling awareness coursing through every inch of her body. The fire his touch had ignited within her had consumed her throughout the night and invaded her dreams.

And this morning it was as if it had never happened. He was exactly the same. Seeing her in that state, holding her in his arms, had had no effect on him whatsoever. If he had seen Ruby Lovelace or Lady Penrose in their nightdress and carried them to bed, would he have made silly jokes the next day? Would he have teased them as if they were children? Daisy doubted that very much.

But then, she wasn't Lady Penrose or Ruby Lovelace. She was little Daisy Chain. He would never see her as anything else and, really, she should be grateful for that fact.

And, fortunately, she would be saved from last night's embarrassing encounter ever happening again. Once had been mortifying enough. If it was to become a nightly routine, she was sure she would die from embarrassment.

This morning, climbing out of bed had been much easier and had only required the assistance of the maid. The maid had informed her that Guy had arranged for the bed to be replaced with a lower one, one she could easily get into without the need to be carried. That was surely a thoughtful act, something else she should be grateful for, yet her first reaction had been disappointment.

That just showed what a naïve little fool she was, getting all excited because Guy had held her in his arms. Thank goodness he could not read her thoughts or he really would have lots of ammunition with which to tease her.

As the cane wheelchair creaked its way along the gravel pathway down towards the river, she gave herself yet another stern talking to. If Guy was incapable of seeing her in the way he saw other women, then she would not shame herself by letting him know that it had had even the slightest effect on her. Although, she knew that was not going to be easy.

It was the third time he had carried her, and each time the intensity of her reaction had increased. But no more. If he happened to pick her up again, she would simply ignore the intoxicating effect of his strong arms surrounding her. She would not notice the masculine strength pulsing through his muscles. She would not let his heady manly scent invade her awareness. Just like him, she would be completely unaffected by the experience. That was as it should be, and that was how it *would* be.

He parked her wheelchair beside a stone bench under a weeping willow tree. They both looked out at the tranquil river, sparkling in the warm summer sun, and paused to watch the quacking ducks going about their busy activities while two majestic white swans glided past.

'Will this spot do for you, m'lady, or would you prefer if I wheeled you to a more salubrious site?'

'No, my man, this will be adequate,' Daisy replied in an equally teasing voice. 'And please, sit down. You're messing up the scenery, standing around like that.'

'Very good,' he said, giving her a mock salute.

Daisy looked down at the letters on her lap, in two minds as to whether she really wanted to read them. It was essential that Guy find out the truth about Horace's letter, and if possible who Boysie actually was, but if she was to maintain her composure in Guy's presence, reading about kissing and courting was going to be something of a trial.

But then, since when had she not been up for a challenge? She would just have to see this as yet another test of her resolve to overcome adversity. Lady Featherstone always said that members of the High-Wheeling Ladies' Cycling Association should never shirk from a challenge, should not run from adversity but face it down and overcome it. Well, that was exactly what Daisy would do now.

She sat up straighter in her chair and handed the pile of his mother's letters to Guy. He opened the first letter, scanned the words, blew out a sigh of annoyance and placed it back in the envelope.

'No.' She picked up the letter and handed it back to him. 'You have to tell me what it said.'

'It's a letter from the time after they were engaged. That's all.'

'But I want to hear what she said.'

He made no move to reopen the letter, so she made a grab for the envelope.

'Oh, all right, if you insist.' He reopened and unfolded it. *'"My darling, Bertie..."'* He rolled his eyes. 'She still hasn't realised that that man was anything but a darling. Perhaps my mother had something wrong with her eyesight.'

'She was in love,' Daisy said quietly. 'And they do say that love is blind.'

'Hmm...' was his unconvinced response before he looked back down at the letter. *'"I can't wait. I simply can't wait to marry you,"'* he said, then folded up the letter.

'That's not all she said. I can see from here that the letter is longer than that. If we're to find the truth, you need to read out the entire letter, otherwise we'll never know whether the letters are in the same style as the one Horace showed you.' She tilted forward in her chair and attempted to take the letter from his hands, but he moved it away.

'Go on, read it.'

He exhaled loudly before unfolding the letter and

continuing. *'"Mother said it would not look right if we rushed our nuptials, as people might question my virtue. If only they knew what we had done, their questions would be answered, wouldn't they?"'* He looked up at Daisy. 'It seems my parents had rather lax morals.'

Daisy shrugged. 'I hardly think you're in a position to judge.'

He stared at her for a heartbeat, his eyes intense, and then he smiled. She so wished he wouldn't do that. While it was good that they were back to teasing each other, and he had apparently taken no offence by her judgement, his smiles were not conducive to her maintaining an air of nonchalance. Not when they caused her breath to catch in her throat and her heart seemingly to skip a beat. Not when it drew her attention to his lips. She quickly looked back up at his eyes, horrified that her gaze might have lingered too long on his soft, sensual lips, and distressed that she might have revealed too much.

'Yes, you're right,' he said, his voice thankfully still containing a teasing note. 'But it is a bit disconcerting to know one's parents—or should I say my mother and her husband—had, you know...' He circled his hand as if unsure of the correct phrase.

'Well, if they did...' Daisy followed his example and circled her hand in the air. '...then there's more chance that the late Duke is your father.'

'Yes, but doing that...' he repeated the circling gesture '...before marriage suggests my mother was a bit free with her favours, and a lawyer could argue if she was free with one man she could be equally free with another.'

'No, not at all,' Daisy shot back, louder than she'd intended. 'If she was in love with your father, and the letters suggest she was, that's different. She's not being free with her favours. She's giving herself to the man she loves and expressing her own love for him.' She crossed her arms to emphasise her point, unsure why it was so important for him to know that sometimes a woman could get caught up in a moment's passion and it did not mean she was loose.

He stared at her and then slowly nodded. 'Yes, perhaps you're right. But that doesn't excuse my father's behaviour. She was an innocent young woman. He should have used more self-control and not risked compromising her reputation. The man was obviously a complete cad.'

'Like father, like son,' she murmured.

'That is not fair,' he retorted, his words clipped. 'I have never compromised a young woman, nor have I ruined any woman's reputation. Unlike my so-called father, I have never seduced a virgin, and I never will.'

Heat exploded onto Daisy's cheeks and engulfed her entire body. She moved uncomfortably in her chair and stared out at the river. So much for trying to be nonchalant and sophisticated.

'I'm sorry, Daisy,' he murmured. 'I should not have said that.'

'No, it's me that should apologise,' Daisy said, her voice equally quiet. 'It's not my place to judge how you live your life.'

He looked down at the letter, breathed in deeply and exhaled loudly. 'But, if you're right, if it is a case of "like father like son", then it looks like I am the true Duke of Mandivale.' He gave a laugh, which to Daisy sounded somewhat forced. 'Perhaps my lawyer can use our equally disreputable behaviour to prove that the old duke, not Boysie, really was my father.'

Daisy forced herself to smile, to let him know she was no longer judging him and that she most certainly was not reacting in any way to his claim that he never seduced virgins.

He looked at the pile of letters on her lap. 'But perhaps I should read the rest of the letters in private after you return to London.'

'You can't do that,' she all but shouted. 'That would be cruel.' She placed her hands protectively over the letters and looked up at him beseechingly. 'Please, Guy, I want to know what happened,' she continued in a less strident manner.

'They are getting a bit too risqué for a young lady's ears. What would your mother think if she knew I was exposing you to such things?'

'Stop treating me like a child!' she said, with more force than she'd intended. 'I am not a child. I am a twenty-four-year-old woman. I'm almost as old as Lady Penrose, and I'm probably about the same age as Ruby Lovelace. I'm not a little girl any more.'

His gaze locked onto hers. 'I know you're not a little girl any more,' he said, his voice a low growl, his eyes burning into hers with an intensity that was both unnerving and exciting.

Daisy wanted to look away, but she couldn't. Her breath becoming shallow, her heartbeat pulsing through her body, she held his gaze. If she wanted him to treat her like an adult woman, not like an innocent child, she would have to act like one. Fighting to keep her breathing regular, she lifted her chin higher and stared deep into those velvet dark brown eyes surrounded by those thick black lashes. Her heartbeat accelerating her gaze moved down his face to his lips, those lovely, full, sculpted lips.

I'm not a little girl any more and I want you to kiss me. That was what she wanted to say to him, but knew she would never do so.

Slowly, she lowered her gaze to the letters in her hands. Perhaps she was still a child after all. A confused little girl who didn't know what she wanted. She didn't want Guy's attention, yet she craved it like a thirsty woman desperate for a cool drink. And, if she did get his attention, what then? She lost all courage, unsure what to do and what to say. She did not know how women made their interest in a man known. She was not like Lady Penrose or Ruby Lovelace, who could make their intentions very clear. Guy was right—she *was* an innocent young lady—but, damn it all, how she wished she wasn't.

Chapter Nine

Guy was emphatic. There would be no more letter reading sessions with Daisy. Finding the answers to his questions could wait until she returned to London. He had not been lying when he'd said he should not expose an innocent young lady to such things. Of course he should not. What on earth had he been thinking? His quest to thwart Horace had blinded him to the effect such letters might have on Daisy.

She had stated that she was not a little girl any more, and that was something he did not need to be reminded of, but she was innocent, and she should remain that way. Yes, as she'd said, she was of a similar age to Lady Penrose and Ruby Lovelace, but their ages were where the similarities began and ended. Charlotte and Ruby were worldly, experienced, while Daisy was chaste, and so she should remain until she was married.

He was on less firm ground on whether or not Lady Daisy would object, not knowing what her opinion might be. But such an excuse suited his purpose and disguised what, deep down, he knew to be his real reason. Reading about such intimacies with Daisy had a decidedly unsettling effect on him. Despite his extensive experience with women, when it came to reading these letters it was as if *he* was the innocent, experiencing emotions and reactions for the first time, unable to control or know what to do with them.

No, that wasn't true. He knew exactly what he wanted to do with his emotions and reactions, but he also knew he mustn't, and that was what was so unsettling.

'Shall we go and find our horticulturists?' he suggested with as much joviality as he could muster, placing the pile of letters back in her lap.

He expected her to put up a barrage of objections, for her to list all the reasons why they should continue with the letters, but she merely nodded, still staring down to where the letters were piled up in her lap.

It was a pleasant day for a stroll. The river was always beautiful at this time of year, with the trees in full leaf and dipping their branches into the gently flowing water and the sun bathing them in warmth. Horace was right about one thing. Guy needed to appreciate the estate while it was still his.

The gravel path turned off and they left the river to make their way towards the large, domed glasshouse surrounded by an array of brightly coloured flowers in their full summer bloom. They passed a gardener, trimming the line of topiary shrubs into perfect spheres, and Guy stopped beside him.

'Please take these to the house,' he said. The man

put down his hedge clippers, wiped his hands on his trousers and took the letters from Daisy's outstretched hands.

'Give them to one of the indoor servants and ask them to place them in the sideboard drawer in the room Lady Daisy is occupying.'

Daisy twisted round in her wheelchair and watched as the man departed. Guy almost expected her to call out to the gardener to return her precious letters but she settled back in her chair and he pushed her through the glasshouse doors.

Fabric rustled, a wooden planting table rattled on the stone floor and Florence and Nathaniel jumped apart. Like startled rabbits, they turned and stared at Guy and Daisy, then Florence smoothed her hands down the front of her skirt to brush away any tell-tale creases. Daisy looked up at him, and once again they exchanged their now familiar knowing looks.

Guy had no concerns for his cousin's virtue. He knew his friend well. While Daisy might believe Guy had no objection to seducing virgins, Nathaniel would never do something so fiendish. If Nathaniel had been kissing Florence—and their blushing faces and furtive manners suggested he had—then his intentions would be honourable. Florence would soon achieve something Guy had dreamed of as a child—becoming part of the Springfeld family—and he couldn't be happier for her.

'How are the orchids?' Guy asked.

Two blank stares greeted this enquiry.

'Oh, yes, the orchids,' Nathaniel said. 'They're most impressive.'

'So, where are they?' Daisy asked in mock innocence.

'Um...' Florence replied, looking round the glasshouse at the array of palms, ferns and the exotic flowering plants acquired by Guy's various ancestors and carefully tended by his gardeners.

'Over there,' they said together as they pointed in different directions.

'Over there and there!' Nathaniel said. 'The greenhouse is full of orchids.'

'Full of orchids and awkward moments,' Guy whispered to Daisy, causing her to giggle behind her hand.

'Well, we've come to drag you away from orchid spotting so we can all take a walk around the estate,' Guy said. 'Or, in Daisy's case, a roll around the estate.'

'What a lovely idea,' Florence said, hiding any disappointment at no longer being alone with Nathaniel. But then, like him, Florence was used to keeping her emotions hidden. While he'd had to suffer life with his father, Florence had endured living with that brute Horace. It had not been so bad when Florence's parents had been alive, but her father had died when she'd still been a child and her mother had passed away the year after the Duke of Mandivale had died and she had been left alone, in the charge of her callous brother.

Guy invited her to stay at Mandivale whenever she wished, and to visit his London townhouse so she could attend balls during the season, but Horace often created obstacles for no other reason that Guy could see but that he wanted to prevent his sister from enjoying herself. Marrying Nathaniel and escaping into the loving warmth of the Springfeld family couldn't be a better outcome for his kind, sweet cousin.

Unfortunately, he too would soon achieve freedom from cousin Horace, but at the expense of losing the Mandivale estate and his title, and it would be his unfortunate tenants who would be forced to live under the whims of that insufferable, insensitive cur.

But for today he would push those thoughts away. He would enjoy the company of three of the people in the world about whom he cared the most and take pleasure in the estate that would soon no longer be his.

Nathaniel took Florence's arm and walked along the path and through the woodlands, followed by Guy pushing Daisy in her squeaking, ancient wheelchair.

'We'll have to show you the turtle dove nest we saw yesterday,' Florence called over her shoulder. Arm in arm, they rushed ahead, as if the birds were about to fly the nest and there was no time to waste.

'It seems your brother has added ornithology to his new-found interests,' Guy observed as they moved off the path, onto the grasslands and towards the woodland area of the estate.

'Ornithology and horticulture, along with a fascination with the intricacies of embroidery. Nate is quite the changed man.'

'People do go through some odd transformations when they fall in love, there's no doubt about that.'

'Yes, as those letters between your parents prove.'

'Mmm...or shouldn't we say my mother and the man she married?'

'We don't know that yet,' Daisy said turning in her chair. 'Horace's letter might still be a forgery.'

'But it seems unlikely. Her letters to the late Duke are getting more and more passionate, and the letter Horace showed me was in a similar style.'

'But I can't believe she would turn her attention from one man to another so quickly. It's obvious that she's besotted with her darling Bertie.'

'But that was before they married,' he said, easing the wheelchair between two trees and lifting it slightly so it could move over an exposed root. 'My father probably changed the moment she became his wife and no longer had the right to object to his behaviour. Once he revealed his real character to her, then she presumably was driven into the arms of this Boysie fellow.' He paused briefly. 'My real father.'

'Well, we'll just have to keep reading them until this mystery is solved.'

'Daisy, I said…'

She turned and reached over, placing her hand on the back of the chair, lightly touching his. 'I know it's a private matter, and if you do want to read the letters by yourself I will respect your decision, but I would like to help.'

'As I said, I don't think it's appropriate.'

'Well, if it's my virtue you're worried about, then I have to say you're being just as old fashioned as Dr Howard. I'm not some fragile little thing who is in danger of swooning because she's reading about a man and a woman kissing and whatnot.'

He stared down at her, trying to formulate an argument to put her off while fighting to ignore the soft touch of her hand on his. Despite her glove, he could feel the warmth of her skin, and could not help but wonder what it would be like to feel those soft, warm hands touching more of his body than just his hand.

She gripped his hand more tightly, and like a naïve schoolboy he almost gasped.

'Please, Guy, I'm sure I'll be a lot of help.'

Was she deliberately making her blue eyes even bigger so she would undermine his resolve? He suspected she was, because it was certainly working.

'Oh, all right, as soon as we're alone again we'll finish reading the letters together.'

She clapped her hands in victory and turned back around in the chair. 'And I suspect we're going to have lots of time alone.'

He looked ahead. Florence and Nathaniel were now nowhere in sight. 'I think you're right. Once we've got this visit to the turtle doves over and done with, shall we leave the love birds alone and get back to reading those letters?'

'Oh, yes, let's,' she said, and leant forward in the wheelchair, as if urging it and time to travel at a faster pace.

Guy was wrong. Several days passed before he and Daisy had sufficient time alone to bring out the letters. He had suggested to Daisy they include Nathaniel and Florence in their quest. After all, there was safety in numbers. But Daisy had said as they had started that it was only right that they complete the job. She also claimed that it was the only fair thing to do. If they did find conclusive proof that Horace was right, and the estate and title were rightly his, then it would be wrong to destroy Florence's happiness any sooner than was necessary.

Guy had to agree with the logic of her reasoning. While he waited for an opportunity to get back to the letters, the two couples passed their time playing cards, chatting and laughing, or in companionable silence reading books and newspapers. They even played a few rounds of croquet and tennis, with Daisy acting as umpire.

As expected, she was a particularly imperious umpire, seated in her wheelchair, shouting out instructions and final decisions about which she would brook no argument. Guy could tell she was just itching to jump out of her wheelchair and show everyone how the games should be played, but for once she was forced to act the lady and remain a spectator. Well, forced to act as much of a lady as she was capable.

Finally, they had their chance when, one morning as they were finishing breakfast, Florence stood up and said with great urgency, 'Let's go and see how our turtle doves are doing.'

'Excellent idea,' Nathaniel agreed, exchanging a secretive smile with Florence. He then turned to Guy and Daisy. 'Oh, would you like to join us?'

'No,' Guy and Daisy said in unison. It was obvious these two wanted to be alone just as desperately as Guy and Daisy, but for quite different reasons.

'Thank you, but I'm not much of a bird watcher,' Guy added.

'And I could never see the point of staring at birds just sitting in their nests,' Daisy added, sending Guy a quick wink. 'But you two go ahead. I'm sure Guy and I can find something to entertain ourselves with while you're gone.'

Nathaniel and Florence exchanged another secretive smile, causing another exchange of winks between Guy and Daisy.

'Quick, get the letters,' Daisy said the moment they left, wheeling her chair towards the sideboard. 'We might not have much time, so we better get straight onto them.'

Guy crossed the room, moving faster than Daisy, took out the letters and handed her the ones from his father.

Guy sat back at the table and waited while the footman cleared away the last of the breakfast dishes before he opened the first letter from his mother. 'All right, let's see what else my mother has to say to her dear, darling Bertie. *"I do love you, my darling Bertie. I did not know it was possible to feel this way. Every time I think of you my body trembles, I can't stop myself from..."*" He stopped and quickly pushed the letter back into the envelope.

'What? What did she say? What can't she stop herself from doing?

'You do not need to hear the rest and it adds nothing that we don't already know.'

'Guy, are you blushing?' She laughed and reached over to take the letter.

'Of course not!' he shot back, pulling the letter out of her reach.

'You are. I never thought I'd live to see the day when something would embarrass Guy Parnell.'

'Well, no son should read that his mother did that.'

'What?' Daisy made another grab for the letter. 'What did she do?'

'And no innocent unmarried woman should read it either.'

'I thought we had already discussed that. You claimed you were not old-fashioned and you promised you'd stop treating me like a child. Are you going back on your word?'

Guy could not remember making any such promises. 'No, it's just…'

'It's just nothing,' she said, making another grab for the letter. 'Your mother was also an innocent unmarried woman when she did whatever it was that's in that letter, so it can't be that bad.'

'Not *that* innocent,' he said under his breath, still holding the letter at arm's length and out of her reach.

'Well, if you're not going to tell me, then I'll just have to see what Darling Bertie thinks about her letter.'

Guy tried to grab the next letter out of her hand, but she placed it low on her lap, under the table. '"*My darling Bella, your letter has made me ever the more desperate to have you as my beloved wife…*"' She looked up at Guy and gave a little satisfied smile. 'That's all rather lovely and sweet. It looks like you're overreacting.'

She looked back down at the letter.

'"Oh, how I long to run my hands over your soft breasts..."'

'Stop. Now.' Guy stood up, turned his back to her and walked to the window. 'I most certainly do not need to hear this and you don't need to read it.'

The strength of his anger took him by surprise. He closed his eyes, took in a few deep breaths then turned back to Daisy, staring up at him with wide eyes and blushing cheeks. 'I'm sorry,' he said with as much control as he could muster. 'I did not mean to raise my voice.'

'No, it's me that should be sorry. I keep getting caught up in wanting to know what they wrote next and forgetting that these are letters between your parents. I should be more respectful of how this is affecting you.'

And it *was* affecting him, causing him to react with such intensity that was unlike him. Nothing his father had done or said had affected him for a long time, but these letters were forcing him to see a different side to the man—a man capable of affection, something he had never shown Guy. They were also causing him to see his mother as a real woman, not the saint-like image he had always had of her.

He walked back from the window and sat down. 'Obviously at the start of their marriage my parents were in love—well, in lust—with each other, but something must have changed, and changed pretty damn quickly, for my mother to have taken up with this Boysie fellow. I was born two years after they married. Presumably, once they wed my mother started to see my so-called father for what he really was—a cold, callous man.'

Daisy slowly nodded, her cheeks still burning. 'But I'm afraid there is only one way to find out.' She looked over at the letters piled in front of Guy. 'And we still don't know if the estate really is yours. Do we really have any choice but to continue reading?'

He didn't answer.

'Guy, we need to know. You must realise that. And if the dispute over the estate goes to court these letters will be read out then anyway. Perhaps you need to prepare yourself for what they reveal.'

He nodded. She was right, but that didn't make it any less painful. 'All right, but skip any parts that get a bit…'

'A bit…' She circled her hand in the air.

'Exactly.'

She nodded and opened the next letter. *'"My dearest, darling Bella, I must apologise for my actions last night. You graciously said I have nothing to apologise for, but you are wrong. My behaviour was appalling. All I can say is that a demon called desire overtook me and made me act that way."'*

Guy harrumphed. 'Here we go. He's now starting to show his true colours. I knew it wouldn't take long before he behaved appallingly.'

'"All I can say to try and excuse my behaviour is that you drive me wild with desire and I can't control myself when I am with you."'

Guy crossed his arms, fury percolating within him. 'I told you. The man was a cad. No wonder he drove my mother away,' he muttered through clenched teeth.

'I'm not so sure about that,' she said. 'Listen to this.

"I had to have you, to touch you, to kiss you, to worship you the way you should be worshipped. But I should have used more restraint, and for that I apologise from the bottom of my heart." He is sorry—that's something, isn't it?'

'It's a bit late being sorry afterwards. He shouldn't have seduced her in the first place.'

'Perhaps you should read her response to see if he really was such a cad.'

He huffed out his disapproval, but returned to his chair, picked up the next letter and quickly scanned it. 'No, there's more gushing stuff about her darling Bertie.' He shook his head in annoyance. His poor, inexperienced mother did not even know what the brute had done. She'd still thought his actions were forgivable, but they weren't. Nothing could excuse such behaviour. She'd been innocent, he'd been experienced. It had been up to him to ensure she remained that way, not take advantage of her naivety and trust for his own gratification.

He placed the letter back in the envelope, took out the next one and skimmed through it, his frown growing with his disapproval.

'What does she say?' Daisy asked, leaning towards him.

'*"My darling Bertie, my darling Naughty Boy..."*' He rolled his eyes again. He hadn't just been naughty, he'd been an unforgivable philander and a scoundrel. '*"You have nothing to reproach yourself for and nor should you be asking for my forgiveness. If you remem-*

ber correctly, it was I who kissed you. When your hand moved to my..."'

He dropped the letter as if it were burning his fingers. 'That will do for today, Daisy,' he said in his most authoritative voice. 'This is getting us nowhere and we're no closer to finding out whether Horace's letter is genuine or not.

He walked back to the window and stared out at the garden, seeing nothing, his rage at his father consuming him. Behind him he could hear the rustling of paper as Daisy continued reading the letters, thankfully in silence.

'Oh, Guy, you're going to want to read this one,' she said.

He turned to face her and she smiled up at him, her eyes sparkling with excitement. 'I very much doubt that.'

Her smile grew wider. 'Yes, you are. Listen to this. *"I love it when you call me your naughty boy..."*'

'That's nothing new. She's been calling him her "*naughty boy*" in the last few letters I've read. All rather ridiculous, if you ask me. He was much more than a naughty boy. He was a scoundrel, a—'

'No, wait, it goes on. *"But you must be careful, my dear, never to call me that again in public. Your parents looked so shocked when they heard you whisper it to me during dinner last night. I knew what you were telling me—that you wanted us to be naughty together..."*'

Guy cringed.

'It goes on a bit about them being naughty, which you don't need to hear.'

Guy huffed out a disapproving sigh. He most definitely did not.

'But then it says, *"In future, if you want me to be naughty, don't call me a naughty boy, call me Boysie. We can tell people that it is your pet name for me. Then you can use it as often as you wish and in public and only you and I will know what you are asking. You are asking your Boysie to be your naughty boy. It will be our private signal."*'

She lowered the letter and they stared at each other, wide-eyed.

He crossed the room, took the letter from her outstretched hand and read it for himself, his excitement mounting with every word. 'Daisy, that's it, you've solved it. You clever, clever girl.'

'You know what this means don't you?' she said, clapping her hands together. 'Horace's letter is genuine, but it's a letter to your father, the Duke of Mandivale—and you're the rightful heir. We did it, we proved it.'

'No, Daisy, *you* proved it. If you hadn't insisted on continuing to read these letters we'd never have known the truth.' Before he knew what he was doing, he knelt down, took her face in his hands and kissed her lips. 'Oh, Daisy, this is wonderful. You're wonderful.'

She looked back up at him, no longer smiling, her face still framed by his hands. Her blue eyes stared into his, her plump lips parting, her chest swelling up and down with each quick intake of breath. Wild desire pumped through him. He lowered his head towards hers, desperate to kiss her again, to taste her again, to lose himself in her.

'Daisy, you're wonderful,' he whispered, his lips so close he could feel her breath, as soft as a feather against his own lips.

She closed her eyes, her lips parted further, her head tipped back, waiting to receive his kiss.

Voices crashed into his consciousness and he jumped back, as if Daisy had done what she should have and slapped his face.

Florence and Nathaniel entered the room, laughing together, their arms entwined. They stopped and stared at Daisy and Guy. Then, like mirror images, they raised their eyebrows, turned to each other and smiled.

'What have you two been up to?' Nathaniel asked, still smiling.

'Nothing, nothing at all!' Guy shot back faster and louder than he intended.

'Actually,' Daisy said, her voice constricted. 'Actually...' she continued after clearing her throat. 'We've got some good news.'

'Oh, that's wonderful.' Florence rushed forward and clasped Daisy's hands. 'Didn't I say my cousin will soon make an announcement?' she said, turning to Nathaniel.

'What?' Guy looked from Florence to Nathaniel. 'How could you possibly know?'

'Women's intuition, I suppose. Women just know these things.'

Guy suspected his cousin was losing her mind, but perhaps that was what falling in love did to you. It had certainly made his mother a bit deranged, and falling in love with Nathaniel was causing his cousin to become a bit peculiar.

'Daisy and I have been reading through my parents' letters, and she's discovered that "Boysie" was my mother's pet name for her husband,' he explained to a still smiling Florence. 'The letter that Horace said was addressed to another man was actually addressed to my father, the Duke, who was going by the name of Boysie.'

Florence stared back at him, no longer smiling. It seemed love was also making her a bit dim-witted.

'These letters prove that the late Duke of Mandivale was my father, and I am the rightful heir to both the title and the estate,' he explained, stating something that should have been obvious.

He waited for his cousin to exclaim with glee. 'Oh,' was all she replied, standing up and returning to Nathaniel's side. Disappointment was not the reaction he'd been expecting. 'Oh,' she repeated, with slightly more excitement.

She approached the table and picked up the letters. 'Oh, Guy, this is excellent news. Horace will not become the Duke of Mandivale. At least, not yet.'

'Yes, that's right,' he said, pleased that she had finally understood what he was saying. Then he frowned, taking in the implication of her response.

'What do you mean, not yet? Has Horace got some other scheme up his sleeve to take the dukedom away from me?' He looked over at the letters then back up at Florence. 'Whatever it is, it will fail, just as this scheme has.'

Florence continued to stare at him, as if he was now the simpleton. 'Horace will become the next duke if you don't get married and have an heir,' she said, slowly enunciating each word, as if trying to make him understand. 'I know you're still young, Guy, but really, that is the only way you can guarantee that Horace will never get the title.'

Guy stared back at her, knowing that horror was written all over his face. It was a terrible fate, but one he knew was waiting for him eventually. Marriage. For a duke, it was inevitable. He had to provide an heir. He'd known he would have to do that one day, but it was something he'd intended to put off for as long as possible. But, damn it all, Florence was right. The sooner he wed and bred, the better, before Horace could come up with some other scheme. He wouldn't put it past that miscreant to put some arsenic in his brandy or arrange for him to be run over on a London street.

He looked at the others. For some unaccountable reason, Florence and Nathaniel were smiling at Daisy, but the look of horror on her face reflected exactly how he was feeling. She too could see what a bad idea this was. But what choice did he have?

'You're right, Florence,' he muttered, his heart sinking even further as he dropped down into the nearest chair. 'There's nothing for it. I'm going to have to find myself a bride.'

Chapter Ten

Guy looked like a condemned man facing the gallows. Of course he was going to have to marry and sire an heir. For a duke, it was as inevitable as night following day. Daisy knew that. She had always known that. And yet, the thought of Guy actually marrying had never really occurred to her.

Florence and Nathaniel continued chattering as if the announcement was the most natural thing in the world—which, Daisy had to remind herself, it was.

She looked over at the now morose Guy, slumped in his chair. He seemed to have forgotten all about that kiss, as if it had never happened. The news of his forthcoming search for a bride now appeared to be all that was on his mind.

Well, what was good enough for him was good enough for her. She too would see it as nothing of importance. After all, it had just been a friendly little peck on the lips, no more passionate than you would expect between almost-siblings. He'd been merely expressing his thanks to her for finding the answer to his questions.

She crossed her arms to underline her defiant determination to believe it had meant nothing to her.

While one couple sat in silence, the other continued quietly talking together, completely absorbed in each other's company, until they eventually rose as one from their chairs and made some excuse to leave—another walk around the garden, to post a letter, to see some birds, or something. Daisy hardly heard what they were saying, too distracted by not thinking about that kiss or Guy's eventual marriage.

They left the room, giggling together like two school children sharing a secret, and sending Daisy and Guy what could only be described as pointed looks. But whatever those looks meant eluded Daisy, and she had more important things to think of, or at least, not think of.

Silence descended on the room broken only by the clock ticking on the marble mantelpiece, highlighting just how slowly time can move.

'I've thought about this carefully,' Guy eventually said, as sombre as an undertaker. 'And I believe that you can provide the solution to my marriage problem.'

She glared at him. Had he gone completely mad? She most certainly would not be marrying Guy Parnell. The mere thought of it was ludicrous, just ludicrous. That fire which kept erupting on her face did so again, although this time it was caused by indignation at his impertinence, nothing more. That would also explain why she had lost the ability to breathe and why her heart had unaccountably stopped beating in her chest.

'I'm going to need that clever brain of yours to solve

this latest problem,' he continued before Daisy could order the list of objections spinning in her mind. 'You must know who would make a perfect Duchess of Mandivale. You can tell me who I should marry.'

Air returned to her lungs and her heart started pounding again, louder than she would have wished. She was wrong. She wasn't even to be considered as a possible bride. Of course she wouldn't be. After all, she was just Daisy Chain, hardly a woman at all, just his best friend's little sister. Someone he could pick up and put into bed without a second thought. Someone he could kiss in a brotherly fashion without it having any ramifications. Daisy was unsure which was more insulting—him expecting her to marry him or not even considering the possibility. All she knew was she was very insulted indeed.

'I have absolutely no idea,' she said with a huff.

'Oh, come on, Daisy, you must be able to think of someone who will fit the bill.'

'What about Ruby Lovelace?' she snapped. 'You two are already rather familiar with each other.'

Guy laughed, as if that was all the response that was required.

'What? Is she good enough to toy with but not good enough to be a duchess?' Daisy knew she was being terse, but she was furious with Guy, and needed to let him know the extent of her anger.

'Ruby would have no interest in becoming a duchess,' he said. 'She's a successful actress who loves the life she leads. She has her own ambitions and the last thing she wants is to play the role of duchess—unless, of course, she's doing so on stage.'

He stood up and began walking up and down on the Persian rug, his face thoughtful. 'No, what I need is a woman who wants a title more than anything in the world. One who couldn't care less that it's a marriage in name only. Someone more than happy to give me complete freedom.'

'In other words, you want to be married but still behave as if you're single.'

'Exactly,' Guy confirmed, turning and nodding, seemingly oblivious to her condemnation. 'You must know plenty of debutantes who would be happy with such an arrangement.'

Unfortunately, in that he was correct.

'What about some of those single ladies in your cycling society? Would any of them want to be a duchess?'

Daisy sniffed. 'They're my friends. I wouldn't inflict you on any of them.'

'No, I suppose not. Who, then?'

She shrugged.

'Oh, come on, Daisy. You know lots of debutantes. What about that Margaret Smythe girl? Her father's only the third son of a baron. Wouldn't her parents be happy to see her married to a duke?'

'But what about what Margaret wants?' Daisy all but shouted. 'Surely you should be considering what she wants, not just what you want or what her parents want?'

He nodded. 'Of course. Well, do you think she'd want to marry me?'

Daisy had absolutely no doubts about that. Guy was rich, titled and handsome. Margaret Smythe and her parents would collectively pull out all their eye teeth if it would help them achieve such a marriage. 'I have no idea,' she said instead.

'Hmm,' Guy muttered, and resumed his pacing. 'I suppose I'm going to have to start attending society balls, let people know I'm looking and see what surfaces.'

It was Daisy's turned to utter a loud, 'Hmm,' but hers was of the disapproving kind, not the contemplative kind. 'You sound like you're on a fishing or hunting expedition, not trying to find the love of your life.'

He raised both hands, along with both eyebrows, as if her statement really needed no comment.

'It's disgusting,' Daisy said, turning her head away as if she couldn't bear to look at him.

'I agree entirely. It is disgusting that I need an heir to ensure the estate doesn't fall into Horace's hands. It's disgusting that debutantes have to seek out a husband for their financial and social survival. It's disgusting that, for all the sophistication of society balls, they are nothing more than a place for mothers to try and catch the best husband available for their daughters. But that is the world in which we live.'

'Well, it should change.'

'Again, I agree entirely, but it's not likely to change in my lifetime. Nor are the rules of inheritance. So, I need to find a suitable woman to become the next Duchess of Mandivale. I was hoping to get your help so I don't make a terrible mistake, either for me or for the unfortunate woman I wed.'

Daisy merely harrumphed again.

'Don't be like that, Daisy Chain,' he said, moving

towards her. 'You must know someone who only wants a title and money, nothing more. That way the wife gets exactly what she wants and no one gets hurt.'

The griping in Daisy's stomach suggested that wasn't so, but it wasn't pain for her own sake, Daisy told herself, it was in reaction to this abhorrent situation.

'Let's make a list.' Guy strode towards the desk, pulled up the roll top and sat down, then removed a pen, inkwell and paper from the drawer. 'Right, who do you suggest?' he asked, turning to face her, his pen poised above the paper. 'Maybe once we've got a good long list I could host a ball here at Mandivale and invite them all.'

'Oh, how wonderful for you. Then you can inspect all the goods on offer and pick the best one.'

He lowered the pen. 'I'm sorry this is upsetting you, but what choice do I have? I'm a duke. I need an heir if I'm to prevent Horace eventually getting the estate. I don't want to do this, but I have to.'

'So what? Do you expect me to feel sorry for you? Poor, poor you, having to…having to…'

He circled his hand in the air and smiled that annoying, slow, seductive smile.

'Exactly,' she shot back. 'And some poor woman has to breed an heir for you. It's disgusting.'

'And I couldn't agree more,' he said, still smiling as if the thought of breeding held no disgust at all. 'That's why I want your help, so the *poor woman* is someone who is agreeable to this arrangement.'

Once again Daisy folded her arms and looked away.

'Well, I can see you're going to be of no help. In that

case, I'm going to have to find someone myself, and if I pick the wrong one you'll only have yourself to blame.'

'How dare you?' she all but spat out. 'It most certainly will not be my fault.'

They glared at each other, then Guy sighed, stood up and went back to pacing, the pen still in his hand. 'I suppose I could always ask Nathaniel and Florence to help, but the two of them are such romantics, they'd actually try and make a love match, and that's not what I'm after.'

A love match? Daisy's breath caught in her throat. Surely that would be the best outcome? If he married a woman he loved and who loved him back wouldn't that remove all her objections? So why was that even worse than him finding a woman who just wanted a title?

'Isn't that what marriage is supposed to be about?' she choked out, pushing aside her objections. 'My parents are in love, as are both my sisters and their husbands.'

He stopped pacing and turned to her, a smile quirking the edges of his lips. 'Why, Daisy Chain, I never knew that deep down you're a bit of a romantic yourself. Haven't you always said that you'd never marry? That it's enslavement for a woman?'

Daisy shrugged. 'I did, and I do, I just think if anyone's going to enter into that arrangement they should do it for the right reasons.'

'And how many people of our class do that, apart from those lucky members of the Springfeld family?'

Daisy shrugged again, surprised to find herself on this side of the argument. Usually, she was the one expressing Guy's view. 'Well, your parents married for love,' she said, pointing to the pile of letters.

'Humph. Were they in love or in lust? It's hard to tell. And my father certainly didn't love the offspring from that arrangement. On the rare occasions when he even spoke to me, it was to remind me that I had killed my mother.'

Daisy could hear not just bitterness in his words but real heartache.

'Loving my mother certainly didn't make him a better man,' he said, gripping his pen tightly. 'It didn't make him a happy man, one who could enjoy life.'

'Perhaps it was loving your mother that made him a tyrant,' she murmured. 'Perhaps when she died he felt he couldn't live without her.'

'Well, if that's what love does to a person then I, for one, am better off without it.'

He sank back down in front of the desk in defeat. 'But, no matter what we think of love and marriage, I'm going to have to marry someone, and I would appreciate your help so I don't make a disastrous selection.'

She refused to answer.

'We made a good team overcoming Horace's attempt to grab the title. I'm sure we'll make an excellent team solving this problem as well.'

He looked over at her and slowly shook his head. 'I have to choose someone and I don't want to get it wrong. After all, once I'm married there will be no going back. I know you think this is appalling, and rightly so, but it has to be done, and with your help I'll avoid making some catastrophic mistake.'

'Oh, all right,' she finally conceded with a deep sigh.

'Good.' He unscrewed the bottle of ink, dipped in his pen, then looked up at Daisy, his pen on the paper. 'Right, who do you suggest?'

'Well, I suppose you should put Margaret Smythe on the list. She would do just about anything for a title and put up with just about anyone to get one.'

'Even me,' he said, writing her name on the page. 'Good.'

'But Margaret Smythe is rather judgemental,' Daisy added. 'I don't know if she'd tolerate your lifestyle. I'm sure she'd be shocked by your liaisons with the likes of Ruby Lovelace.' Daisy had no idea if this was true, but as *she* had been shocked, then surely so would other women, particularly ones who wanted to marry Guy.

'Hmm,' was all Guy replied. 'So, who else is there? Someone who couldn't care less how I lived.'

Daisy placed her hand on her chin, considering the young women who had made their debuts this year, and immediately dismissing each one in turn, even the ones as desperate for a title as Margaret Smythe.

'What about Eugenie Welsh?' Guy asked. 'She's rather comely, and if I'm going to be siring a line of heirs that would be an asset.'

'She's horrid,' Daisy shot back, her temperature rising dangerously high. 'She's vain, foolish, superficial... and I doubt that woman has ever had an original thought in her life.'

'She sounds perfect. Does she want to be a duchess and would she give me complete freedom?'

'I have absolutely no idea.' Something Daisy knew

to be untrue. Nothing would give that high-and-mighty young woman more pleasure than to be married to Guy Parnell, the dashing Duke of Mandivale, and no sacrifice would be too great if it meant becoming a duchess.

'I think we should add her to the list,' he said, his pen scratching across the page. 'So, who else?'

Daisy folded her arms tighter. 'I've no idea.'

'Well, I can hardly host a ball and invite only two debutantes. Perhaps I should just invite as many as we can think of and see what happens.'

Daisy knew exactly what would happen. As soon as word got out that the Duke of Mandivale was seeking a wife, there would be a stampede of mothers and daughters vying for his attention. Any ball he hosted would turn into a cattle market, with well-dressed, polite young women being thrust in front of him for his inspection, their attributes listed, their defects downplayed. It wasn't often a duke came on the marriage market, so it would be an opportunity no mother of an unmarried daughter would let slip through her fingers.

'It's disgusting,' she muttered under her breath.

Once again, the room descended into silence, broken only by the ticking clock, Daisy's occasional disapproving sigh and the scratching of Guy's pen. It seemed he no longer needed her approval, or more accurately her disapproval, and was perfectly capable of compiling his own list.

When Florence and Nathaniel returned, Daisy smiled at them, not so much in pleasure but in relief, pleased for the distraction from Guy and that damned scratching pen.

'How was your walk?' she asked, hoping that they would prattle on happily about turtle doves or orchids or something, anything other than marriage and heirs.

'It was lovely, thank you,' Florence said as she walked over to the desk and looked down at the paper in front of Guy. 'What's this? "Margaret Smythe, Eugenie Welsh, Lillian Dankworth, Isabella Farnsley, Alma Fitzherbert, Bertha Huntington..." What are you doing?'

'I'm compiling a list of potential brides.'

Florence's eyes grew wide and her hand shot up to cover her open mouth. 'Are you sure you're making the right choices?' Florence asked, looking from Guy to Daisy to Nathaniel and back again.

'Yes,' Guy said, holding up the list. 'As I explained to Daisy, I need someone who wants the title of duchess above all else.'

Florence clenched her hands together in front of her chest, as if Guy's words were causing her heart to ache. 'But what about love?'

Guy laughed. 'Something best avoided. I have no intention of causing the future Duchess of Mandivale any pain. If she does love me, it will be a disaster.'

'But what about you loving her?' Florence insisted, her eyes enormous.

'I suspect there's little danger of me falling in love with anyone on this list,' he said, his gaze scanning down the paper.

'Then perhaps you should throw away the list and direct your attentions to more appropriate young women.'

'What?' Daisy squeaked as Florence turned to look at her.

Guy looked over at Daisy, then scoffed. 'You're not suggesting I marry Daisy Chain, are you?'

Florence blinked rapidly and looked over at Nathaniel for help.

'I agree with Florence,' Nathaniel said. Daisy would have been amused by Nathaniel's answer if she wasn't so annoyed with everyone in the room. It was exactly the response her father would give to her mother, non-committal yet completely supportive.

'If anyone is interested in *my* opinion, I have no interest in being placed on Guy's list. Nor do I want to be used to breed the future Duke of Mandivale.' Daisy had blushed before, but the level of heat now flaming on her cheeks was an entirely new experience.

'I think the whole thing is disgusting!' she blurted out, trying to cover her embarrassment with indignation.

'I agree,' Florence added, while Nathaniel nodded his support. 'You should not be making lists, Guy. You should only marry for love.'

That hadn't been what Daisy had said, but she let it go, not wanting to draw further attention to herself or her burning cheeks and squirming body.

Guy released the letter and it fluttered back to the desk. 'I think you're being overly sentimental and romantic, Florence. And Daisy, you're being overly judgemental. I think we all agree I have to ensure Horace doesn't get the title. To do that, I have to marry. I have to sire an heir. Those are the facts and nothing can change them. If you're going to put obstacles and objections in my way, then I'm just going to have to do this all by myself.'

'Well, you can't find yourself a bride until Daisy's foot is better,' Florence said. 'So, put that list away for now. I'm sure you can wait a few weeks before you start looking for a wife. Once Daisy is better, then I promise I'll do everything I can to help you find a suitable wife, one who will be perfect for you and exactly the woman you need.'

'Thank you, Florence.' Guy nodded, capped his pen, screwed the lid back on the bottle of ink and put everything away in the desk drawers. While he was distracted, he did not notice the conspiratorial smiles exchanged between Nathaniel and Florence, but Daisy did.

Those two were up to something—but if it involved match-making between Guy and her, then they had better brace themselves for disappointment.

Chapter Eleven

Florence was right. Guy had but a few weeks to relax and enjoy himself before the onslaught would begin. And he could think of no better way to start off his last period of freedom than informing Cousin Horace that his delusions of grandeur were just that—delusions. He was not the Duke of Mandivale, never had been and, once Guy had sired an heir and a spare, never would be.

Excusing himself from his guests, he set off towards the village. It was a glorious day, made even more glorious by the task he was about to perform, so he chose not to ride in his carriage. The thought of ruining that bully's day seemed to make the sun shine brighter, the sky appear bluer and the air smell fresher, and he was almost tempted to whistle as he walked along the country lane.

He reached the cottage and was about to knock, then thought better of it and walked in unannounced, startling the maid. She made a fruitless attempt to halt his progress, then rushed down the hallway to try and inform her master that he had a visitor, but before she could do so Guy burst into the parlour.

'Good morning, Horace. Beautiful day, isn't it?' he said, taking the chair opposite to his cousin.

'What…what on earth is the meaning of this?' Horace spluttered, lowering his newspaper. 'How dare you barge into my house uninvited? Bessie, show this man out.'

The maid hovered at the doorway, her hands anxiously clasped together.

'It's all right, Bessie. I'm quite within my rights to burst in here, as Horace well knows.'

'I know nothing of the sort.'

Guy stretched out his legs. 'If you can riffle through desk drawers at the Mandivale estate and steal my parents' private correspondence, then I believe I have the right to enter your house without knocking.'

Horace signalled for Bessie to leave them. 'Now, listen here,' he said the moment the door closed. 'I'll have you know, I would never—'

'Don't lie, Horace.' Guy brushed away his words with the sweep of a hand. 'And don't worry, I'm in a benevolent mood, so I won't be having you charged with theft.' He looked up at the ceiling and tapped his chin, as if in thought. 'Is theft still a hanging offence? I can't remember.'

He looked back down at Horace, and with increasing pleasure watched as his face turned from its usual ruddy red to a painful shade of scarlet. Even if found guilty, he would not hang for such an offence, but where was the fun in enlightening Horace about that particular legal detail?

'How dare you?' he spluttered, his eyes bulging. 'It's not theft. I have every right to look at anything I want at the Mandivale estate. After all, it is rightfully my home.'

'Ah yes, that reminds me of the real reason I've come to visit you. It wasn't just to threaten you with the hangman's noose.' Guy sat up straighter in his chair. 'I have some good news for you, Horace. It seems your letter wasn't a forgery after all.'

Horace continued to glare at him, but the narrowing of his eyes showed the man had enough intelligence to know that there must be more to this than what Guy had so far revealed.

'The other piece of good news I have for you is I am going to save you the enormous expense of paying lawyers' fees by not challenging its authenticity in court.'

'What?' Horace gasped out. 'Are you going to relinquish the dukedom to me without a fight?'

'No, what I am saying is you don't have a case worth fighting in court. I have proof that my mother's pet name for her husband was Boysie. Boysie, Hubert, the Duke of Mandivale and even...' he gave a mock shudder '...Darling Bertie are all the same man, and that man was undeniably my father.'

Horace's eyes once again bulged, growing so big Guy wondered whether they might pop out of his head. 'I don't believe it!' he spluttered.

'If your thieving fingers had rummaged through the rest of the letters in the desk drawer you might have found this one.' Guy held out the letter towards Horace. He reached forward to take it, but Guy snatched it back. 'You can read it but not touch it. Isn't that how you showed me the letter you stole from my house? After all, I wouldn't want you to tear it up, would I?'

Horace scanned the letter and then sat back in his chair, his crimson face clamped as tight as a fist.

'Don't look so disappointed, Horace. I have a third piece of good news for you.'

Horace folded his arms and turned his head, as if refusing to acknowledge anything Guy had to say.

'You might not be about to gain a title, but I suspect Florence soon will.'

Horace made no reaction.

'Yes, I thought you'd be pleased to hear that. She's being courted by my best friend—a viscount, no less. If, or more likely when, they marry your sister will be a viscountess, and one day a countess.'

Horace turned to face him, his nostrils flared, like a bull about to charge. 'I want Florence to return to this house immediately. She will be marrying no friend of yours.'

'No, Horace, you're wrong,' Guy continued, perhaps enjoying Horace's torment a little too much. 'Florence will not be returning to this house any time soon. As much as you enjoy using her as your unpaid housekeeper, once her role as chaperon is over, should she choose to, she can accompany me to London when I leave in a few weeks so she can enjoy what's left of the season.'

'She will not,' he said, his voice rising, his hands gripping the edge of the arm chair, as if barely restraining himself from attacking Guy.

'Yes, she will,' Guy insisted, his calm voice a deliberate contrast to Horace's fury. 'If she doesn't, then I will have to inform the constabulary that there has been a theft from the Mandivale estate and that I want them to prosecute the offender to the full extent of the law. And, as the Duke, I do have rather a lot of sway in this community.'

He sent Horace a mock frown. 'Oh, sorry, I shouldn't use words like "sway", should I? Not when we're discussing someone dangling from the hangman's noose.'

Horace swallowed and rubbed his neck.

'So, am I to assume that Florence has your permission to join me in London, and that you will put up no objections to her being courted by the viscount?'

Horace nodded, staring straight ahead.

'I'm pleased that you're being so amenable.' Guy stood up. 'Well, I leave you to enjoy the rest of your day in peace.'

He walked back down the hallway, passed the horrified maid, then stopped and turned around. 'Bessie, if you ever want to leave Horace's service, there will be a position for you up at the Mandivale estate.'

'Thank you, Your Grace.' The maid bobbed a curtsey as she took off her apron. 'I'll pack my things immediately.'

Smiling to himself, Guy took his leave, and this time he did whistle as he strolled back home.

The problem of Horace now settled, and the problem of finding a bride thankfully delayed for a few weeks, Guy could now focus on the immediate problem of Daisy and that kiss. If they were to spend more time together while she recovered, it surely must be discussed? But how do you discuss something you hardly understand yourself?

Days passed, without either mentioning the event. Guy decided to take Daisy's lack of reaction as a good sign. It showed she had taken it for what it was—a kiss between friends, nothing more. If she had been offended, he had no doubt that she would have let him know in no uncertain terms. After all, Daisy always let people know what was on her mind.

Despite that, the kiss should never have happened and would never happen again. He should not even be thinking about it. Each time he looked at her he should not be thinking about the touch of her lips on his, should not be remembering how she tasted, sweet with an underlying spicy tang, just like the woman herself. Instead, he should be reminding himself that their kiss meant nothing.

He had been caught up in the excitement of the moment, that was all. Daisy had found the solution to his problem and proved that he'd been the legitimate Mandivale heir. How could he not get excited? And kissing Daisy had been the natural way to express that excitement. That was all. And it had only been a quick peck. No one could be offended by that.

And, if he *had* been tempted to kiss her more deeply, so what? He hadn't, and that was all that mattered. No man could be judged by what they were tempted to do, only by their actions. If they could be judged by their thoughts, then the Springfeld family would be calling for him to be hanged, drawn and quartered, and rightly so.

The kiss remained their unspoken secret. No more was said about his need of a bride. Instead, the two couples passed four companionable weeks together. To begin with, Guy continued to push Daisy round in her wheelchair, taking her on outings to the river, around the gardens, even down to the local village.

Then she progressed to using two canes, further relics from Aunt Myrtle's visits. Soon, she was down to one cane. Eventually, all she needed was his assistance and she could walk about on her own, although she still took his arm whenever they went on strolls around the estate, much to his pleasure.

Nathaniel and Florence, as expected, disappeared as often as they could. It was obvious they not only wanted to be alone together but that they also wanted to ensure Guy and Daisy spent as much time in each other's company as possible. Their plan was so blatant it was almost amusing. But it was doomed to failure. He did enjoy spending time with Daisy but being with her only confirmed his belief that she was not for him. Florence's misguided aspiration that Daisy become the next Duchess of Mandivale was ludicrous.

Daisy deserved more, so much more. She deserved to be married to a good man. A man for whom marriage, fidelity and fatherhood came naturally. Just like her sisters, she deserved to be married to a man who loved her. He could never be that man. The Springfelds had all grown up in a loving home. They knew instinctively what love was, how to give it and receive it.

He was not like that. He had never been in love and had no idea what that elusive emotion felt like. He had not experienced it as a child, and had certainly not experienced it as an adult, despite the countless women who had moved in and out of his life and his bed. He needed to marry a woman who could accept a loveless marriage, and that would never be Daisy Springfeld.

To that end, and with a somewhat heavy heart, the moment Daisy was fully recovered trunks were packed, train tickets were bought and the two couples were off to London. If all went well, before the season was over Guy would be engaged to the future Duchess of Mandivale.

It had been fun, but now it was all over. Despite the pain in her foot, despite being incapacitated, Daisy had found the last four weeks enjoyable, particularly as no further mention had been made of Guy's eventual marriage. Daisy always enjoyed her brother's lively company and was coming to hold Florence in great affection. There was little doubt that she would soon be joining the Springfeld family. Nathaniel's announcement that Florence would be returning with them to London could mean only one thing. He wanted to introduce her to the family. Guy also said he would come to London, supposedly to act as Florence's guardian, but they all knew the real reason, the one they had chosen not to talk about.

As they waited at the railway station, Daisy tried to join in with Florence and Nathaniel's excited chatter but struggled to share their enthusiasm either for the train journey or the return to London. The last time she had been at this station, Guy had been farewelling Ruby

Lovelace. Now he was setting off to find a bride, and her reaction to both events was the same. She disapproved but knew it was not her place to do so.

She sent him a quick sideways look. As he stood on the platform, staring up the empty track and waiting for the London train, she could only wonder what he was thinking. He certainly looked pleased with himself, as if about to set out for a pleasurable outing. But then Guy Parnell was a man who always looked pleased with himself, as if about to indulge in some enjoyable activity—often of the forbidden kind, the sort of activity that would cause most respectable people to tut-tut.

The train arrived with much hissing of steam, blowing of whistles, waving of flags from the station master and bustling from the passengers and railway staff. The two couples found their first-class compartment and, while the women sat down on the plush leather benches, the men placed their top hats and the ladies' parasols on the overhead netted shelving and settled themselves for the journey.

'It feels like such a long time since I've been to London,' Florence said. 'I'm so looking forward to it.' And in her excitement, she actually took Nathaniel's hand and gave it a squeeze, which elicited a smile from Nathaniel and an exchange of knowing looks between Daisy and Guy.

'And are you looking forward to it as well?' Daisy asked Guy with feigned innocence. What she really wanted to ask was, *will you be seeing Ruby Lovelace again? What plans have you got regarding finding a bride? Who is on your list now?* But she would ask none of these questions and was determined to keep her voice and her manner nonchalant at all times.

'I always look forward to visiting London.' He turned to the window for a moment then back to Daisy. 'Although, this time I have somewhat mixed feelings.'

Florence looked over at Guy and frowned. 'You mean because you intend to find a wife?' It was the first time the quest had been mentioned in four weeks and it momentarily caused a brief frown to flick over Guy's face.

'Let's not talk of that now,' he said. 'Let's discuss all that you'll see when you're in London, Florence. All the balls, parties and other social events you'll attend. And I suspect you'll be attending them all as well, won't you, Nathaniel?'

Daisy stared at her brother, who had the most surprising expression on his face, one that could only be described as sheepish. Oh, yes, those two really were in love. While Guy was off searching for his bride-to-be, Nathaniel would be entertaining the cousin. It was all working out rather well for Guy. He would have complete freedom to do whatever he wanted, find a wife, visit his mistress—anything at all. But didn't he always? And from what he had said, his life would continue in exactly the same manner when he married.

Disgusting. Daisy turned to look at the passing countryside.

While Florence and Nathaniel discussed what they planned to do and see in London, Guy stared out of the window, uncharacteristically silent.

'Don't you agree, Guy?' she heard Nathaniel's voice, slightly raised. 'Guy?'

Guy turned towards her brother. 'Sorry, Nate, what did you say?'

'I said, the next ball on the social calendar will be Lady Danton's. You should escort Florence to that ball. It is expected to be quite an event. She always makes them rather special. She spares no expense, and they tend to be the talk of the season.'

Well, she has three daughters to marry off, so needs to flaunt the family's wealth to attract the best suitors, Daisy wanted to say, but kept her opinion to herself, not wanting to dampen Florence's and Nathaniel's enthusiasm.

'Yes, of course. Florence must attend that,' Guy said. 'And I assume you will be as well, Nate?'

'Oh, yes, I wouldn't miss it for anything in the world.'

Daisy raised her eyebrows at her brother, but he failed to notice her questioning look and continued smiling at Florence. Nathaniel had about as much interest in going to balls as she had, and in the past had only attended when forced to escort one of his sisters. But it seemed, now that Florence was in his life, that too had changed.

'And you, Daisy?' Guy asked. 'Will you be gracing us with your presence at Lady Danton's ball?'

'Yes, I plan to go as well.'

What was she saying? She'd had no intention of going to that ball or any other on this season's calendar. At twenty-four, she was in most people's minds already a spinster, someone who might as well give up trying to find a husband, and apart from chaperoning other young ladies there was no reason why she would be expected to put in an appearance.

'I will be going, if for no other reason than to make sure Guy doesn't trap some unfortunate young woman into marriage. I wouldn't want any poor girl to think she is getting more than a mere arrangement.'

'Kind of you, Daisy,' Guy said, and Daisy was unsure whether he was being genuine or facetious.

Nathaniel and Florence smiled at each other, but Daisy told herself it meant nothing. Those two were always smiling at each other, although their smiles did look suspiciously like the knowing looks she and Guy often exchanged over something the two dewy-eyed love birds had done or said.

The train pulled into Victoria Station and the hustle and bustle they had experienced at the village station repeated itself, just multiplied by swarms of people disembarking from a multitude of trains, while white steam filled the air, porters shouted instructions, guards blew whistles and waved flags, and people of all classes made their way on and off the platforms.

They boarded a horse carriage and travelled through the bustling streets to Nathaniel and Daisy's Belgravia home. After a month in the quiet of the country, London seemed even more chaotic than she remembered. Carriages, carts and omnibuses jostled for places in the crowded streets, while a cacophony of horses' hooves and carriage wheels rumbled over cobbled roads, and shouting voices assaulted her ears. In among this mayhem, several people were riding bicycles, including a few women, braving the traffic and the looks of disapproval from pedestrians. Daisy waved to them, to show her support.

When they arrived at the Springfelds' townhouse, her parents rushed out to greet them. Throwing propriety to the wind, her mother hugged Daisy, Nathaniel and Guy on the footpath, where anyone could see, as if Guy too were part of the family, then she turned to Daisy, anxious to assure herself of her full recovery.

Nathaniel introduced Florence and her parents exchanged quick glances, nodded imperceptibly then smiled in delight at Florence. Florence might not realise it, but Daisy knew from experience that her parents had just conducted a lengthy conversation in that quick exchange of looks, and Florence had received their wholehearted approval.

'You must dine with us while you are in London,' her mother said to Florence. 'Oh, you too, of course, Guy,' she added. 'But that goes without saying. I'd be disappointed if you didn't dine with us as often as you could while you're in town.'

'And we're all going to the Dantons' ball on Saturday night,' Guy said.

'What, all of you?' her mother said, looking at Daisy.

'Yes, even me, Mother,' Daisy said with a sigh.

'Oh, well, that's good.' Her mother's eyebrows drew together, as if Daisy had imparted some confusing news she was having difficulty comprehending. 'Then you'll all be able to go together, won't you?' she said, smiling at Nathaniel and Florence.

'Indeed we can,' Guy replied, also looking at his cousin, who was blushing rather attractively.

'I think you'll discover a few things have changed with our Daisy while she was staying at the Mandivale estate, and I don't just mean her new-found desire to attend balls,' Nathaniel said, smiling at their mother, one eyebrow raised.

'Really?' Her mother tilted her head as she waited for Nathaniel to explain.

'Oh, yes,' Nathaniel said. 'And Guy has been most attentive while Daisy recovered from her injuries.'

'Thank you, Guy,' her mother said. 'You always were such a kind boy to Daisy, helping her when she got into all those scrapes when she was a child, and it seems you're still doing it.'

'Very attentive indeed,' Nathaniel added, an addition which Daisy considered completely unnecessary.

Her mother paused, stared at her smiling son then turned to face Guy. 'That's very good of you, Guy. I'm sure Daisy appreciated it.'

'I'm more than happy to be of service,' he responded with a small bow.

Her mother's smile grew into a beam, almost as large as Nathaniel's, and Daisy wondered how long everyone was going to stand around on the pavement for all the world to see, smiling at each other like ninnies.

After a bit more polite conversation, Guy and Florence departed in the carriage and the Springfelds entered their home. The moment the door closed, her Daisy's mother turned to her, her face now serious.

'There's only a week until the Dantons' ball. We need to see my dressmaker this afternoon and get you something appropriate to wear.'

'I've plenty of gowns in my wardrobe, Mother, some of which I've never even worn,' Daisy assured her, moving toward the drawing room, her progress halted when her mother grabbed her arm.

'I said something appropriate. I've never before insisted that you do as I tell you, but this time I must. You *will* accompany me to my dressmaker. You *will* wear a gown I deem to be suitable—one that shows you off to your best. Is that clear?'

She had never seen her mother like this, and it must have been shock that caused Daisy to nod.

Nathaniel gave a small cough and the two women looked in his direction, her mother still gripping Daisy's arm. 'Mother, I would like to have a word with you and Father on an important matter,' he said, his voice formal.

'Yes, yes, Nathaniel. Florence is lovely and I thoroughly approve. Talk to your father about it. He knows that you have my blessing, but for now I have a ball gown to order.'

Before Daisy even had a chance to freshen up after the train journey or change out of her travelling clothes, her mother was bundling her out of the door, leaving an equally stunned Nathaniel standing in the hallway.

Chapter Twelve

Like a leaf caught up in a gale, Daisy was pulled from one side of the dressmaker's studio to the other, while her mother and Madame Blanchard unwound rolls of silk, tulle and satin, draped them over Daisy's shoulder and stood back to discuss whether the colour highlighted her eyes, flattered her skin tone, was too daring or not daring enough.

Eventually, after discarding a mounting pile of fabric her mother selected a pale lemon silk, and Daisy breathed out a sigh of relief. Finally, it was over. But no. Still draped in the lemon cloth, various laces were wound around her neck, discarded and replaced with alternative styles of lace, all of which appeared exactly the same to Daisy.

Once Madame Blanchard and her mother had agreed on the lace, chiffon was discussed in minute detail before a suitable fabric for the train was decided upon. Daisy was then dragged over to the wooden shelves lining the cluttered studio and a selection of sashes was tied around her middle, and an animated discussion ensued on which type would best emphasise Daisy's slender waist and highlight the curve of her hips.

In amongst all this mayhem, the dressmaker's assistant attempted to take Daisy's measurements. Tape measures were rapidly run across her shoulders, from shoulder to waist, waist to ground, and each measurement listed in the assistant's book. When she took Daisy's waist measurement, she stopped and turned to her employer, confusion in her eyes.

'What is it, Madeline?' Madame Blanchard asked in an accent Daisy doubted was genuinely French.

'My lady is not wearing a corset,' Madeline whispered, trying and failing to keep the shock out of her voice.

Dismay briefly crossed the dressmaker's face before she smiled politely. 'What size waist do you 'ave when you are suitably— I mean, when you are wearing your undergarments?' she asked Daisy.

'I don't wear a corset and I won't be wearing one to the ball.' Daisy was making enough concessions to her mother already. She would not go completely against the principles of the Rational Dress Society and bind herself up in one of those hideous garments of chafing whale bone, restricting laces and overly starched linen.

The dressmaker looked at her mother, who sighed but nodded. 'I'm afraid Lady Daisy doesn't believe in wearing a corset.'

A frown briefly flitted across the dressmaker's face, but she signalled to the assistant to continue taking measurements.

'And yet, she still 'as a fashionably small waist,' Madame Blanchard observed, looking at the measurements in the assistant's book.

'She rides a bicycle,' her mother explained, causing Madame Blanchard's arched eyebrows to rise momentarily.

'All that exercise affects the shape of a woman's body,' her mother continued. 'Luckily no one at the ball will be able to see her legs, which are rather too muscular for a young lady. When she wears her riding bloomers you can see her calves through her stockings and my, oh my, they look like the legs of a dairy maid!'

'Riding bloomers?' Madame Blanchard gasped before remembering herself and smiling politely.

'Yes, riding bloomers. They're the most rational clothing to wear when cycling,' Daisy stated before turning to her mother. 'And I'll have you know my legs are strong from riding my bicycle and there is nothing wrong with a woman being strong.'

'Yes, dear.' Her mother sighed heavily and went back to inspecting a roll of ivory silk.

'If women spent as much time getting out in the fresh air and exercising as they did selecting clothing—'

'This fabric is stunning,' her mother interrupted.

As if pleased the outlandish conversation had come to an end, the dressmaker went back to discussing fabrics with her mother, while the assistant continued taking Daisy's measurements.

Once the assistant had finished, and the lace, fabrics, buttons and threads had been selected, Madame Blanchard spread some sketches on the table for mother and daughter to inspect.

Each dress looked as unnecessarily fussy as the next, so Daisy moved over to the window to watch the busy London street and let her mother make the selection.

As she observed the fashionably dressed couples strolling along the pavements, the servants rushing by on errands and the delivery carts unloading goods to the adjacent shops, she wondered what on earth she was doing.

Throughout the last five seasons she had done her utmost to avoid attending balls. She hated the way the debutantes, trussed up in their finery, were paraded in front of the men for their inspection, and how the mothers oh-so-politely jostled with each other to secure dance partners and ultimately marriage partners for their daughters.

And yet she was about to submit herself to that ordeal again, and now she would have the added distress of watching Guy Parnell assessing the young women on offer so he could select the best available to be his duchess. She picked up a piece of ribbon and wound it round her fingers as she continued to stare blankly at the outside street.

She wanted to condemn Guy for what he was doing, to hold him personally responsible for the appalling situation where young men and women were forced into marriages for family advantages, to advance their position in society and to ensure family titles and wealth were passed onto future generations. But could she really hold him accountable? He had not created this terrible situation and was caught up in it as much as the debutantes.

Pulling the ribbon off her fingers, she returned it to the counter. No, she would not feel sorry for Guy Parnell. He was a man and, even if as a duke he did have no choice but to marry, he could still continue to live like a single man, and she knew exactly what that would mean. She was just lucky she would not be the young woman he took as his duchess. He had made it perfectly clear that she was out of contention, and thank goodness for that. She would hate to join the ranks of debutantes desperate to capture a duke and then end up as the poor wife, stuck away in the country while he enjoyed himself in town with whomever he wanted.

'That one,' her mother proclaimed.

Daisy looked over her shoulder to see her mother stabbing her finger at one of the sketches. Reluctantly, she returned to the desk to inspect the fluffy concoction she would be expected to wear, but was pleasantly surprised. There were no flounces, no enormous sleeves, no tight neck that would almost choke the wearer.

Instead, her mother was pointing to a simple gown with a low neckline that left the shoulders bare and with a fitted bodice held in place by delicate lacy straps. From the waist it gently flowed to the ground, and as it would be made from silk it would not restrict movement. The long train was Daisy's only objection, but she knew if she made a fuss about that her objections would go unnoticed, so she might as well make the best of things, and her mother was quite obviously delighted with her choice.

As was Madame Blanchard. 'Excellent selection, my lady,' she said, clapping her hands together. 'That is the latest style from Paris and will look *très* fabulous in the lemon silk. Most young women are not confident enough to wear the sweeping décolletage and I'm sure your daughter will attract many favourable comments.'

'My darling daughter's clothing always attracts comments. At Lord and Lady Danton's ball, I hope she also attracts compliments.' A remark directed more at Daisy than Madame Blanchard.

'Well, if other people don't like the rational manner in which I…'

Before she could continue, her mother and the dressmaker turned back to the sketch and continued their conversation, something about threads and how a sweeping line of embroidered flowers would accentuate Daisy's curves.

What was the point? They wouldn't listen to anything she had to say, so she wandered off to stare back out at the street. It was all a lot of bother about nothing, she thought as she picked up a piece of silk and let the soft fabric run through her fingers.

Although, her mother was right. In that dress, she was likely to stand out, and possibly get compliments rather than just comments. Perhaps even from Guy.

She dropped the silk. Not that she wanted any compliments from him, and anyway, he'd be too busy assessing all the other young women on display to pay attention to her. Not that she'd want it if he did.

Once her mother had finished, she bundled Daisy back into a carriage.

'Right, now we've got you all organised, let's get home and see to organising the other marriage in the family. I hope Florence will allow me to choose her wedding gown. That ivory silk would look wonderful on either you or Florence, but you can't both wear it. I've asked Madame Blanchard to save enough for one wedding gown and I suppose it depends which of you gets married first.'

Daisy stared at her mother in disbelief. 'I agree that Florence and Nathaniel are likely to marry, Mother,' she said slowly, as if talking to someone who had trouble understanding simple concepts. 'But, as I am not even courting, and have no intention of doing so, then I believe it's rather premature to start choosing material for my wedding gown.'

To Daisy's intense infuriation, her mother patted her hand as if she were the one who did not understand. 'No man will be able to resist you in your new ball gown, and I am certain that before the end of this season we will be having two more Springfeld weddings.'

All Daisy could do was shake her head in pity at her poor mother's deluded state.

Daisy stood in front of the full-length mirror and hardly recognised herself. Under instruction from her mother, and ignoring Daisy's own demands, her lady's maid had swept her hair off her neck high onto her head and had intricately woven it into the voluminous style favoured by fashionable young ladies.

She swung her head from side to side, pleased that her hairstyle didn't impede movement. That would be taking things too far and would have caused Daisy to demand it be restyled in a simpler fashion. It would never have done if one had been riding into a head wind on one's bicycle, but, as her mother had pointed out ceaselessly, she was going to a ball, not hurtling along the road on one of those contraptions.

She took a step forward, pleased that the light, silk fabric did not curtail her ability to take longer strides, should she choose. Unlike many of the gowns young women wore, this one would not weigh her down by the excessive draping of heavy fabric. Her clothing would not constrain or restrict her. She wanted nothing to hamper her ability to keep an eye on Guy as he hunted for his bride.

Only the embroidered train was in encumbrance but, as the chiffon was light and it swirled around her legs when she stopped, Daisy decided she could cope with such frivolity.

As for the low-cut top and the lacy straps, Daisy had to admit they were rather flattering, if a bit daring, with so much décolletage on display. Her mother had overcome her daughter's objections to exposing so much flesh by arguing it was the liberated thing to do. She was showing the world what an independent young woman she was by not hiding herself away under layers of material.

Daisy suspected her mother was making fun of her and her beliefs but, as the gown was rather beautiful, she'd chosen not to argue. She had, however, put her foot down when it came to the corset. Under no circumstances would she wear one. Her mother had eventually relented but had instructed the lady's maid to tie the sash as tightly as she could around Daisy's waist.

'You look stunning, my lady,' her maid said, lifting the train and circling it round Daisy's feet, which were encased in white satin evening slippers. 'You will be the belle of the ball, I'm sure.'

Daisy said nothing. She wasn't about to point out to Annette that the only reason she was going to this ball was to keep an eye on Guy Parnell. She pulled on her elbow-length gloves and picked up her feathered fan, not sure whether such an accessory was entirely necessary, and walked down the hallway to the stairs. Guy and Florence had just arrived and were chatting with Nathaniel and her parents at the bottom of the staircase.

Daisy paused and rubbed her quivering stomach. While Annette continued to fuss around her, she pulled at her gloves, moved her fan from one hand to the other, then gripped the wooden banister to steady her jangling nerves. They were all waiting for her so, despite her unexpected anxiety, she was going to have to descend the stairs eventually.

She paused to take in a few more breaths. She should not keep them waiting but her feet would not move.

Everyone turned and stared up at her. All were smiling. All, that was, except one. Guy Parnell was not smiling. He was staring at her, his brown eyes intense, unblinking. Daisy could not look away from his captivating eyes. The others seemed to float away and disappear. She could hear their voices, but only as a muffled background noise. It was Guy, and only Guy she was aware of.

She continued to grip the banister tightly, suddenly

dizzy as heat simmered through her. He was not looking at her like a little sister now, or an annoying pest. He had the same expression she had fleetingly seen after he'd kissed her, the one she was uncertain whether she had imagined, as if he wanted to devour her.

And her body was responding in the same manner, her skin tingling, her lips suddenly sensitive. There was no denying, she liked it when Guy looked at her that way. Lifting her head, she swept down the stairs, every inch of her body aware that he was staring at her, assessing her—and that look told her loud and clear that he liked what he was seeing.

'Daisy, you are beautiful,' he said quietly when she reached the bottom of the stairs.

She smiled at him, suddenly bashful and unsure of herself, unsure what to say. Daisy was never lost for words, even if sometimes those on the receiving end of her sharp retorts wished she were. But what could you say to a man who was looking at you with such intensity it was causing your body to melt and your heart to flutter like a bird trapped within your chest?

Perhaps she could return the compliment, as he too looked wonderful. But then Guy always looked magnificent, and he certainly did tonight. Dressed in a black evening suit, dove-grey brocade waistcoat, white shirt and white bow-tie, he had never looked more elegant, more masculine or more irresistible.

Instead, she murmured a small, almost coy, 'Thank you.'

'Shall we?' He extended his arm and she lightly placed her gloved hand on his forearm.

As if in a daze, Daisy heard her parents say their goodbyes, and Guy led her out the house and into the carriage. Then the London streets passed by in a blur as they made their way to Lord and Lady Danton's Park Lane home.

The others were talking, about what Daisy was unsure, but she nodded, smiled and hoped her responses were appropriate. Instead of adding to the conversation as she normally would, she played with the fan in her lap, picking at the white feathers, grateful that she had such a diverting accessory.

This was not like her at all. She did not enjoy balls, but they never made her anxious. Bored, yes. Anxious, never. At every other ball she had attended, it had always been a case of getting the tiresome thing over and done with as quickly as possible. And she'd only gone to those balls to keep her mother happy so she could be left alone to pursue her real interests.

The carriage arrived outside the Danton home and the driver jostled for a space among all the other carriages offloading their passengers. The footman opened the door, and Guy and Nathaniel jumped out. Guy held out his hand to help the ladies out of the carriage and Daisy waited for Florence to take his hand, but she remained seated. Florence was obviously waiting to take Nathaniel's hand.

She placed her hand in Guy's. The moment their hands touched, a jolt rippled up her arm, causing her breath to catch in her throat and her heart to race. It was the same sensation she had experienced when he had picked her up and placed her in bed, except all that was touching her now was his gloved hand lightly holding her own gloved fingers.

She looked up at him and once again he was looking at her in *that* way. The same way he had looked at her when she had descended the stairs. The same way he had looked at her when he had kissed her. She froze, unable to move, unable to think. All she wanted to do was stare into those deep brown eyes, to drown in them, lose herself in them. Had they always been so dark, so deep, so mysterious? He had to be the most captivating man she had ever…

'Get a move on, can't you? There's other carriages waiting!' Daisy heard the gruff voice of a hackney cab driver call out to Guy's coachman. 'Don't take all blimmin' night about it.'

Daisy rushed down the steps, shocked at her own foolishness. *Drowning in his eyes, for goodness' sake—what on earth was the matter with her?*

'Shall we, Lady Daisy?' Guy asked, offering her his arm.

Her lips quivered slightly as she smiled at him, which had to be a reaction to foolishly causing the arriving carriages to become backed up. She was never shy, never coy, but tonight that was exactly how she was behaving.

She looked over her shoulder at Nathaniel. It would be more appropriate to enter on her brother's arm but, as he was seemingly oblivious to her, and only paying attention to Florence, she placed her hand lightly on Guy's.

They entered the crowded house and moved through to the mezzanine above the ballroom, where a large number of guests had already assembled, waiting to be announced.

As she looked down at the beautiful room, Daisy's sense of anticipation rose. She had been to balls at the Danton home before but had never seen the ballroom looking more glorious. They must have bought up every flower in London, because the room was awash with white roses, blue delphiniums, sweet peas in an array of pastel shades and vibrant pink lilies, and their floral scent was captivating.

The large chandelier suspended from the ornate, engraved wooden ceiling sent light glittering around the room, giving it a magical appearance, and several couples were already dancing to the orchestra, which was seated above the ballroom floor on a balcony.

A thrill of excitement rushed through her. She wanted to be on the floor, wanted to be in Guy's arms, wanted to be whirled around, to feel like a giddy young woman dancing with a handsome gentleman.

The footman announced them and every head in the room seemed to turn as one as they descended the stairs. Daisy's foolish smile died and her fluttering heart sank to her stomach as reality hit her hard.

Every mother in the room was staring at them. Every unwed young lady was smiling at Guy. How on earth did they know? Did they have some sort of telepathic sense that alerted them to when a duke came on the market?

There would be no dancing with Guy for her, no

twirling around the floor. Guy was here for one purpose only—to find a bride—and, judging by the eager looks on those smiling faces, he was about to be spoilt for choice.

Chapter Thirteen

It was a long time since Guy had experienced real fear. He had forced himself not to show fear in front of his father. That determination had stood him in good stead throughout his childhood. Eventually, he had learnt to stop fearing the man and had been able to remain calm and detached no matter what insults or punishments his father dealt out.

But this overwhelming desire to turn tail and flee felt suspiciously like fear. As the mothers grinned up at him from the ballroom floor, the magnitude of what he was about to face became a daunting reality. The mothers all knew why he was here—knew he was an eligible duke looking for a wife. They could somehow sense it, smell it on the wind, like lions detecting the presence of their prey.

He still had Daisy's arm and was grateful for it as they descended the stairs down to the circling mothers. Under normal circumstances he would assume that everyone was staring at the woman on his arm, and that would be understandable. Daisy looked beautiful tonight. Well, she always looked beautiful, even when dressed in her ridiculous cycling clothes, but tonight she seemed to be almost glowing, as if her beauty was coming from within and shining out for all to see. But he knew it wasn't Daisy's beauty that had caught the mothers' attention.

He should be pleased. He *was* in want of a wife, and if the mothers were keen to foist their daughters onto him then it shouldn't be too hard to find a young woman who would make an appropriate Duchess of Mandivale. And he should be enjoying himself. As a red-blooded man, there were few things he enjoyed more than looking at young ladies, and tonight no one would stop him from scrutinising to his heart's content. In fact, such behaviour would be actively encouraged.

But he wouldn't be scrutinising them for their beauty and desirability. If that was the case, then he already had the most beautiful woman in the room on his arm. No, he would be assessing them for their marriageability. He was after a woman who wanted a title which, judging by the sea of smiling faces, was every young lady present. He also required someone who had no real interest in him and would let him live his life however he wanted. A woman who would not love him and did not want love in return.

How did one go about finding such a woman? Guy still had no idea.

'You seem to be in great demand tonight,' Daisy said as they reached the bottom of the stairs. 'Perhaps I should leave you to find yourself a duchess.' Her arm slid out from his, but he grabbed it before she could escape.

'Don't leave me,' he said. Hearing the desperation in his voice, he laughed. He was being ridiculous. 'Don't leave yet,' he repeated in a softer tone. 'Not until we've had at least one dance.'

Lady Danton approached him, her arms outstretched in greeting, three young ladies trailing behind her. Guy's mounting panic notched up a few degrees.

'You must dance with me,' he whispered to Daisy, holding her arm tighter. 'Please.'

A dance would give him time to collect himself before the onslaught began. She tugged lightly on his arm, but he would not let her go. He needed her like he had never needed a woman before.

'But what about all those other young women?' She nodded towards the growing line of ladies assembling behind the trio of young Danton daughters.

'Exactly,' he said and, before she could disappear and leave him to his fate, he placed his hand on the small of her back and moved her through the crowd and onto the dance floor.

The orchestra struck up a waltz, and he guided her around the floor. His initial relief disappeared as he became conscious that he was holding Daisy in his arms. He had never noticed before how waltzing was so sensual. No wonder it had caused such a stir when it had first been introduced. It was impossible for him not to be aware of the woman in his arms, of how close she was, how their bodies were all but touching. It was just a dance, he told himself. He'd waltzed with many a young woman in such a manner. It was certainly nothing to get excited about.

He inhaled deeply, catching her subtle scent of lilacs, and memories came flooding back of lifting her up and placing her in her bed, of taking her face in his hands and kissing her lips.

Slowly, he exhaled, trying not to think of such things, trying not to remember how he had felt her soft curves through her nightdress, how her lips had tasted or how he had reacted when he had first seen her descending the stairs this evening, definitely no longer a child but all woman—all luscious, desirable woman.

No, that was not what he should think of. He should remember her as little Daisy Chain, skinning her knees, climbing up trees, using a sling shot to prove she was just as proficient as any boy. But he was asking the impossible. With his hand around her slim waist, he could not ignore her womanly curves, nor could he ignore the effect she was having on him.

Perhaps small talk would drive out any improper images. He smiled down at her in what he hoped was a casual, friendly manner, racking his brain for something, anything, trivial to say. She looked up at him and his mind went blank. All he could think of was the blue of her eyes. Deep blue like the ocean, and just as beguiling. Had they always been that colour? Had they always glittered, like sunlight on a cool blue lake? And had her lips always been so inviting, like soft pillows drawing you in?

He had never felt such a desperate urge to kiss any woman the way he wanted to kiss her right now. And yet, she was the one woman he should not kiss. He was here to find a wife, not to seduce Lady Daisy Springfeld. In fact, the words Daisy and seduction should not have entered his mind. Even thinking them must be a sin. So why was he still staring at those inviting lips?

As if wrenching himself free from an almost unbreakable force, he looked over her head at the other swirling couples.

Think of something else...anything else.

Instead, he had somehow managed to pull her even closer, so close her breasts were almost touching his chest. He swore to himself that it had not been deliberate. How could it be deliberate when it was exactly what he knew he shouldn't do?

He did not need to be enticed by her warmth, by her scent. Did not need to have her so close that she could easily place her head on his shoulder. And yet, irrationally, that was what he wanted, what he hoped she would do. Fortunately, she was more rational than he, and her head remained where it should be, upright and nowhere near his shoulder.

The dance ended and, still in a state of confusion, he led her off the floor. Would it be inappropriate to ask her for another dance? Could he trust himself if he did so? Before he could answer his own question, two mothers bustled up to them, edging Lady Danton and her three daughters out of the way. In the hunt for a husband, it seemed even basic good manners towards one's hostess could be dispensed with.

'Why, Your Grace, it is wonderful to see you here. I do hope you will be dancing with as many young ladies as possible tonight,' Lady Clifford said. 'My daughter, Cecilia, was just saying what a marvellous dancer you are.'

'Oh, what a coincidence,' Lady Forsythe butted in, all but elbowing her friend out of the way. 'My youngest, Beatrice, said exactly the same thing. She's only eighteen, you know. This is her first season, and she's thoroughly enjoying it, as she is so much in demand.'

'If you'll excuse me,' Daisy said and slipped away from him before he could grab hold of her and beg her to protect him.

The two mothers grinned up at him, waiting for his reply. 'Then I must dance with both of your daughters,' he said, causing them to flutter in a manner that reminded him of hens ruffling their feathers. Lady Clifford immediately gripped his arm and all but dragged him across the room to her smiling daughter, and he had no option but to escort the young woman onto the dance floor.

While making polite conversation, he looked over the young woman's head to search for Daisy, but she was nowhere in sight. Had she disappeared into the ladies' retiring room? Was she in the supper room? She most definitely was not on the floor in the arms of another man. He smiled, pleased by that realisation, then squashed that smile. She should be enjoying herself and dancing with as many men as possible.

The dance came to an end, and Lady Forsythe appeared as if by magic with her daughter Beatrice in tow. After much smiling, and another mention from the older woman of how in demand Beatrice was, Guy escorted the younger lady onto the dance floor. As soon as that dance was over, Lady Danton got her chance and he danced with each daughter in turn. Once that duty was done, another mother and daughter appeared in his path, giving him no option but to lead yet another potential duchess around the floor.

Dance after dance was the same until he had danced with what he assumed to be every available young woman in the room. This was what he had come for, and he should have used the dances to ask questions, make assessments and comparisons, but he could hardly remember what any of the young women had looked like, what they had said and certainly not whether they would make an ideal duchess.

Finally, the orchestra stopped for the supper break and he made his excuses to the warring mothers. He needed to take stock, to pull himself together and focus on his task. Instead, he looked around the room for Daisy. She was nowhere in sight. Was she hiding? Had she gone home? Nathaniel and Florence were ensconced in an alcove, looking lovingly into each other's eyes and whispering sweet nothings. They would have no idea what had happened to Daisy, and Nathaniel was obviously not taking his role as chaperon at all seriously. It would be up to Guy to find her, then, and ensure that she was safe and being looked after.

She wasn't in the supper room. Nor was she up on the mezzanine floor or seated in the room reserved for card playing. Eventually, he found her, all alone on the small outdoor balcony that led off an empty upstairs drawing room.

'There you are, Daisy. I've been looking for you everywhere.'

She turned slowly to face him and he stopped in his tracks. Had she grown even more beautiful than when they'd arrived at this ball? Of course not. He was being absurd. But in the reflected glow of the full moon, she was simply breath-taking. The naked alabaster skin of her shoulders seemed to glow and the desire to run his lips over her silky skin was oh, so tempting.

His gaze moved lower to the mounds of her breasts, on display above the lace of her gown. If he had any doubts that Daisy was now a woman, those beautiful round breasts were all the proof he needed. But, despite her beauty, despite the temptation of that exposed flesh, she was still Daisy Chain, his best friend's little sister, the child whose cut knees he had bandaged. The little girl he had helped find a way down when she had become stuck in a tall tree. She was not for him.

'Well, you've found me,' she said, turning to look back out at the garden which was bathed in the black velvet of the night. 'And how is the pursuit of the duchess going?'

'What? Oh, that. Yes, it's going as well as can be expected, but I'm taking a much-needed rest before I return to the fray.'

'I'm not surprised you need a rest. After all that dancing, flirting and carrying on, you must be quite exhausted.'

She continued to stare out at the garden and he moved closer to her, joining her on the balcony. 'I didn't see you dancing. How did you know whether I was flirting or carrying on?'

'I was watching from the mezzanine floor. Then I got disgusted at the way those mothers were all but throwing their daughters at you. It was like watching an appalling ritual where sacrificial virg... Where sacrificial young ladies were being placed on an altar for your selection. So I retreated to this balcony. Do any of those young ladies know what you're up to, what you expect from them?'

'I imagine they all know exactly what I'm up to and that is the precise reason their mothers are all but throwing them at my feet. But the more important question is, Daisy, what are you doing out here? You should be dancing.'

She merely shrugged one of those enticing, naked shoulders.

'You're not going to try and tell me you've had no offers? Dressed like that, I have little doubt that you had the men falling over themselves to put their name on your dance card.' As she still had her back to him, his gaze was free to roam over the delicate pale skin of her shoulders and exposed neck.

'I have no interest in dancing.'

'Then why did you come to a ball—the main point of which, if not the only point, is to dance?'

'I came to keep an eye on you, if you must know. I don't want you marrying any poor young woman who doesn't know exactly what she's getting into.'

'You seem to have a very low opinion of me. Do you really think I would do such a thing? Trick some innocent young thing into thinking we're marrying for love, rather than letting her know exactly what the deal is? The woman I marry will know exactly what arrangement they are entering into. There will be no false promises, no unrealistic expectations.'

She shrugged one shoulder and he wished she'd stop drawing his attention back to her naked skin.

'But you're going to have a hard time monitoring my behaviour from this balcony.'

She shrugged again. Was she deliberately trying to torture him, to make him think of running his fingers over her skin, touching her naked flesh with his lips?

He coughed lightly. 'Your mother will be very disappointed if she hears you spent the ball hidden away from sight.'

She turned towards him, the moonlight making her blue eyes glisten. She was now breathing faster, luring his gaze back to her breasts. He forced himself to look back at her angry eyes and not imagine cupping those lovely mounds.

'I'm perfectly happy out here.'

She looked anything but happy.

'If you don't want to dance for your own sake, then do it for those men in the ball room. I doubt I'm the only man who has noticed how beautiful you look tonight. It would be so unfair if you hide yourself away,' he said, trying to keep his voice light.

She continued to stare at him, and her breasts continued to rise and fall, but he forced himself not to lower his gaze.

'And you are a beautiful woman,' he whispered, more

as an admission to himself than as a compliment to her. An image invaded his mind of her body not covered by a silk dress, but by silk sheets. Of her lying in his bed, her long hair loose and curling around her naked breasts, looking up at him, waiting for him, eager for him.

He coughed and looked over her shoulder out into the darkness. What on earth was wrong with him? He needed to get away from this balcony, from the subdued light that was causing his mind to go off into areas where it should not go.

'I think we should return to the ballroom,' he said, annoyed at his constricted voice.

'You return. As I said, I'm quite happy here.'

He should not stay. He should return to the bright lights of the ballroom, to the safety of company. It was too dangerous to stay out here, alone in the dark, where he was free to think inappropriate thoughts. He needed other men to dance with her, men more appropriate than he could ever be. He huffed out a hard, course breath as the thought of some other man touching her, holding her in his arms, entered his mind. He didn't want that either.

'I wish to dance with you,' he said as he swallowed down his irrational jealousy. 'You wouldn't be so cruel as to deny your old friend a dance, would you?' He emphasised 'old friend' as much to remind himself that he was merely her friend, nothing more. One she had known for so long that she should be able to trust him not to have inappropriate thoughts of her, and most certainly never to act on those thoughts.

'Oh, but if you danced with me you'd disappoint all those potential duchesses, wouldn't you?'

'Let them be disappointed. I want to dance with you.'

She looked up at him and gave an almost imperceptible nod.

He took her hand before she changed her mind. 'I don't care who I disappoint,' he murmured. 'As long as I don't disappoint you.'

He gently kissed her cheek. 'I never want to disappoint you, Daisy.'

It was merely a friendly gesture or, if not that, then the light kiss that a brother would give his sister. Nothing more. No one could remonstrate with him for that, not even himself.

His lips lingered, hovering close to her cheek. He wanted to kiss her cheek again, wanted to kiss her lips. But that would be wrong.

Slowly, her head lifted and turned until it was her lips, not her cheek, that were almost brushing against his lips. Her lips were so close he could taste them. A light kiss on the lips. That would be all right. It would mean nothing, merely a friendly, almost familial gesture. His lips stroked hers, the touch as light as a gentle caress. They were just as he had remembered, soft, warm and delicious.

His lips lingered, just as they'd done when he had kissed her cheek, so close, so tantalisingly close. She moved in closer towards him, her lips pressing onto his more firmly, her body almost up against his. He should stop this now. It was lasting too long for a friendly kiss. Her hands encircled his head. All was lost. He was lost. How could he possibly stop now?

So he didn't. With all pretence stripped away, his

arm wrapped tightly around her waist, pulling her in towards him, and his lips crashed onto hers. His kiss was no longer friendly but intense, fierce, demanding. He wanted her kisses too much to continue pretending. And the way she was kissing him back showed that she wanted him too, just as desperately.

Needing to taste her, he ran his tongue along her bottom lip, savouring the mix of sweetness and spice. When her lips parted, it was all the encouragement he needed. He plunged inside her, savouring, probing, plundering, unable to stop the kiss even if he'd wanted to—but he didn't want to. He would not stop, not until he had fully satisfied his need for her.

All control now stripped from him, his hands ran over those curves he had been desperate to explore. A moan of appreciation escaped his lips. His caresses were not impeded by a stiff corset, her body was not shaped by such artifice, and he could explore her natural, womanly body. He slowly traced a line along her waist, over the gentle curve of her hips, down to the rounds of her buttocks.

She put up no objection to his touch. Her only reaction when he cupped her buttocks was to mould herself closer to his body, her breasts touching his chest, her hips and legs hard up against him. And she continued to kiss him back with a passion that was as surprising as it was arousing.

'My beautiful Daisy,' he murmured as he withdrew from her lips, looking down at her. She was indeed beautiful, more beautiful than any woman he had ever seen. Her eyes were closed, her head tilted back, her full red lips parted and her breath coming in small, ragged breaths, drawing his attention back to the rise and fall of her swelling breasts.

Unable to resist temptation, he kissed a line along her naked shoulders, relishing the taste and touch of her soft skin. He had wanted to kiss her naked flesh from the moment he had seen her standing at the top of the stairway, looking so bewitching. He ran his tongue lightly over her skin. It was as silky as he had imagined. No longer thinking, just acting, his kisses moved lower, closer to those enchanting breasts.

Her breath came in faster, shorter gasps, those enticing mounds rising and falling more rapidly as if swelling towards him, urging him on, giving him permission to do what he was aching to do. He kissed a slow line across one then the other, wishing that he could do more than just kiss her. That he could take her to his bed, free her of all her clothing and kiss every inch of her luscious body before his demanding, pulsating need found release deep within her.

This is wrong, so wrong, a small, insistent voice nagged. He should stop.

His gaze left those lovely breasts and looked down at her face. She was so exquisite, like a priceless art work. He could spend an eternity staring at that lovely face, appreciating its beauty and perfection. Slowly, her eyes opened and she looked up at him, her blue eyes dark, her parted lips glistening.

'Daisy, I…'

'Don't talk,' she whispered and, before he could order the confused words circling in his mind, she took his hand and moved it to her breast, her back arching towards him.

Guy released a soft moan as his hand slid inside the soft fabric of her gown, his palm stroking the tight nub of her nipple. Slowly, he teased her bud, watching her face, loving the way she surrendered herself to his touch. With each stroke a gasp escaped her parted lips, as if urging him on.

He kissed her gasping lips, then her neck, her shoulders. Her hands encircled his head, her fingers curling through his hair as his kisses moved closer to her breasts. She was as lost as he was, and he knew exactly what she wanted him to do.

Pushing the straps off her shoulders, he gently pulled down the soft fabric of her gown, exposing her full, round breasts to his gaze. In the soft moonlight her breasts were as beautiful as he had imagined, the tight, pink nipples pointing up at him as if begging to be caressed, to be nuzzled.

She gasped. He had gone too far. He reached for the lacy straps to pull them back onto her shoulders. She took hold of his hand, lightly kissed his fingers then moved it back to her breast.

'Are you sure?' he whispered in her ear.

She didn't answer, merely nodded.

Cupping both breasts, he gently stroked and teased each bud, watching her face as he did so, loving the reaction. Her swollen red lips parted wider and her breath came in faster, shallower gasps until she was all but panting...panting for him.

'Oh, Daisy. My lovely, beautiful Daisy,' he murmured, before taking one nipple in his mouth, nuzzling and licking the tight nub, loving the sound of her rapidly gasping breaths.

This was wrong. He knew it was wrong. But wrong had never felt so right.

'Guy, oh, Guy,' Daisy whispered. With each uncontrolled gasp, her body burned as unbridled pleasure mounted within her. Her hands clasped his head tighter, desperate for him not to stop until he had taken her to the top of the peak where his tongue and lips were leading.

'Oh, Guy!' she called out, her voice louder, her body convulsing in reaction to his tormenting tongue. Her fingers dug into his skin, holding him in place, refusing to let him go until she had reached the zenith she was rushing towards. He did as she commanded, cupping her neglected breast, his thumb and finger caressing the sensitive tight nub while his tongue, lips and teeth continued to nuzzle, suck and torment its twin until she was sure she could hardly bear the mounting excitement building within her, consuming every inch of her body.

Her breath coming in louder, faster gasps, she lost herself in the delicious sensations, no longer caring what she was doing, where she was and if anyone could hear...until an explosion of ecstasy flooded her body and the muscles deep in her body contracted with a wildness she had not known possible.

His lips left her breast and found her waiting mouth. Wrapping her in his arms, he kissed her, deeply, passionately, her body hard up against his. If it was possible to die from pleasure, Daisy was sure she must be in mortal danger.

She pulled back from his lips, swallowed and tried to make sense of what had just happened.

'Guy, that was, that was…' Words defied her. None were adequate to describe such ecstasy. Despite the euphoria still coursing through her, it wasn't enough. She wanted more. Sliding her hands down his body, she cupped his buttocks and pulled him in towards her, rubbing herself against his body as the throbbing intensity that had overtaken her returned. She needed more. She needed what only he could provide. Needed him to fill her, to complete her, to take her as his own.

His hands moved down to her buttocks again, holding her tightly against him. He groaned lightly as she continued to rub herself against him, and the heat coursing through her intensified until every inch of her body was ablaze. It was as if she had secretly waited a lifetime for this, and she wanted him to take her, right here and right now.

The pounding deep in her core, the pulsating tension between her legs, increased its demand for release, a release that she knew only he could give her. This might be wrong, so very wrong, but she wanted Guy Parnell to seduce her, to take her on this balcony, and to hell with the consequences. And she knew enough about male anatomy to know that seducing her was exactly what he wanted as well. The evidence was pushing against her, hard and insistent.

'Please, Guy,' she whispered. 'Make love to me.'

'Oh, Daisy, we can't,' he mumbled, kissing her neck, his arms wrapped around her waist, holding her tight.

'We can,' she gasped back. 'No one would know. You've done it with other women. Now do it with me.'

He drew back from her as if pushed hard by an invisible force, then stared at her with a ferocity that would have been unnerving if she wasn't so intoxicated by what he had done, what she wanted him to do.

'Guy, seduce me,' she whispered, her voice barely audible as she rose up on her toes to kiss his sweet lips again.

'Daisy, I'm sorry,' he whispered, his voice husky.

He did not need to be sorry. He could put things to rights by kissing her back, harder and deeper, by caressing her body again, by giving her release from the pounding need building up within her.

'Don't be sorry,' she murmured,

'This should not have happened. I'm so sorry,' he repeated, stepping back and disentangling her hands from around his shoulders. 'I should never have kissed you, should never have… I just shouldn't have.'

As if emerging from a fog, Daisy tried to take in his words, barely aware that he was pulling up the neckline of her gown, restoring the straps to her shoulders.

What was he doing? He should be kissing her, stroking her body, making love to her. When her gown was restored, he exhaled a held breath and stood up straighter. 'Please, forgive me.'

Slowly, she shook her head. He had done nothing that needed to be forgiven—nothing, that was, except what he was doing now. She looked at him in disbelief.

He stared out at the garden, as if not wanting to look at her, his jaw tense, his lips tight. He would not be kissing her again, would not be caressing her, and certainly would not be making love to her. He had given her a small sample and that was all that she was going to taste. She had all but begged him to make love to her, to do with her what he had done with countless other women…but he had rejected her.

Chapter Fourteen

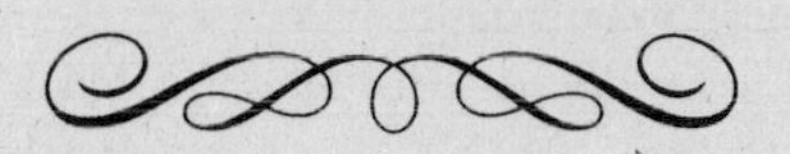

'We should return to the ballroom. People will be starting to wonder where we have gone,' Guy said.

If he had disappeared for such a long time with anyone other than Daisy, questions would have been asked, assumptions made. He just had to hope no one had noticed or, if they had, that they thought he was merely taking a brotherly interest in his best friend's little sister's well-being.

Shame consumed him like a physical illness. That was what he *should* have been doing. He had a reputation as a rake but had always believed that to be unjustified. Yes, he'd had a lot of women in his life, but he still had morals that set him apart from many men who were labelled rakes. He'd never seduced anyone, ever. Every woman who came to his bed did so under her own instigation. And he had never made love to a virgin. They were off-limits.

Tonight, he had ignored all those self-imposed rules and, not only that, had tried to seduce a woman who was more off limits than most.

He was a cad of the worst kind, a man capable of acting in a debased manner, a manner which was unforgivable. He had put his carnal desires before a woman's reputation. He had betrayed himself, his best friend and a family who had taken him in as a child and provided him with the warmth and love he had never received in his own home. They had cared for him like a son, and this was how he repaid them.

'I don't want to go back to the ballroom. I want to stay here, with you,' she whispered into the dark air.

The pain clenching Guy's stomach intensified. What had he done? Had he corrupted her? Despite her innocence, her kisses had not been chaste but had contained an unexpected passion. That too was his fault. That passion should not have been unleashed by him, and not here. It should have been saved for her wedding night, when she'd be in the arms of a man who loved her, a man she was in love with, a man worthy of that love.

'Daisy, please, for the sake of your reputation. We have been absent for too long. People will talk. You know that they will.'

'As if I care about such things.'

How he wished to take her at her word. But, despite her claim to be independent, she was wrong. Society would forgive him anything—he was a man and a duke—but it could be cruel to a woman who transgressed its strict moral code.

'You might not care, but your mother will care. And I care.'

She pulled back from him, as if repulsed by his words, her eyes defiant. 'You care about your reputation, do you?' She gave a harsh laugh. 'Now that you're after a bride, you suddenly care what people think about you?'

She had misinterpreted his words. He did not need to care about his own reputation. His position in society meant he could get away with almost anything. It was Daisy, and only Daisy, he cared about. But he had to get her back into the ballroom, back in public, before people started to speculate about their prolonged absence, and the gossiping women started to discuss Daisy's good name behind their fans. If it took her believing he was doing it for his own selfish reasons, then so be it.

'That's right. I'm sorry, Daisy, but you know that the only reason I am here tonight is to find a bride. It will not help my cause to be absent for a long time and then reappear with a woman I have no intention of marrying.'

She gasped, and this time it was not a gasp of ecstasy. He didn't want to hurt or offend her, but it was for her own good. And if she was angry with him, if she thought badly of him, despised him, then it was no more than his behaviour deserved. He was a cad who had come perilously close to doing the unforgivable. Such a man *should* be despised.

'Perhaps you should have thought of that before you kissed me,' she said through clenched teeth.

'You're right. But you know me, Daisy, and you know my reputation.' He forced a light laugh. 'I can't resist any available young woman.'

A slap stung his face. Her gloved hand hardly hurt, not physically, but it still stung him deeply and her anger left him reeling.

'You're despicable.' She pushed past him and stormed off the balcony.

Guy gripped the railing and looked out at the dark night. She hated him. He did not want her to hate him, but he had brought this on himself and had no right to self-pity. And as long as she hated him there was no likelihood of her ever allowing him to kiss her again, or do more than just kiss her. He gripped the iron railing tighter, drew in a deep breath and repeatedly reminded himself that, if she hated him, it was all for the best.

After what he hoped was sufficient time for no one to notice that he and Daisy had been absent together, he re-entered the ballroom. The volume of the chatter increased markedly with his reappearance. Hopefully, Daisy's re-entrance had been more discreet than his. But a duke who was seeking a bride could do nothing discreetly. As with his arrival every mother noticed that he was back, and he was greeted with a sea of smiling mothers and daughters.

Even Florence and Nathaniel were smiling at him from their private alcove. Although, those two seemed incapable of doing anything but smile. Their happiness with each other was all but palpable. That must be what love looked like—all smiling and soppy, as if the world was a wonderful place and everyone in it was good and kind. But if Nathaniel had known what Guy had just been doing with his little sister, what he had almost done, he would not have been smiling. He'd be taking Guy outside and giving him a thrashing, and rightly so.

While one mother grabbed his arm, and another prattled on about her daughter's charms and accomplishments, he looked around the room for Daisy. She was on the floor, in the arms of Archibald Fitzsimmons. As if punched in the stomach, Guy exhaled explosively. Fingernails dug into flesh as his hands curled into tight fists. Breathing slowly and deeply, he forced his hands to unclench, forced his rigid jaw to relax and lowered his tense shoulders.

This was what he'd wanted. Daisy was in public. No one was talking about her. She had not been shunned and she was dancing with another man. A man who could offer her all the things that he could not. He should be happy for her. But if the bile burning up his throat was happiness, it was an emotion he could live without.

The babbling mothers' voices faded away as he watched the couple move around the floor. Fitzsimmons was a good man, he reminded himself. A bit dull, perhaps, but certainly not a rake. He would make any woman an excellent husband and provide everything that Guy was incapable of: love, fidelity, a comfortable family life. That was what he wanted for Daisy: for her to love, be loved and be happy. So why did he want to rip her out of Fitzsimmons' arms and carry her off into the night?

He turned back to the mothers and tried to concentrate but, as if directed by a power over which he had no control, his attention kept being drawn back to the dancing couple. The dance came to an end and Fitzsimmons led a solemn Daisy off the floor.

Ignoring the chattering mothers, ignoring the voice in his head that was telling him not to do this, Guy pushed his way through the milling crowd. It was only right to dance with her again, he argued with himself, trying to shout down that other, niggling voice that was telling him to turn round and walk away. Dancing together would show that they were still merely good friends, he argued with himself, just as they had always been.

'I believe you promised me the next dance, Lady Daisy,' he said with a formal bow. He had tried to keep his voice light, but the restriction in his throat made the request sound more like a command.

She arched one eyebrow and he expected her to put up an argument, to tell him that she had promised him no such thing, but she placed her hand on his arm and allowed him to lead her out onto the floor.

The orchestra played the first notes and, damn it all, it was another waltz. A quadrille, a gallop or a polka would have been preferable—anything where they would have had little physical contact. He placed his hand on her waist and took her hand in his, fighting not to remember holding her in his arms in the moonlight, caressing her body as if he'd had every right to do so.

He drew in a deep, controlling breath and glided her across the floor. Despite the tension between them, dancing with her felt so right, as if she was meant to be in his arms. Although, that must be down to the skill of her dance instructor and Daisy's natural grace, and nothing to do with any compatibility between them. He twirled her around and she followed his lead.

He had to smile. It was one of the few times Daisy followed anyone. She had grown into such an independent young lady, rebellious, feisty and, as he had now discovered, passionate. He exhaled slowly. The last of those attributes was something he should not know and should try and forget.

'So, you only kissed me because I was available?' she asked, interrupting his thoughts. 'If there had been any other young woman out on that balcony, you would have kissed them instead?'

He tried to laugh off her angry questions. 'Any young woman looking as beautiful as you did in the moonlight. Any young woman dressed like you.'

Any young woman who was you.

'It was all my fault, then, was it?'

'None of it was your fault,' he said, staring down into her eyes, hoping she would know it to be true. 'It was all my fault. I told you the reason why I kissed you so you would know the sort of man I am.'

'As if I didn't already,' she murmured under her breath, looking away.

He tried not to flinch, tried not to hate himself any more than he already did. He was once again tempted to beg for her forgiveness, but what would be the point? She knew what sort of man he was, had always known it, and now he had proved it.

They moved through the circling couples and once again silence descended between them.

'So, how did kissing me compare to kissing Ruby Lovelace, Lady Parnell or all those other women you have kissed?' she finally asked, making him long for the return of silence.

He looked down into her angry blue eyes, glaring

at him as she waited for his answer. But what *could* he say?

Kissing you was unlike anything I have experienced before. I have never known such intensity, such closeness. With other women, part of me always remained detached, but with you it was different. All boundaries between us seemed to melt away, as if we had become one.

That was what he wanted to say, but he could not, he must not.

'Daisy, don't,' he murmured instead. 'I should not have kissed you and I am profoundly sorry that I did. I know that I am a cad, but until tonight I hadn't known just how much of a cad I could be. I know that I have no right to your forgiveness, so I won't ask for it, but I promise I will never take such liberties with you ever again.'

Guy Parnell had kissed her. It should mean very little—after all, she was not the first woman to have been kissed by a charmer—but it meant more to her than she could articulate. It wasn't her first kiss, although that was the way it had felt. The other times she had been kissed it had been nice, but Guy's kisses could never be described as 'nice'. Until tonight she had not known it was possible to be consumed by such surging ecstasy, to lose oneself so completely in a sensual experience. Even the thought of it was causing that throbbing intensity to well up inside her, causing her to long for him to kiss her again, caress her again, complete what her body had desperately desired of him.

As if under the power of an uncontrollable compulsion, she moved closer towards him, wishing he was kissing her now. But he was right. It should not have happened, and it should never happen again. She cared not a fig for her reputation. If society wanted to gossip about her, that was no concern of hers, and certainly would not be the first time she had earned the disapproval of society ladies. Riding a bicycle alone through the London streets while wearing bloomers had already made her the subject of many a disapproving discussion.

But gossip over a ruined reputation would reflect badly on her family and shame her mother. She could not do that to them. Nor did she want to be merely one more woman in Guy's long list of conquests. And she most certainly did not want to become his mistress after he had found that sought-after wife.

Did she?

She looked up into those coal-dark eyes and for a brief moment her resistance melted before returning, stronger and fiercer. No, of course she did not. The fact that he was going to offer a title to some woman who was prepared to let him have a mistress was bad enough. She most certainly would not *be* that mistress.

She sighed lightly. It was all so confusing both to want something desperately and be equally determined not to want it. But it made no difference what she wanted or did not want. He had made that clear.

He would never kiss her again. He would never make love to her the way he had made love to so many others. She knew now exactly why Lady Parnell had looked like a satisfied, purring cat, and why Ruby Lovelace was so eager to return to his estate. They had experienced that rapture, and more. With his mistresses, he had not stopped but had taken them to heights of excitement of which she could only dream.

And some other young woman present tonight, the one he chose to be the Duchess of Mandivale, would also experience such heady pleasure. But Daisy never would.

She looked round at the dancing couples, and the crowds lining the dance floor, and wondered which one he would take as his bride. Almost every woman present was staring at them. No doubt many were jealous of her, but they had no need. She was the one woman Guy had rejected.

'So how has the hunt for the next Duchess of Mandivale been going?' she asked, pleased that her voice betrayed nothing of her agitation.

'As expected,' came his vague reply.

'So, what did you expect? That the perfect woman would present herself and fall into your arms?' Her attempt to keep her voice neutral failed, and she silently cursed herself for sounding jealous. She would not be jealous.

'Is there such a thing as the perfect woman?'

'No, but if there was I doubt if she'd want to marry you.'

He smiled at her and she wished he wouldn't do that either, not when it caused her icy anger to thaw and undermined her determination not to be affected by his charm or good looks.

'You're quite right,' he continued. 'But so far I have not found the *im*perfect woman who would make the perfect Duchess of Mandivale.'

She harrumphed her disapproval.

He whirled her around and, damn it all, she almost slipped, so tense was her body. His hand moved further round her waist to steady her. Their bodies were now closer than propriety permitted. So close she could feel his thighs against hers. Thoughts of him holding her tightly rushed back, more a physical memory than an image, and a sigh escaped her lips, a sigh that was almost a groan.

He looked down at her, his expression the same as it had been before he'd kissed her, as if he was hungry, as if he needed her, wanted her. But he did not need or want her. He might be hungry, but wasn't that typical of a rake? Weren't they all like hungry wolves always on the hunt? And like a fool she had succumbed. She had been the available woman alone on the balcony just waiting for him to kiss her.

She moved further away from him. She would never be that available woman ever again. The waltz came to an end and he took her arm. Before they had even made it to the edge of the floor he was surrounded. He held on to her arm as the swirling mothers tried to edge her aside like a drowning man clasping at a straw.

'I'll leave you to your pursuit,' she said, firmly pulling her arm from his grasp. The moment she was free of him, the mothers surged forward. He was swallowed up by the crowd of fawning women and Daisy found herself on the outside of the pack surrounding Guy.

She turned abruptly and strode across to the other side of the ballroom. While he was admired and adored by a coterie of women, she would spend the rest of the night dancing with as many other men as possible. He would see just how unaffected she was, that their kiss meant as little to her as it did to him, and that she wasn't giving him or his caresses another thought.

Chapter Fifteen

Somehow Guy found himself dancing with Lady Constance Dudley. Despite the energetic nature of the polka, she managed to keep up a steady stream of chatter and appeared satisfied with a few nods of agreement and the occasional smile from Guy.

Which was fortunate, as it allowed him the opportunity to observe Daisy as that buffoon Arnold Carruthers bounced her around the floor. He was almost as boring as Fitzsimmons, but then, he was also as dependable, and the sort who would make a faithful husband. But, really, Carruthers? He would have thought she had better taste.

Not that it was his role to ensure Daisy found a suitable husband. That was the role of her brother, the man who should be acting as Daisy's chaperon. The man who was doing a very lax job. If he'd been doing his job properly, he would never have allowed his sister to disappear onto that balcony, and would never have allowed her to be alone with Guy.

Florence and Nathaniel skipped past. They were staring into each other's eyes, still with those matching smiles on their faces. Guy suspected that the roof could fall in and those two wouldn't notice, so it was no surprise that Nathaniel hadn't noticed that his sister's virtue had been in peril. Guy wanted to blame his best friend but knew that would be unfair. There was only one person to blame. Himself.

He looked back at Daisy. She was talking and smiling at Carruthers, and Guy forced himself not to react. If he *was* going to react, it should be with happiness. No one knew what had happened between them. It had not affected Daisy's reputation. They could move on and pretend it had never occurred, and hopefully one day, when Daisy was happily married with several children, it would be a distant memory that had disappeared from both their minds.

Daisy caught his eye and sent him an angry scowl, reminding him that for now she had not forgotten what had happened. He suspected it would be a long time before she could forgive or forget his transgression, and he would have to bear her disdain with as much forbearance as he could muster. After all, he should expect no less.

Lady Constance looked up at him. She was no longer speaking, and her expectant look suggested she had just asked a question, but what? He had no idea. He nodded and her face lit up with pleasure.

Damn, what had he just agreed to?

'Mother will be so pleased,' she said.

Damn again. He knew exactly what would please Lady Constance's mother.

'Will she?' he probed.

'Oh, yes.'

'And why is that?' he asked, bracing himself for the answer.

'She had wondered whether you would be attending our ball, as the invitations were sent out some weeks ago but we are yet to receive your reply. Mother told me to make sure that you accepted.' She gave him a coquettish smile. 'And you have.'

'I'm looking forward to it,' he said with relief, as he lifted her up in the air as the polka step demanded, causing her to giggle. Agreeing to another ball was so much better than agreeing to a marriage. Although, wasn't that the whole point of him being here tonight?

He looked down at the young lady in his arms who was still smiling fit to burst. She would make a perfect Duchess of Mandivale. Her family might have had a title but little in the way of property. As an obedient younger daughter, he knew she would marry whomever her parents selected for her, with little expectation of love or happiness.

He sighed and looked across the room at Daisy. She had every right to be disgusted by what he was doing. This ball really was little more than a very refined, very polite cattle market.

But he would not be marrying Lady Constance and he hoped, when a husband was selected for her, she would be one of the lucky few and that they would be happy and would grow to care for each other.

The dance ended and he led Lady Constance off the floor. Once again, the mothers swarmed around him. Smiling politely at them while taking quick glances over their heads, he noticed that Daisy was also getting a lot of attention. It was obviously not due to lack of interest that she had remained single. Perhaps she was waiting for the perfect man just as he was waiting for the perfect duchess. But what sort of man would be the perfect husband for a woman like Daisy? Someone who admired her independent spirit, who loved her humour, who adored her and treated her respectfully.

Fitzsimmons took her hand and led her out onto the dance floor.

Oh, please, not Fitzsimmons again—you don't want to give that man ideas that he's in with a chance! Guy wanted to shout across the ballroom.

As if able to read his thoughts she looked in his direction and frowned at him. She was right. It was not his place to judge Fitzsimmons, to care who she was dancing with or who she eventually married. So he smiled back at her, as if giving his approval, which was also not his to give. Her lips pinched tighter, her eyebrows drew closer together then she beamed a smile at Fitzsimmons and blinked rapidly in a coquettish manner.

That was not like Daisy. Was she flirting with Fitzsimmons? She was neither a flirt nor a coquette. While contemplating this unusual behaviour, he discovered that he had somehow asked another young woman to dance and was back on the floor. How had that happened? How had Lady Agatha Ratliffe ended up in his arms while her mother looked on encouragingly from the edge of the floor?

He looked over at Daisy again, whose smile was starting to strain at the edges as Fitzsimmons chatted on and on. Fitzsimmons was under the delusion that everything he said was fascinating and was oblivious to the glazed expressions that quickly came over the faces of the people he spoke to. If Daisy married Fitzsimmons, it would sap all her spirit as she died a slow death by boredom.

Perhaps he should ask her for the next dance to save her from the likes of Fitzsimmons and Carruthers.

When the dance was over, he returned Lady Agatha to her delighted mother and attempted to extract himself from the hovering pack. But he was not adept enough, and they were too experienced at trapping dukes. Before he could get away, Daisy was back on the floor, lining up for the quadrille with Gilbert Townsend.

Gilbert Townsend—how could she?

Was she deliberately trying to dance with the most unsuitable men in the room? Townsend was worse than Fitzsimmons or Carruthers. He might not be a bore, but he was a notorious scoundrel with even fewer morals than Guy, if that was possible. This, he had to stop.

A young woman's hand somehow appeared on his arm. He was unaware that he had asked anyone to dance, but the mothers had him trapped. He had no choice, so he escorted her onto the floor, but ensured he was in the same set as Daisy and Townsend.

The dance began. He took his partner's arm, bowed and circled around her, then passed her on to Townsend and took Daisy's hand.

'What are you doing with that scoundrel?' he whispered.

'I'll dance with whomever I wish!' She seethed before moving off to join the third male in the set.

He danced with the other three women in turn, all the while his gaze flicking between Daisy and Townsend. *Was he holding her too closely? Was he looking at her too intently, with too much meaning?*

Fortunately, Daisy was not giving him the coquettish look she had given Fitzsimmons. That was all the encouragement a man like Townsend would require. Instead, she was mainly looking in Guy's direction and frowning. Good. As long as she was preoccupied with her anger at Guy, there was little danger of her falling for Townsend's seductive charms.

Daisy took his hand again, and they circled round each other.

'Be careful. Townsend has an appalling reputation,' he said quietly, causing Daisy to roll her eyes and move onto the next partner.

Damn it, she was not taking his warning seriously. And, even worse, when she returned to Townsend she sent him a beaming smile that caused Townsend to give an appreciative smirk in response. This had to stop. Daisy was playing a dangerous game.

'Daisy, I beseech you to be careful,' he said when she spun back towards him. 'Gilbert Townsend is a notorious womaniser.'

She looked up at him, her eyes narrowed. 'Nanny had a saying for such things.'

He nodded and waited for Nanny's words of wisdom.

'She would always say, "Well, my dear, that's a case of the pot calling the kettle black". It comes from pots and kettles both being placed in the cooking fire and getting covered in soot.'

'I know what the saying means, I'm just…' He called out as her hand slipped out of his and she danced off towards Townsend. *Worried for you,* he added to himself.

But she was right. There were definite similarities between the way he and Townsend lived their lives, although he was nowhere near as soot-covered as that rake. His teeth gritted together and he watched helplessly as Townsend leered down the front of Daisy's dress in a blatant signal of what he wanted. Daisy had to know he was a lecher and to be avoided, but she actually smiled at him. What on earth was wrong with her? Did she want to encourage his leering? Did she want to destroy her reputation?

'Daisy, I'm warning you. That man is not to be trusted,' he pleaded when she once again took his hand.

'I'm perfectly capable of looking after myself. Perhaps you should be paying more attention to Lady Matilda. I think she'd make an ideal duchess.'

She danced away and he looked over at his partner. Lady Matilda—was that her name? He had not caught it when she had been thrust into his arms. Lady Matilda sent him the same smile that Daisy had sent Fitzsimmons and Townsend, all simpering and coquettish. Would these young ladies never learn? They should not behave in that way with cads—or bores, for that matter.

The dance over, he escorted Lady Matilda off the floor. While he did so with correct decorum, the same could not be said of Townsend. Rather than take her arm, he placed his hand around Daisy's waist, dangerously close to her buttocks, led her to the side of the floor and stood too close to her for Guy's liking, his hand still on her waist.

This was going too far. That man needed to be taught a lesson on the correct way to treat a young lady. He excused himself from Lady Matilda, extricated himself from the circle of mothers and strode towards Daisy and that bounder.

Before he arrived, Daisy made her excuses and walked to the opposite end of the room to join Florence and Nathaniel. Good. Hopefully, Nathaniel would finally take his role as chaperon seriously and do what he had failed to do so far—keep his sister away from all cads, including himself.

As if following the Pied Piper, the mothers streamed across the room behind him. When he turned round, there they were, and another young woman's arm appeared on his. How were they managing to do that? Once again, he led an unnamed young woman out onto the dance floor, made polite conversation then returned her to her waiting mother.

And so it continued, until he was sure he'd danced several times with every available young lady, and unfortunately given hope to every mother present with a daughter of marriageable age.

Like him, Daisy was on the floor for the rest of the evening, dancing with a succession of young men, including Carruthers and Fitzsimmons again. One thing for which he was grateful—Gilbert Townsend had disappeared, presumably to the card room, or perhaps to one of London's so-called gentlemen's clubs, where no young ladies of a certain type would refuse him and he could do much more than just leer down the front of their dresses, provided he paid them handsomely.

When the ball finally ended, he had to concede that he was no closer to finding his duchess. But then, he had been too distracted. Perhaps at the next ball he should try to discourage Daisy from attending. Then he could focus on the task at hand and not be constantly monitoring her dance partners.

Not that Daisy would do anything he told her to. If he suggested she not attend a ball, then he could guarantee that that would be exactly what she would do, whether she wanted to or not. He made his way towards the door, where servants were desperately trying to pair guests with the correct coats, shawls, scarves and hats. With a smile, he thought that, if he didn't want Daisy to go to the next ball, perhaps the best thing to do would be to try and encourage her to attend.

He joined Florence, Nathaniel and Daisy waiting outside on the pavement where carriage drivers were jostling for space, horses were neighing their disapproval at the congestion and the departing guests were talking loudly and animatedly. Or, more accurately, most of the guests were talking loudly and animatedly. Daisy stood beside her brother, her body rigid, her faced pinched. Had Townsend offended her? Had Fitzsimmons or Carruthers literally bored her rigid? Guy would like to think that was the case, but he knew there was only one man to blame for her unhappiness, and it was the man now racked with guilt.

He spotted the carriage bearing his crest and the driver and footman in his livery of purple and gold. Nathaniel escorted Florence through the milling crowd, leaving Guy with no choice but to extend his arm to Daisy.

She looked down at it as if it were an offensive object, then reluctantly placed her arm through his. No one watching them would ever believe that they had recently been wrapped in each other's arms locked in an embrace, that he had kissed and caressed intimate parts of her body. They must appear like people who could barely tolerate each other's touch.

But that was for the best, wasn't it?

The carriage doors closed. With a jolt, the carriage moved forward and they were soon travelling at a brisk trot through the quiet, early-morning streets. Guy looked at the couple on the opposite seat. Florence and Nathaniel's expressions were the complete opposite to Guy's and Daisy's. Those two were still wearing identical smiles, and happiness seemed to shine out of them.

'We've got something to ask you,' they said at the same time, then looked at each other and laughed, as if talking together was the funniest thing anyone had ever done.

Nathaniel took Florence's hand. 'You ask him, if you wish.'

She smiled at him, a shy yet flirtatious smile. 'No, you ask him. That's more appropriate.'

'But he's your cousin.'

'Yes, but he's—'

'Will someone please just ask me?' Guy butted in. It was only a short journey from the Dantons' home to the Springfelds' but he suspected those two could go on like this all night.

Nathaniel sent Florence another smile, then adopted a more serious expression. 'Florence and I would like to wed. My parents have already given us their blessing, and we would like to have yours.'

'Of course, of course,' Guy said, taking Nathaniel's hand and giving it a hearty shake, then leaning over and kissing his cousin on the cheek. 'Although, shouldn't you be asking Horace for his blessing?'

Florence's smile died momentarily, then returned as bright as before. 'Perhaps, but you've been more of a brother to me than he has ever been, so it is your blessing we seek.'

That unfortunately was true. 'Well, I'm very happy to give my blessing, and I'm sure when Horace hears of your engagement he will be delighted.' Guy wasn't going to add that Horace would have no choice but to be delighted, not if he wanted to avoid a charge of theft.

'I'm so happy for you,' Daisy said, leaning over and kissing Florence's cheek. 'And I can't wait to introduce you to my sisters, Hazel and Iris. I know they're going to love having you as part of the family as much as I will.'

The two couples continued chatting about the forthcoming nuptials as they drove back through the quiet London streets. Throughout the journey Florence and Nathaniel held each other's hands as if they couldn't bear not to touch each other for a single second.

The carriage pulled up in front of the Springfelds' home and the footman helped the ladies down the steps. While Nathaniel and Florence remained talking quietly in the shadow of the carriage. Guy escorted Daisy up the path to the front of the house where a waiting footman held open the door.

Unsure how to say goodbye after such an evening, he took her hand and made a formal bow. She bobbed the quickest curtsey he had ever seen and disappeared inside without saying goodbye, leaving him standing on the doorstep.

He retraced his steps back to the carriage, his body suddenly leaden, his feet dragging and waited for Florence and Nathaniel to exchange a seemingly endless stream of farewell endearments. They would see each other again soon, probably the next day, but anyone would think they were saying goodbye at the dockside, with one of them about to embark on a long voyage.

While he waited, he looked up at the Springfeld house and pondered what this engagement would mean for him. He couldn't be happier for his cousin and his best friend, but it presented one rather unfortunate problem. It meant engagement parties, family dinners and other social events, not to mention the wedding and probable christenings. At all of which, Guy's and Daisy's attendance would be mandatory.

Eventually, Nathaniel departed.

'I'm so happy for you, Florence,' Guy said as he sat on the carriage bench. 'Nathaniel is a capital man, and I'm sure he'll make the perfect husband.'

She nodded, still smiling. 'I know, I know. And, oh,

I love him so much.' She gave him what he would have described as a sly look if it had come from anyone but his honest and open cousin. 'And it looks as though you've found the perfect future Duchess of Mandivale.'

He gave a false laugh. 'No, I'm afraid not. I met lots of sweet young women tonight, but I came to no decision.'

She shook her head slowly. 'Oh, Guy, you are such an idiot. It's so obvious. The next Duchess of Mandivale should be Daisy Springfeld.'

Chapter Sixteen

Love made you insane. That was the only explanation. Or perhaps when you were in love you thought everyone else should be too, that they should all be equally as eager to rush to the altar as you were. That could be the only explanation for Florence's bizarre statement.

'Don't look at me like that,' Florence said. 'Nate and I agree. You two are made for each other.'

The insanity had seemingly affected his usually level-headed friend as well. Had Nathaniel forgotten that Daisy was his little sister? Had he forgotten what sort of man his best friend was? This *had* to be insanity brought on by being in love. If Nathaniel had been in his right mind, he would never have considered Guy to be *made for* Daisy or for Daisy to be made for him.

Although, if he knew what Guy had done to his little sister out on the balcony, he would indeed be forcing Guy up the aisle, but it would have nothing to do with how right or wrong they were for each other.

'We both noticed it,' she said, causing Guy to cringe.

He would have expected those two not to to notice anything, so obsessed were they with each other, but perhaps they had been aware that he and Daisy had been absent for an inordinate amount of time, and when a man like Guy was absent with a woman it could mean only one thing.

'You couldn't keep your eyes off each other the whole night,' she continued and the tension in Guy's shoulders released slightly. His cousin and Daisy's brother had only noticed it had been his eyes that he couldn't keep off Daisy, not any other body parts. Thank goodness for that.

'You're wrong. And if I was watching Lady Daisy it was to monitor who she was dancing with and that she was being treated respectfully.'

Florence raised her eyebrows as if she didn't believe him.

'And, of course, I was concerned about her ankle. I would not have liked her to over-exert herself.'

Florence's eyebrows moved even further up her forehead.

'It was all just brotherly concern,' he said, his voice sounding as pathetic as his argument.

Florence stared at him, as if waiting until he had exhausted all his excuses, then adopted a school-mistress posture.

'So, answer me this. Do you enjoy her company?'

'Yes, Daisy is delightful company,' he conceded. That was perhaps an understatement. They'd had such fun together while she'd been recuperating at his estate. He enjoyed being with her, loved talking with her, loved laughing with her, even enjoyed arguing with her, because she was never slow to give her opinion on anything. He couldn't remember a time when he had taken so much pleasure in a woman's company.

'And it's obvious you find her attractive.'

Guy didn't answer, preferring to stare out of the dark window at the passing London streets.

'Admit it, you find her attractive.'

'Yes, I suppose she has grown into a rather pretty young woman.' That too was down-playing the truth. She was simply beautiful, the most stunning woman he had ever seen. He mixed with actresses, and other society ladies considered to be the most beautiful women of their age, but they paled in comparison to Daisy. It was not just her looks. It was her spirit. That spark within her that lit up her eyes, made her skin glow, that seemed to affect the very air around her.

'You're smiling in rather a dopey manner, Guy. I think that says a lot more than words ever could.'

Guy stopped smiling. He wouldn't have a so-called 'dopey smile' on his face. Expressions like that were for deranged lovers like Florence and Nathaniel.

'Well?' Florence asked.

'Well, what?

'Wouldn't she make the perfect Duchess of Mandivale?'

'No,' he stated emphatically. 'I admit she is attractive. And, yes, I enjoy her company. But that is all, Florence. I will not be marrying Daisy Springfeld.' He hoped his stern tone would alert her to the fact that he did not wish to discuss the subject any further.

'Why not? You plan to marry, so it makes sense to marry someone who makes you happy.'

'I'm not denying she would make me happy.' Memories of that kiss flooded into his mind and he coughed to drive them away. Daisy could make him more than happy. She could send him into a state that could only be described as euphoric.

'Exactly. She'd make the perfect duchess for you.'

'No. Well, yes, in many ways she would make a perfect duchess, but I wouldn't do that to Daisy.'

Florence shook her head slowly to indicate she did not understand.

Guy huffed out a breath, unsure whether he should be having this conversation with his cousin, but she continued to stare at him, waiting for an answer. She was not going to let this go until he had made it clear why he would not be marrying Daisy Springfeld.

'I plan to marry for one reason, and one reason only. I want an heir. I want to save the title and estate from ever falling into Horace's hands.'

Florence nodded. 'Yes, I know. But…' She raised her hands palms upwards to indicate that she expected more of an explanation.

'I don't intend to change when I marry.' He looked into her eyes to see whether she got the full meaning of his words. She continued to stare back at him, uncomprehending.

'I want a wife who will accept me for who I am, who will let me continue to live my life exactly as I live it now—as if I am a single man.' He watched as the realisation of what that meant dawned on her.

'Oh!' she squeaked.

'Oh, exactly. I would not inflict such a life on Daisy. Daisy should be with a better man than me, a man who will love her and do what the marriage vows say: forsake all others. That is not in my nature, is it, Florence?'

Sadly, she shook her head.

'I require a wife who is content with being a duchess and a mother but expects nothing more from me.'

Florence continued shaking her head, her brow furrowed, as if he were telling her a tale full of woe. Guy knew that he could also add that he wanted a wife who did not love him and whom he did not love. With Daisy Springfeld he knew he would have the first of these requirements but, despite what he had said to Florence, he was starting to fear he was in danger of failing to achieve the second.

The Springfeld household was always noisy and chaotic, but never more so than when another wedding was imminent. As soon as Nathaniel had informed everyone that he was soon to wed, Hazel and Iris rushed back to the family home bringing with them their husbands and, in Hazel's case, her two children.

Iris also had her own good news to impart. She was pregnant with her first child, which caused the volume of raucous celebrations at the family home to increase exponentially.

Daisy was of course delighted for her brother. She adored Florence, was looking forward to having yet another sister and she couldn't have been more pleased for Iris and her husband. But she couldn't shake off a ridiculous melancholy that had descended on her since Lady Danton's ball. She knew exactly what had caused it. It was that damn kiss that damn Guy had given her, leaving her with a taste of something heavenly, something which had then been taken away, something which she knew she would never experience again.

Within the chaos of having the entire family back at home, including Iris's noisy, excitable pug dog and her husband's rather large Irish wolfhound, Daisy's mother was organising a dinner party for the two families. She was discussing her plans for the wedding with anyone in the family who would listen, including the busy servants, and making constant suggestions on what style of gown Florence should wear.

Daisy would have thought that such organisation would take all her mother's time, but she had added getting another gown made for Daisy to her list of jobs to do. It was something Daisy could not understand. Surely she had enough gowns already hanging in her wardrobe? But her mother would not be persuaded otherwise.

'For the engagement dinner, I want a gown that really brings out your beauty,' her mother said as they rode in the carriage to the dressmaker for another round of selecting fabric, lace and all the other paraphernalia that went into such elaborate clothing. 'Something that highlights the colour of your eyes, and your lovely chestnut hair.'

Daisy couldn't see what all the fuss was about. This gown wasn't for another ball, at which her mother was hoping to foist her onto a potential husband. It was for a dinner which only the family would attend, and they had all known for some time that she had blue eyes and brown hair.

Well, the family plus Florence, who would soon be part of the family, and Guy, who was almost family anyway. Daisy's breath caught in her throat and she slowly turned to face her mother, who was chattering on about whether satin or silk would best flatter Daisy's figure.

'Mother!' she said, her words coming out as a shocked gasp. 'You're not trying to match-make are you?'

Her mother looked at her with wide-eyed innocence. 'Me? You know I'm not like other mothers who force their daughters onto unsuitable men just to get them married off. I've always said that, when my children marry, I want it to be for love and love alone. If not, then they can remain unmarried.'

'You didn't answer my question,' Daisy said, still hardly able to breathe. 'Are you trying to match me up...' She swallowed, her hand on her fluttering stomach. 'With Guy Parnell?'

Her mother gave a small laugh, which sounded false to Daisy. 'Don't be silly, my dear.' She patted Daisy's knee. 'I just want you to look your best for the engagement dinner. And, if Guy happens to realise just how grown up you now are, and just how beautiful you have become, well there's no harm in that, is there?'

Daisy didn't know where to begin in enlightening her mother as to the full extent of the harm there would be in *that*. Guy was a rake—surely her mother knew that? Daisy certainly did, and now knew it not just through his reputation. Worse than that, he was a rake in search of a compliant wife who would sire him a son but let him continue in his rakish ways. That could not be the sort of husband her mother wanted for her.

'Guy is wholly unsuitable as a husband.'

Her mother shrugged. 'Well, I've always been very fond of him. Despite his childhood, he was a delightful boy, and he's grown into such a handsome and charming young man.'

'A bit too charming and handsome if you ask me,' Daisy muttered.

'There's no such thing,' her mother said in that familiar voice she adopted when she believed her opinions to be indisputable.

'Mother,' Daisy said, slowly enunciating her words. 'Guy is *too* charming. He is a...well...he has had rather a lot of women in his life.' She stared at her mother to assess whether she understood the full extent of what she meant by *had*.

Her mother gave what could only be described as a wicked smile. 'And what woman doesn't appreciate a man with a bit of experience? Why, before I married your father...'

'Mother, no,' Daisy cut in, her hands flying to cover her ears.

'All I'm saying,' her mother continued, pulling Daisy's hands back down, 'Is there's nothing wrong with a man who knows what he's doing, and a man can always change once he meets the right woman.'

'I doubt that very much,' Daisy said, crossing her arms firmly. 'The man's incorrigible. Do you know he's planning to marry some unfortunate woman who will have to do her duty and provide him with an heir while giving him complete freedom to do as he pleases?'

Her mother tilted her head. 'Oh, he's thinking seriously about marriage, is he?'

Daisy glared back at her. 'Didn't you hear what I said? He wants a wife who will bear his children but let him do exactly as he wants. And I would never be such a wife.'

'No, I know you wouldn't, my dear,' her mother said, as if that meant their future marriage was more, not less, likely.

'Please, Mother, don't try and match me with Guy. I couldn't bear it.'

Her mother patted her arm. 'I would never do anything to hurt you, Daisy, you know that.'

Daisy stared at her mother, trying to assess the meaning of her words. 'Promise me you won't match-make. Go on—say it.'

'I promise. But there's no harm in you having a new gown and looking your best, and there's certainly no harm in letting nature take its course.'

'Mother, do not—'

'Oh, we're here—good.'

The carriage pulled up in front of the dressmaker's premises and Daisy reluctantly followed her mother into the work room where silks, satins, tulles and laces were once again thrown over her shoulder while her mother and the dressmaker discussed styles and textures.

Daisy played no active part in the process. She did not care what she looked like at the dinner and was dreading seeing Guy again. She knew he had no meaningful interest in her—he had made that plain

Those words ran through her mind once more: *I can't resist any available young woman.* And she had made herself available to him. She had exposed her own longings to him in such a blatant way—had let him know just how easy it would be for him to seduce her, had asked him, all but begged him, to do so. It was so mortifying, she could hardly bear it.

Like so many women before her she had succumbed to his charms and good looks, something about which her mother was so wrong. They were qualities of which a man most definitely could have too much.

And the last thing she wanted was her mother adding to her humiliation by actually trying to encourage Guy. What if he thought she had told her mother she was interested in him? What if he thought she was one of those women who were desperate to marry him? She was not like those women. She never had been and never would be.

Daisy was tempted to wear her cycling bloomers to the engagement dinner just to prove that she did not care one fig whether Guy thought she looked attractive or not, and to show him she had no intention of trying to attract his interest ever again. She had made one mistake. She would not be making another.

'Oh, don't look so churlish,' her mother said as they finally climbed back into the carriage. 'Don't think of it as dressing up to impress Guy. Think of it as dressing up in honour of your brother and his new fiancée.'

Daisy's lips became more pinched. 'Mother, you promised.'

Her mother patted her knee again. 'I know you, my dear. And I know that without my guidance you're just as likely to turn up in those silly…in those rational bloomers of yours…but you mustn't. It would take the attention away from Florence and Nathaniel, and you wouldn't want to do that, would you?' Her mother smiled at her in satisfaction. 'So, you're just going to have to wear that lovely blue gown I've chosen for you.'

Daisy merely huffed out her disapproval, refusing to discuss the subject any further. Fortunately, once they returned from the dressmaker, her mother's attention was once more caught up in organising the dinner and discussing wedding arrangements, so no further mention was made of Guy Parnell. Hopefully, her mother would be true to her word and would just let nature take its course without any interference or attempt at matchmaking and, given her nature and Guy's nature, that would mean they would most certainly not be marrying.

On the evening of the engagement dinner Daisy was uncharacteristically nervous. She dressed with studied care, telling herself that she was doing so out of respect for her brother and his fiancée. She even agreed to allow her lady's maid to style her hair in the latest ornate fashion once again, telling herself it had nothing to do with what Annette said about the style being both flattering and feminine.

Observing her reflection in the full-length mirror, Daisy had to admit, despite her annoyance at her, her mother had chosen a gown that did flatter her figure and was rather becoming.

Once again, her mother had selected a soft fabric that clung to the body, ending with a train that gently swept around her feet. Delicate embroidery in silver thread contrasted with the deep-blue silk. As she twirled in front of the mirror, the fabric shimmered and the silver embroidery twinkled like stars in a dark blue sky.

Her mother really did have good taste in fashion, if not in men—or at least, in future husbands for her youngest daughter.

As with the gown she had worn to Lady Danton's ball, this one was cut low, exposing her naked shoulders and her décolletage. A small shiver rippled through Daisy as she continued to stare at herself in the mirror.

Guy had told her he couldn't resist her when he had seen her standing in the moonlight, and hadn't been able to stop himself from kissing her. Rightly or wrongly, he had been attracted to her, and had wanted to kiss her—not just her lips, but all of her.

She gently placed her hands on the exposed swell of her breasts, remembering the touch of Guy's hands, his lips kissing her breasts and his tongue caressing them, his lips nuzzling and sucking… She pulled her hands away, fire exploding on her cheeks. Now was not the time to think of such things. She had to get through this engagement dinner and celebrate her brother's engagement, and she would not be able to relax and enjoy herself until she put all thoughts of Guy firmly out of her head.

She entered the drawing room where the family

had assembled before dinner was to be served. Florence looked incandescent with happiness and Nathaniel seemed incapable of not smiling and constantly stared at his bride-to-be. There could be no doubt that they were in love. That was what love looked like, and it was not what Guy felt for her. He had gone from seeing her as a child, as little Daisy Chain, to seeing her as just another woman—an available woman with whom he could toy—and she wasn't sure which was worse.

Her gaze moved over to Guy standing beside the mantelpiece. Damn him, he was looking his usual handsome self. Dressed in a formal black swallow-tailed suit, white shirt and tie and a silver waistcoat, he was far too attractive for his own good—or, rather, for *her* own good. He smiled at her and her heart did a disturbing flip inside her chest that was almost painful. The weakness of her legs as she walked across the room, the dull pain in her chest and the difficulty she was having breathing, made it obvious that putting all thoughts of Guy out of her head was going to be no easy task.

While Guy did not love her, there was no denying she felt something for him, but it could not be love. He made her feel uncomfortable, almost dizzy, and that was a stark contrast to the easy, loving manner between Florence and Nathaniel. That was love. She did not know what it was she felt for Guy, but it most certainly was not love.

She reached the family group and forced herself to greet Guy and Florence in a manner that gave away none of the agitation stirring inside her.

'I see you're continuing to dress in an irrational

style,' he said in that familiar teasing manner, while slowly looking her up and down.

If her mother had expected Guy to suddenly succumb to her beauty at the sight of her in yet another new gown, and throw himself down onto one knee and propose, she would be very disappointed. Despite the effort that she had taken, her clothing was having no effect on him at all, unless her mother considered teasing to be a desirable outcome. And, damn him, he was right– she *was* becoming less rational—and she didn't just mean in her clothes. Since that kiss she seemed incapable of being at all rational over anything. But that was going to have to change. She needed to be rational if she was to stop herself from acting like even more of a fool than she already was.

'Mother insisted that I dress appropriately. She said it would be disrespectful to Nathaniel and Florence not to do so for their engagement dinner,' she said, unable to keep a huffing note out of her reply.

'Well, you look beautiful, but I don't think those two are capable of noticing what anyone else is wearing or doing,'

They both looked over at Nathaniel and Florence who were laughing together at some private joke while gently touching each other's arms.

'It's good to see one member of the Parnell family is going to marry for the right reasons,' Daisy said. 'So, have you found the Duchess of Mandivale yet?'

'No, not yet,' he said with that infuriating smile. 'No young lady has yet been singled out for that fate worse than death.'

Heat exploded onto Daisy's cheeks. She did not want to think of the fate that awaited his bride. Why did he have to remind her that the main reason he needed a wife was to produce an heir? The fate of the future duchess was not something Daisy would consider worse than death, not if their time together on the balcony was anything to go by. The young lady he took as his duchess would no doubt walk around with the same satisfied smile on her face that she had seen on Lady Penrose, or would be giving him top billing the way Ruby Lovelace had.

'I still think it's morally wrong,' she said with a disapproving sniff, unsure what she was really objecting to.

He shrugged. 'Yes, but I'm not like you, Daisy. You're lucky. You have choices.'

She glared up at him. Surely he didn't really believe that? 'Choices? What choices do I have?' she all but spluttered. 'No woman truly has choices. Unless you think the options of marrying and losing all freedom and rights, or remaining unmarried and being seen as some sort of social pariah, are choices? Whereas for you, even though you say you are being forced to marry and father an heir, it will change nothing. You will still have the same freedoms and maintain all the same rights and privileges as you do now. You can still live the life of a bachelor. No woman would ever be able to do that.'

'Is that what you want? To marry but live your life as if you were still unmarried?'

'Yes...well, no. I don't know. All I know is it's unfair

and you have no right to say your situation is anything like mine. You won't have to sacrifice anything when you get married. All you have to do is get some woman with child and then you can carry on just as you please.'

She could tell her voice was getting louder and she looked around, slightly embarrassed at losing her temper during a happy family occasion. But no one had noticed. They were all busy talking and laughing in their usual exuberant manner.

'Neither of your sisters had to sacrifice anything when they married.'

They turned to look at Iris and Hazel, both holding onto the arms of their husbands, their laughter showing how happy they were with their married status.

'Neither of them married just so they could sire an heir or save a title. Neither of them was used by the man they married for his own purposes.'

He looked suitably chastened by her outrage. As he should be.

'I will be honest about what I'm offering the woman I eventually marry,' he reminded her quietly.

She continued to scowl at him but was somewhat pleased he had the decency to look a bit shamefaced about it, although that was hardly suitable consolation.

'And she will be using me as much as I am using her,' he continued. 'You saw the way those young women behaved at Lady Danton's ball. They wanted the title of duchess and I doubt they would care who they married to get it.'

Daisy sniffed again, although she knew that for those aspirational young women his stunning good looks, masculine countenance and immeasurable charm would be an added incentive.

'It's still not right, and I still think marriage is a terrible institution and unfair to women.'

Daisy waited for his objections and prepared herself to give him a lecture on how women lost everything when they married—how they became almost the property of their husbands and how that was an intolerable situation that had to change.

But he merely shrugged and looked across the room at his cousin. 'Despite what you say, the thought of marriage is making Florence happy. I've never seen her looking more beautiful and I couldn't wish for a better husband for my cousin than your brother.'

She followed his gaze and looked at the happy couple. Her anger evaporated and she remembered that tonight was supposed to be a celebration. 'I know. I'm so pleased for them, and everyone in the family simply adores Florence. Another sister. It's just wonderful.'

Guy smiled at her and her irritation instantly returned. Damn him. Why did he have to have such a glorious smile? Why were his teeth so perfect? Why did the edges of those brown eyes have to crinkle up in that infuriatingly attractive manner? And why did a smile have to make her feel as if she were melting internally?

His smile faded but the effect on Daisy remained no less intense. His deep-brown eyes stared into hers, capturing her gaze and preventing her from looking away, as she knew she should. As if pulled by an invisible thread, she leaned closer to him, her body aching to feel his hands on her again. Her lips were tingling, desperate for his kisses.

The dinner gong resounded loudly in the room, causing Daisy to blink rapidly as she tried to drag herself back to reality. What on earth was she doing? Surely she wasn't falling under Guy's spell yet again, and so easily? The same spell that had captured all those other women he was rumoured to have had? Well, she would not succumb to a man who was too charming and too handsome by half. She would not succumb to Guy Parnell. Not tonight. Not ever.

Chapter Seventeen

Guy took Daisy's arm and joined the line of couples moving from the drawing room to the dining room. As they walked arm-in-arm, he fought to get Florence's words out of his head. There were so many reasons why Daisy Springfeld *would* make a perfect duchess, but there were even more compelling reasons why she would not—including that she did not want to be married to him, or any man. No, Florence and Nathaniel were wrong, but they were too blinded by love to realise it.

Despite adhering to protocol, the Springfeld family couldn't stop their constant chatter, laughter and playful teasing as they paraded down the hallway. This was what a happy family looked like. This was the world in which Daisy had grown up. Should she ever marry, this was the type of world in which she should live.

His own home had been bleak, cold and unloving. He could not guarantee that the home he made with his wife would not resemble the one in which he had been raised. Any woman who married him would need to be aware of what she was getting into, and he would never inflict such a fate on Daisy.

No, Florence was wrong. Even if he did love Daisy, and he was starting to suspect that he might, hadn't his father loved his mother? Loving his wife hadn't stopped him from being a mean-spirited, heartless man, and that too was something to which he would not risk subjecting Daisy.

Florence believed Daisy was right for him. His father had presumably met the right woman, but it had not changed him. He had been a tyrant. No doubt if his mother had not died giving birth to him his father would have ceased to be the devoted, love-struck young man he'd appeared to be in his letters, and would have treated his wife with the same callousness with which he had treated his only son.

No, he would not marry Daisy. He would marry someone who would accept him as he was, someone who wanted nothing from him, not even his love.

The noisy family entered the dining room, and he led Daisy to her seat and pulled it out for her before the footman could do so. With a rustling of her silky gown, she sat down, looked up at him and smiled her thanks.

He wished she wouldn't do that. She was beautiful when she smiled, so feminine and enchanting. Damn it all, she also was beautiful when she scowled. She was just plain beautiful under all circumstances. But the effect on him was so much worse when she smiled. It caused something unexpected to pulse through him. It wasn't lust. He was very familiar with the effects of lust. That was most certainly something Daisy could arouse in him. But this was different, unfamiliar, as if he wanted to care for her, protect her, be her champion.

He pulled out his chair, sat down and huffed out his annoyance as he shook out his napkin and placed it on his lap. The best way he could be her champion, protect and care for her was to leave her alone and let her find happiness with another man. But that was something he seemed all too easily to forget every time he looked into those blue eyes.

Footmen served the soup as the family continued to talk and laugh in the buoyant manner they always did. Only Daisy and Guy remained quiet. He looked along the table at the four happy couples. The family had always welcomed him into their home, and he would miss spending time with the Springfelds, but if he was to free himself from Daisy he was going to have to see as little of them as possible.

Although he wondered just how welcoming they would be if they knew he had kissed Daisy, caressed her and caused her to reach a peak of ecstasy under his touch. Would they be so welcoming if they knew that he had run true to form? That he had acted like the cad everyone said he was, and had done so with a member of their family?

He glanced at Daisy, now chatting to her sister Iris, knowing that he would miss gazing at her beauty. She really was lovely, with full, soft hair he longed to release and let flow over her shoulders, delicate cheeks he longed to stroke and blue eyes that sparkled in the reflected light of the candles. And she had the most divine lips he had ever seen, soft, plump and red, just made to be kissed.

He lowered his head and stared at his soup plate, reminding himself that he was not here to admire Daisy's lips or to think about kissing them or stroking any parts of her body. He was here to celebrate his best friend's and his cousin's engagement.

He looked back along the table to where the engaged couple were sitting and caught Lady Springfeld's eye. She beamed at him, raised her wine glass in toast then actually winked. She'd always been an exuberant woman, but this was most peculiar. He smiled at her, uncertain if that was the right response, and raised his own glass.

'Your mother just toasted me,' he whispered out of the side of his mouth to Daisy.

'Oh, just ignore her,' she said tersely.

He looked at Daisy. That too was an odd response. 'What's going on?'

'Nothing,' she retorted, then sighed. 'Look, I'm sorry about this, but Mother has got it into her head that you would make a good husband.'

He stared at her. 'For whom?'

'For me.'

He continued to stare at her in shock.

'I know. I know,' she repeated with a small shrug of her shoulder. 'It's ridiculous. I suppose it's because I've gone through five seasons without getting married. Now that my sisters are married and Nathaniel is engaged, she's turned the full force of her match-making on me. And, well, you are convenient.' Those lovely lips pinched and she scowled. 'Just as I was a convenient woman when you found me alone on the balcony.'

He flinched as if she had slapped him and wished he could take back those insulting words.

'You'd never be just a convenient woman,' he said quietly.

'Anyway,' she continued, either not hearing him or ignoring his denial. 'I think Mother is starting to get desperate.'

'So desperate she's sunk as low as me.'

She placed her hand on his arm. 'Oh, no. I didn't mean that.'

Guy looked down at her hand, at the long, slim fingers, and fought the temptation to place his own hand over hers just to feel her soft skin one more time.

'It's me she's desperate for.' She looked down at her hand, then pulled it away and placed it on her lap, as if it needed to be kept under control. 'But Mother is wasting her time, as we both know.'

'And we both know you can do much better than me.'

She sent him a quizzical look. 'I don't want to do better than you.'

A surge of expectation shot through Guy. 'You don't?'

'I mean, I don't want to marry anyone—you or anyone else—that's all.'

He gave a dismissive laugh, either directed at her statement or his unwanted reaction. 'But I was right,' he said. 'You can do a lot better for yourself than marrying me.'

'Well, Mother doesn't seem to think so.'

He shook his head. 'I never thought I'd say this, but

I'm afraid Lady Springfeld is wrong. If she had seen the attention you were getting at Lady Danton's ball she would not be so desperate as to pair you off with me,' he said, fighting not to scowl as he remembered all those men who had held Daisy in their arms on the dance floor.

'That's part of the problem,' she continued in a whisper, leaning in so close he could feel her soft breath warm on his cheek. 'Nathaniel told her I danced nearly every dance with you, and you were paying me an inordinate amount of attention.'

Once again, Guy flinched, remembering just how much attention he had paid Daisy, although thankfully neither Nathaniel nor Lady Springfeld were aware of what that attention had actually entailed.

'Didn't he mention that you also danced several dances with Fitzsimmons and Carruthers?' He unclenched his tight jaw before continuing. 'And you danced with Gilbert Townsend and several other men.'

She shrugged and nodded her thanks to the footman as he removed the soup plates and served the fish course. 'No, he didn't.'

'And have any of those men called since the ball?'

She put her hand over her wine glass to indicate she did not want the footman to refill it. 'They've all sent flowers and invitations to take rides in the park or walks, or have made requests to visit.'

He gritted his teeth. 'Even Townsend?'

'Yes, even Townsend, although my mother threw his card away and told me I was to have nothing to do with him, as he was not to be trusted.'

'I've always said your mother was an eminently sensible and intelligent woman,' he said with satisfaction. 'She can recognise a scoundrel when she sees one.'

Daisy turned and looked at him, her eyes wide. She did not need to speak. What she was thinking was written on her face. *She can recognise a scoundrel when she sees one, and yet she wants me to marry one.*

They ate their fish in silence as the noise of the family circled around them. As the footman took away their plates and replaced them with plates of roast beef, he once again looked down the table at Countess Springfeld. She was watching him closely. If it hadn't been for Daisy's words, he would have assumed she was keeping an eye on him to make sure her precious daughter was safe with a man like him.

That was what she should be doing, not harbouring foolish notions of marrying Daisy off to the likes of him. Carruthers and Fitzsimmons had made their intentions clear, so Countess Springfeld should be setting her sights on those respectable men.

Daisy followed the direction of his gaze and Countess Springfeld beamed at both of them, causing Daisy to sigh, neither quietly nor discreetly.

'Mother also has this irrational belief that you are capable of changing your ways, even though I told her that you want a wife who will guarantee that you do not have to change at all. She's such a deluded romantic.'

Change his ways. Was such a thing possible?

Since he'd returned to London, he had not contacted Ruby or any of the other delightful young women he usually spent his time with. Lady Penrose had left her calling card, but he was yet to respond. Was it the pursuit of a duchess that had caused him to abstain from the company of other women? Yet, it could be some time before he found her. And he was seeking a woman who did not expect him to *change his ways.*

A possibility hit him like a blow to the head. Had he *changed his ways* because of Daisy? Since she had unexpectedly arrived back in his life, he had not sought out any other woman. Even now, having returned to London where there were almost endless opportunities for a man seeking feminine company, he had not even thought of doing so. Instead, he spent his nights alone, lying awake, thinking of Daisy.

Was Lady Springfeld right? Could a woman make a man change his ways? No, it was ridiculous. As the saying went, a leopard could not change its spots. He was a womaniser and always would be. This was merely some sort of aberration in his behaviour that he was certain would soon pass.

'Is there something wrong with your meal?' Iris asked from across the table.

He lowered his fork, realising it had been suspended in mid-air for some time. 'No, it's delicious,' he assured her, even though he had no idea how it tasted.

The dinner proceeded through more courses and, once the cheese boards were served, Daisy's father stood up and signalled for the chatter to stop. Eventually, after he'd asked several times, his voice getting louder with each request, the family stopped talking and laughing and turned to face him.

'We've already welcomed Florence into our family,'

he said. 'But I'd just like to officially announce that my lovely wife and I will soon have another daughter, something about which we are extremely happy.'

Everyone raised their glasses towards a smiling Florence and added their agreement and calls of, 'Welcome.'

'We've been connected to the Parnell family for many years, thanks to Guy.' He looked down the table, his glass still raised. 'We were delighted when he joined us as a young boy and always knew that he'd grow into an exceptional young man.'

Guy smiled politely, grateful for his words, but he knew the Springfelds had taken him into their family out of charity and because of their love of Nathaniel, not because of any virtues he might or might not possess.

'And now Guy has brought the lovely Florence into our hearts, something else for which we have him to thank.'

As one the family now turned towards him and raised their glasses, as if he had done anything except be lucky enough to have a cousin like Florence.

'And we must remember Daisy's contribution,' Nathaniel added. 'If it hadn't been for Daisy, her bicycle and a twisted ankle, I might not have met the love of my life.'

Another toast was made to Daisy. 'Well, I'm just pleased you found each other,' Daisy said, laughing. 'And I hope I don't have to twist my ankle for the sake of anyone else's happiness.'

'No, I suspect one sprained ankle will be enough to marry off the last unmarried member of this family,' her mother added from the end of the table. Everyone at the table laughed as if it was a joke they were all in on. Everyone except Daisy and Guy.

Was the entire family expecting him to marry Daisy, not just her mother? And were they all accepting of that idea? He would have thought they'd all have more sense. After all, they had always struck him as sensible people. Perhaps they too had got caught up in the madness which was Florence and Nathaniel's love, and a state of mass delusion had descended on the entire family. Guy could think of no other explanation for their bizarre behaviour.

'Anyhow,' her father continued. 'I'd like you all to raise your glasses and drink a toast to Florence and Nathaniel.'

They all loudly toasted the happy couple, then resumed their cheerful, boisterous conversations.

After dinner they all repaired to the drawing room. Once again Guy felt absorbed into the family, but it wasn't the same. He was now here on false pretences. They were hoping he would marry Daisy, but that was something he knew he could never do. He did not want to disappoint a family that had given him so much, but if he did marry Daisy the disappointment he would cause them would be even greater. They would all see him for the man he really was and would hate him for it.

There was nothing for it. Once this dinner was over, he would retreat to his country estate. Florence no longer needed him. He knew the Springfelds would take care of her as if she was now one of the family, which she very nearly was. He also knew he should spend the rest of the season seeking out a suitable duchess, but his heart wasn't in that. All in all, he had made a complete hash of things since he'd decided it was time that he wed. But then, wasn't that to be expected when a rake decided to find a bride?

Chapter Eighteen

Daisy was not in love. What she felt was not how her sisters had described love. There was no exhilaration, no intoxication, nor was she excited. All she felt was miserable. But then, she had done something so foolish, something no rational, intelligent woman would ever do. She had become desperately in *something*—not love, but something—with the wrong man, a man she didn't love, couldn't love, and whom she knew didn't love her.

She'd found herself in a foolish situation, but it was something she had to accept. The question now was, what did she do about it? As she moped around the house, picking up books then putting them down, wandering from room to room, leaving the house then forgetting where she planned to go, she continued to ponder that question. But she could come up with no satisfactory answers.

The most obvious solution to her plight was to get on with her life and just put him and all that had happened between them well and truly behind her. She tried that. She failed at that. Nothing seemed to distract her mind from going over and over what had happened between them. Nothing could drive the memory of him holding her, kissing her, caressing her, from her mind. Nothing could stop her thinking about his captivating face, the way his eyes crinkled at the edges when he smiled, the way he laughed, and most of all the way he had looked at her before he had kissed her.

She was such a fool. While she was pining, he would be off in pursuit of a wife who would give him exactly what he wanted, and would not have given her another thought.

Occasionally, she wondered if she should become the sort of woman he wanted. Perhaps it would be worth it if it meant having him in her life. He wanted heirs. She knew from what she had experienced that making love to Guy, even if it was just for the purpose of producing those heirs, would be heavenly. In exchange for such pleasure, she would give him his freedom and expect nothing more from him. It was tempting, but ultimately it would never be enough. Not for her. She might not love him, but she could never share him with any other woman.

Many women of her class accepted their role as wife and provider of heirs while never expecting fidelity from their husbands. As long as the man was discreet, he could do as he chose. But Daisy could never agree to that. It wasn't in her nature to be a compliant wife, and even the thought of him with someone else caused every muscle in her body to tense, her stomach to churn and rage to surge up inside her.

Nor could she be his mistress, although that too was

sometimes a tempting prospect. Many a night she lay awake thinking about what such a life would be like. He would provide her with a place to live and she would be available to him whenever he wanted her. Those thoughts would send delicious thrills coursing through her body. She would imagine him arriving, her waiting for him, perhaps already in bed, dressed in a manner that would please him. He would join her in the bed and kiss her as he had when they'd been alone on the balcony, caress every inch of her body and introduce her to the act of love-making.

While that was a delicious fantasy, she knew she could not do it. She could never play the role of an available woman. Nor would she agree to be part of such an arrangement, where the convenient wife was left behind in the country while he enjoyed himself in London with his mistress.

What she wanted she could never have. She wanted all of Guy Parnell. She wanted him to commit to her and her alone, and he had already said that was something he would never do. Instead, he wanted it all—a wife and as many mistresses as he chose. She should despise him for that. She tried hard to despise him, and sometimes she succeeded.

Sometimes her anger would consume her. She would rant and rave inside her head, claiming that if she ever saw him again it would be too soon. Then her anger would wear her out, and the thought of never seeing him again would send a great wave of loss and despair crashing over her, leaving her gasping, as if she were drowning.

But whatever she wanted, whatever she felt, it was of no account. He had disappeared. At least, he had disappeared from Daisy's life, and had returned to his estate.

She had no idea whether he had taken Ruby Lovelace with him, or some other woman, and she told herself she did not wish to know. Nor did she know whether he had made a promise to any of the young ladies he had danced with at the ball.

Fortunately, her mother was busy with the wedding preparations and had all but given up on her deluded attempts to marry her off to Guy. The closest she'd come to referring to it was when she had suggested that Daisy get over her melancholic state by going for a nice bicycle ride in the Kent countryside. Was her mother hoping that she would fall into another ditch, or even suggesting she contrive another accident so she could spend time at the Mandivale estate?

Such a suggestion was shocking enough, but even more shocking was Daisy's reaction. For a brief moment she had actually thought the idea held some merit, before catching herself, and telling her mother in no uncertain terms that she would be doing no such thing.

But her mother was right about one thing. If she was to get over Guy, she needed to throw herself, not into a ditch, but back into the activities she enjoyed.

The members of the High-Wheeling Ladies' Cycling Association had welcomed her back with much excitement and many questions about her ankle and her recovery. A few of the young women asked her about Guy Parnell, but she managed to flick off their questions with as much nonchalance as she could muster.

She also threw herself back into attending meetings of the Rational Dress Society and made a point of pushing all her gowns to the back of the wardrobe and returning to wearing her riding bloomers, divided skirts and other practical fashions. If men like Guy Parnell liked their women dressed in frippery, well, so what? She dressed to please herself and certainly did not care what any man thought of her.

As much as she enjoyed spending time with the cycling club, going on excursions, and generally shocking the populace with her outlandish costumes and reckless independence, it was no longer enough. She found it impossible to return to that happy, carefree state in which she had lived before she developed foolish notions about Guy Parnell. Was she going to spend the rest of her life like this? Surely this annoying pall that constantly hung over her would eventually leave.

Her sisters had told her what it was like to have a broken heart, and now she knew exactly what they meant. But she knew it would eventually mend. It had to. It would be ridiculous to carry on feeling like this, especially as she just knew that Guy wouldn't be the slightest bit sad.

In fact, she doubted he had ever given her a second thought since *that* kiss. Unlike her, he would be living a life full of pleasure, the life he would continue to live even after he married and became a father. It was so irrational, silly and pointless to waste time even thinking about him, and yet, irrational as it was, thinking about him was all she seemed capable of doing.

* * *

Guy was unsure what was wrong with him. He had lost interest in everything, did not want to attend his club, had no desire to visit the theatre, had turned down numerous invitations to parties, and certainly put aside his plans to find the next Duchess. In fact, he was starting to agree with Daisy that searching for a woman prepared to marry for nothing more than a title was morally repugnant.

Instead, he had retreated to his estate and buried himself away in the country, alone with his thoughts. And those thoughts were of one thing and one thing only. Daisy Springfeld.

All day and throughout the night memories of her blue eyes, her smile and lips tormented him. The image of her partially naked in the moonlight never left him. His lips could almost taste hers. He could almost feel the soft skin of her cheeks, her neck, her shoulders and her breasts. It was torture, pure torture.

It should never have happened, but it had, and he should not constantly relive it in every exquisite, unforgivable detail. All he had done was kiss and caress her, for goodness' sake. How many other women had he kissed, caressed or made love to? He had absolutely no idea. There had been so many, and yet all those women had quickly faded from his memory. As pleasurable as his time with them had been, as much as they'd laughed together and sated each other's bodies with their love-making, once they'd departed his bed they'd also departed his mind. But not Daisy Springfeld. She was there in his head day and night. He had to free himself of her.

Fleeing to the country so he would not see her again had been the most sensible thing to do. Florence no longer needed his services as a chaperon. As a respectable, engaged young woman, she could spend time in public with Nathaniel without tongues wagging. The Springfelds, as expected, had embraced her into the family, so she was never short of alternative chaperons, and was now spending so much time at their home she was all but living there.

He'd been certain that with time he would drive Daisy out of his mind but, damn it all, if anything he was becoming more obsessed with thoughts of her. Every time he drove past the ditch where she had fallen from her bicycle, he remembered how sweet she'd looked, wearing those funny bloomers that displayed her lovely calves and slim ankles. With dirt on her face, grass in her hair and her clothing dishevelled, she had looked simply delightful.

As he walked round the house and gardens images kept coming back to him of her sitting in her wheelchair, holding court and making her pronouncements on the way the world was—or, rather, on the way she believed the world should be—and making judgements about his and other people's behaviour. Every time he thought of her little lectures, he couldn't help but smile with affection and admiration.

Every look on her expressive face was imprinted on his memory—her anger, her disapproval and her stubbornness. But most of all he remembered how she had looked when he had kissed her, how her eyes had shone in the moonlight, how her lips had parted as she'd gasped under his caresses, how she had shuddered when his tongue had brought her to the peak of ecstasy.

That was one memory he suspected he would never be free of.

As the weeks and months passed, it got no better. But it had to, eventually. He just hoped he was no longer mooning over her like a love-sick schoolboy when the family arrived for Florence and Nathaniel's wedding.

But, as the time approached, he realised that that was wishful thinking. If anything, he was getting worse.

Perhaps he had made a mistake leaving London. Perhaps, in his mind, he had come to idealise Daisy Springfeld. Maybe seeing her again would be the solution. Maybe then he would realise she was just a woman, no different from the many other women who had warmed his bed over the years.

With mixed feelings he realised that when he saw her again on the day of the wedding he would be able to put this theory to the test...and he could only hope he was right.

Chapter Nineteen

Like a whirlwind, the family descended on Guy's estate. Lady Springfeld and her two married daughters, the self-appointed organisers of the wedding, took over, creating a state of organised mayhem. He had expected Daisy to arrive as well, but when he tentatively asked the family informed him that she had decided to remain in London until the wedding day.

While his house and gardens were being turned upside down, no one paid him much attention, and he wandered aimlessly, like a visitor at his own estate. Every time he looked round, as if by magic another enormous display of white flowers appeared in the hallway, the ballroom or the dining room, until his home resembled a flower market. His staff had also joined in the frantic organisation. He often found his housekeeper, butler or chef deep in conversation with Lady Springfeld or one of her daughters, discussing arrangements for the guests, the menus or table decorations. The maids and footmen ran about the house, performing some task or other assigned to them by the organising committee.

In amongst all this, a happy Florence seemed to float on a cloud while the hive of activity spun around her. It had been decided that Guy would escort his cousin down the aisle, and Lady Springfeld had duly informed Horace. Lady Springfeld told Guy that this was Florence's wish, but she had been reluctant to make the suggestion to her brother, fearing that he might be deliberately obstinate.

However, Horace, the man who bullied everyone he came into contact with, was no match for the tactful determination of Lady Springfeld. When she informed him that it would be more prestigious for both families to have a duke give his sister away, a young woman who was about to marry a viscount, he relented.

Although still smarting from his failed attempt to seize the dukedom for himself, the calculating look Horace always wore when they met in the village suggested he still remained confident that he would one day be the Duke of Mandivale. Guy assumed it was this belief which had caused him to acquiesce so easily. He had no doubt heard about Guy's failed attempt to find a duchess. Doubtless he believed that, should Guy die before him without an heir, and in the end he became the Duke, he would be mixing socially with the likes of Countess Springfeld, so wanted to remain on good terms with her.

On the day of the wedding Guy was racked with nerves. Not because he would be leading his cousin down the aisle, which was something he was looking forward to, but because it would be difficult to completely avoid spending some time with Daisy. It was ridiculous, absolutely ridiculous.

She had arrived the night before with her father and brother, along with countless cousins, uncles, aunts and friends of Nathaniel and Florence. In the pandemonium it had been easy for them to avoid each other. She had been seated across from him at dinner, but they had exchanged no more than a few pleasantries. Then she had disappeared immediately afterwards, presumably to her bedroom.

But he would not think of that now. Today belonged to Florence and Nathaniel. He would not ruin their special day with his own concerns.

The wedding was to take place in the local church and, after much toing and froing, everyone drove off in a train of carriages accompanied by a great deal of laughter and loud talking, leaving Guy alone with his cousin.

'Florence,' he said, taking hold of his smiling cousin's hand as they left the house. 'I've never seen you look more radiant. You're all but glowing.'

'Oh, Guy,' she said, tears making her eyes sparkle. 'I would not have believed such happiness was possible. Love really is wonderful!' She laughed as they walked down the steps towards his open-top carriage, which had been transformed with garlands of white flowers and ribbons.

'I'm just a bit disappointed that it isn't to be a double wedding.'

He took her gloved hand and helped her into the carriage. 'The way things are going, I suspect it will be a long time before I find myself a duchess,' he admitted with a light laugh as he seated himself beside her.

Her eyebrows drew together. 'You know what I think of that, don't you? You should marry Daisy. You two are perfect for each other.'

He didn't want to spoil his cousin's happiness, so he merely smiled. As he went to signal to the driver to drive on, she placed her hand on his arm to halt him.

'Guy, I'm serious. You and Daisy are meant for each other, just as Nathaniel and I are meant for one another.'

'Florence, let's not talk about this now. Today is your day. Let's just get you to the church and get you married.' He smiled at her, hoping that would be the end of it, but her smile faded and she adopted a serious expression.

Guy braced himself, knowing what was about to come. His cousin was in love, and wanted everyone else in the world to be in love too, but things were not as easy as that.

'I just want to say, Guy, if you don't marry Daisy, you will regret it. It's so obvious you're in love with each other.'

That was something he did not wish to discuss. 'Let's talk about this another time, shall we? After all, you have a wedding to get to.'

He started to reach up again to signal to the driver, but once again she stilled his hand.

'No. We're going to stay here until we discuss this.'

He turned towards her. She could not be serious. She could not be planning to keep everyone waiting at the church, including her husband-to-be, while they discussed something about which nothing more needed to be said. But her expression was certainly serious, and she still had hold of his arm, so he resigned himself to getting the conversation over as quickly as possible.

'I believe you mean well, but I'm afraid you're wrong. Maybe I wouldn't regret being married to Daisy, but I know she would soon come to regret being married to me. She deserves a man who…' He paused.

'I know what you're going to say. You think Daisy deserves a man who will love her, be faithful to her, do as the wedding vows say and forsake all others.'

Guy merely nodded.

'Someone like you.'

He stared at his cousin, speechless. If he had forgotten how love made people somewhat insane, her statement would have reminded him. How was he supposed to convince a young woman who was delirious with happiness and madly in love that she was talking nonsense?

Florence sent him a smug smile, as if certain that she had already won this argument. 'You said that you couldn't change, and once I might have believed that, but not now. And I can prove that you have indeed changed.' She held up one finger. 'Have you, er, entertained any young ladies since Daisy stayed here to recover from her accident?'

'No, but…'

A second finger was raised. 'Have you thought of entertaining any young ladies?'

'No, but…'

Three fingers were raised. 'Do you want to entertain any young ladies other than Daisy?'

'No.' He looked out into the distance then back at his

an. She had won that round. How could he possibly, entertain any other young ladies when all he thought about was Daisy? But his situation was an aberration. It was not who he really was. Was it?

He turned back to face Florence and she smiled in satisfaction. 'See? You thought you couldn't change, but you were wrong. So that proves you are right for Daisy.'

'I know that was what I said, but it's not the only reason why I'm not right for Daisy. She should be with someone who knows how to provide a loving home for a wife and family. She deserves the type of life she is used to. One full of happiness, laughter and kindness.'

'Oh, Guy.' Florence shook her head then laughed. 'Is that the best you can come up with?'

He stared at her, both shocked and affronted.

Florence stopped laughing. 'You mean she deserves the life you provided for me after my parents died. You supported me, both emotionally and financially, gave me a refuge from Horace and protected me from him. You have always known how to be loving and kind.'

He stared at his cousin. 'But…but…'

'But but…what?' she pressed, smiling in triumph.

'But…' He pulled in a deep breath and exhaled slowly, his chest suddenly tight. 'What if I become like my father? I could never subject Daisy to such a life.'

'And you never would. You love Daisy and would never mistreat her.'

Guy took hold of Florence's hand, desperate for her to understand. 'My father had loved my mother—his letters proved that—and yet he turned into a tyrant. I love Daisy, so what is to stop me from becoming just

like him? Nothing,' he concluded, answering his o
question before Florence could. 'And I couldn't do th
to Daisy.'

Florence gently placed her hand on top of his. 'My mother told me how your father changed when your mother died. It was grief that made him behave the way he did. He grieved for the rest of his life and, yes, he treated you appallingly because he blamed you for her death.' She looked into his eyes as if imploring him to understand. 'That was unforgiveable. He should not have blamed you for something that was not your fault. But you are not like your father, just as I am not like Horace. You are a good man. You have every right to be happy, and you should be spending your life making Daisy happy.'

He stared at his cousin, trying to formulate an argument to counter her claims.

'Anyway,' she said. 'I think we've made my future husband wait long enough. Shall we get to the church?'

As if in a daze, Guy finally signalled to the driver while he tried to take in all that his cousin had said. He was certain that she must be wrong but was no longer sure how.

They arrived at the church and Guy could only hope that no one had been alarmed by the delay or thought that Florence was having second thoughts. If they had been, the way his lovely cousin was beaming and staring at her husband to be with such adoration would dispel any such assumptions.

He escorted his wonderful cousin down the aisle and passed her into the arms of his best friend, knowg that it could not be possible to give her away to a better man.

During the service, he couldn't help himself flicking a few glances across the aisle to where Daisy was sitting with her sisters and the other members of the Springfeld family. If he needed any reminder of the differences between them, the scene in church would provide it.

Daisy was surrounded by her sisters, their husbands and children, her parents and assorted aunts and uncles and cousins. On his side of the church, he was sitting with Cousin Horace and a few distant family members he hardly knew. The rest of the pews were filled with Florence's friends and people from the local community.

While the Springfeld women were all crying, smiling and gazing at the happy couple as if enraptured, his relatives were sitting bolt upright, their faces stern, looking as if they'd just eaten something which hadn't quite agreed with them. How much more proof did Florence need that he was not like the Springfelds?

After the couple was pronounced man and wife and had left the church, the Springfelds rushed after them, tears streaking their faces. They laughed, hugged and kissed each other repeatedly.

It was just how he remembered them from his childhood—a warm, loving and close family. Although they had done everything they could to include him, he'd never been able to help but feel like an outsider. That was how he felt now. And it was how he would always feel, despite what Florence said. He was not like them. He did not know how to give love so easily, the way they did.

Later, during the ball held after the wedding, he danced with Florence and all three Springfeld sisters, as protocol demanded. The dance with Daisy was rather awkward, to say the least. They made stilted conversation while Daisy held her body stiffly, as if reluctant to talk to him and disliking having him touch her.

It was further confirmation that Florence was wrong and he was right. There was no future for Daisy Springfeld and him. He had ruined any chance he might have had by his actions on the balcony and his harsh words afterwards. If he told Florence how he had behaved on the night of the ball, then she would cease to see him as a good man who could make Daisy happy and realise exactly what he was like, and what he would always be like.

But of course, he would do no such thing. Florence did not need to know of such things. Nor would he besmirch Daisy's reputation by discussing what should remain private.

As the couples swirled around the ballroom floor, and joyous music, laughter and loud conversation filled the air, a melancholic mood descended on Guy. He would never marry Daisy Springfeld and now, due to his actions, they would not be friends either. They would no longer share the easy companionship they once had. They would now be relatives by marriage, nothing more, people who saw each other at family functions but had as little to do with each other as possible.

Reluctant to put a damper on the proceedings with

his sombre mood, Guy edged his way out of the crowded ballroom. He would spend some time alone until he was once again able to force a happy mask back on his face, put aside his confusion and instead focus on celebrating this joyous occasion.

Passing a curtained alcove in the hallway, he heard Daisy talking quietly and with some urgency. He knew it was unforgivable to stop and listen, but then it wouldn't be the first unforgivable thing he had done. Compared to kissing her, a bit of eavesdropping was by comparison a minor crime.

'You could try and be civil to him,' Daisy's mother was saying.

'I am. I danced with him. That's enough, isn't it?'

'Well, you looked like you wanted to box his ears.'

'I can't help the way I look,' Daisy said.

'Yes, you can. And would it hurt you to smile? It's obvious the man is in love with you. That should be sufficient to put a smile on your face.'

Guy stood up straighter and looked up and down the corridor, as if unsure he had heard correctly. Then he leant back in to hear what Daisy would respond to such a surprising statement.

'Guy Parnell is not in love with me.' The terse sound of her words suggested she had made this statement through gritted teeth.

'Well, I beg to differ. I know what men look like when they're in love. I've seen it on your father's face, on the faces of Iris's and Hazel's husbands, on Nathaniel's face and now on Guy's face.'

That claim was greeted with a, 'Humph,' and Guy

could imagine Daisy crossing her arms defiantly and lifting her nose in the air.

'But with Guy it's not love. It's…'

'It's what?' her mother asked.

He moved his ear closer to the alcove, worried he might miss what *it* was.

'It's lust,' Daisy said in a quiet voice.

Guy gritted his teeth together, his muscles tense. He cared greatly about Lady Springfeld's opinion and knew how much she would despise him for lusting after her innocent youngest daughter.

'Oh yes, well, it's probably that as well,' she said with a small laugh.

'Mother!' Daisy blurted out in a manner that matched his own surprise.

'Well, you certainly need lust in there with the love otherwise it wouldn't be much fun on your wedding night, would it?'

'Mother!' Daisy repeated, even louder. 'If you think Guy is so wonderful—' She stopped and lowered her voice. 'Then you'll be disappointed to know that he's acted on the lust part, even if he hasn't acted on what you mistakenly believe is the love part.'

'Really?' Lady Springfeld asked, but her voice did not contain the outrage Guy had expected.

'Yes. At Lady Danton's ball. We were alone on the balcony and he kissed me, and he…'

'He…?' Lady Springfeld prompted.

'He…' Daisy's voice was so low Guy had to lean in even closer to the curtain to hear what was said—so close, he was in danger of toppling forward and revealing his unwanted presence.

'He caressed intimate parts of my body.'

'Hmm...' was her mother's considered reply. 'And did you tell him to stop?'

There was silence for a moment. Then he heard the murmured reply. 'Well, no...'

'And why not?'

The silence continued. 'Well, if you must know, I didn't want him to stop. I rather liked it.'

Her mother gave a little laugh. 'I should think so too. But are you telling me that Guy seduced you? Are you saying that you are no longer chaste?'

'No!' Daisy cried out. 'All he did was kiss and caress me.'

'Hmm,' Lady Springfeld said again. 'Did he try to seduce you and you rejected him?'

'No, not exactly. If I'm being completely honest. I suppose if he had tried to, you know—have his wicked way, as they say—I wouldn't have rejected him.' He heard Daisy's long intake of breath and a slow exhalation. 'But surely all that proves is how experienced he is? He was able to make me forget all about propriety, forget what was right and wrong. If he had wanted to seduce me on the balcony, I would have gladly given myself to him. That's the sort of man he is.'

'So, what you're saying is, he could have seduced you but he didn't. You had lost all ability to think, but he didn't take advantage of you. You were no longer caring about the damage you were doing to your reputation, but he was. Is that what you're telling me?'

'Yes…well, no. Well, I don't know.'

'Oh, my dear. All Guy did was prove to you how much he respects and cares for you.'

Guy nodded his agreement.

'That sounds a lot like love to me,' Lady Springfeld continued.

'You're wrong, Mother. Guy Springfeld is a bounder. He always has been and he always will be. People don't change.'

Guy listened carefully to hear what words of wisdom Lady Springfeld would have on that subject.

'Hmm. Perhaps you're right.'

His shoulders dropped in disappointment as if the final judgment had been past.

'After all,' Lady Springfeld continued. 'You've always been stubborn, opinionated and judgemental and I suppose that will never change.'

Guy had to suppress a laugh, knowing the look of outrage that would pass across Daisy's face at that statement.

'Nonsense,' came Daisy's mumbled reply. 'I'm not like that at all.'

Her mother laughed. 'Oh, Daisy, Guy Parnell is a good man. He was a lovely, kind, considerate boy and that is something that definitely has not changed. You couldn't find a better husband and if you continue to ignore him, treat him with disdain, then you're going to regret letting him get away. The man is in love with you, and you're just too stubborn to see that. And you're also too quick to judge him. You are refusing to see how perfect he is for you.'

Guy didn't wait to hear Daisy's response, although he was sure it would be a vehement denial. He walked away, out through the front doors and into the garden. He needed a long walk in the cool night air to think about all he had heard and what he was going to do about it.

Despite everything he had said to Florence, she still thought he would make the perfect husband for Daisy. And despite everything Daisy had said to her mother, Lady Springfeld believed he would be the perfect husband for her youngest daughter. They were two women whose opinions he respected—could they both be right and he be wrong?

Could Daisy be wrong?

He wanted Daisy, he loved Daisy, thought only of Daisy and wanted her happiness more than anything in the world. Could he do the seemingly impossible and be a good husband? Guy knew that he wanted to, and suspected that he could. If he were married to the most glorious, most wonderful woman in the world, how could he not change?

All he needed to do now was prove that to Daisy. He needed to show her that he was not the man she thought he was—that loving her had made him the sort of man that deep down he had always wanted to be but thought he never could be. But that left one problem: how was he going to do that?

Chapter Twenty

Silence descended on the Springfeld home. Florence and Nathaniel were on their honeymoon, travelling around Europe for a month. Daisy's sisters had returned to their own estates, taking with them all their noise and cheerful family chaos.

And Guy had once again disappeared out of Daisy's life. It would be a long time before she had to see him once more. Perhaps Christmas would be the next family occasion he would attend, although he would be under no obligation to do so. Maybe Nathaniel and Florence would return from their honeymoon with some exciting news and the family would be gathering in nine months or so for a christening.

Not that Daisy was thinking about when she would see Guy again. Well, at least not all of the time. Well, perhaps she did think about him all the time, but at least she was not pining for him…at least, not all of the time.

On those rare moments when she wasn't pining, she was formulating a plan of action, one titled *Getting over Guy Parnell*. It involved keeping active and trying to get her thoughts under control. To that end, she would tell herself that for the next five minutes she would not think of him at all. Then, once she had conquered five minutes, she was sure she could extend the time to ten. And she was certain that before she knew it she would be not thinking about him for entire days at a time, maybe even weeks. And then, eventually, she would find that she never thought of him.

The only problem with this plan of action was that telling herself to not think about Guy involved *actually* thinking about him, which made it all so difficult and frustrating.

Constant activity seemed an easier goal to achieve. The season was coming to an end, but the remaining balls, parties or soirees did not tempt her. They had never interested her and now there was always the danger of seeing him again—or, even worse, seeing him in active pursuit of a bride.

Instead, she intended to spend her days walking, cycling and attending meetings. And that was what she planned to do this day. A vigorous cycle through the busy London streets was enough to focus anyone's mind. It was hard to think about your broken heart when you were dodging carriages, omnibuses and carts.

The ringing of a bicycle bell outside her window drew Daisy's attention away from her introspection. She had not organised to go cycling with any of the other members of the High-Wheeling Ladies' Cycling Association, but she could do with some diverting company.

Daisy looked out at the street below and wondered

whether her fevered imagination had conjured up a bizarre apparition.

Guy Parnell was standing on the pavement two storeys below, looking up at her window and, of all things, dressed in men's cycling clothes. The usually debonair man was dressed in red-and-green-checked knickerbockers, jacket blue-and-white-striped socks and a cloth cap.

Daisy blinked several times to clear her vision, sure that the ludicrous image would disappear. It didn't. Instead, he lifted his cloth cap and smiled at her. She closed her mouth, which had inexplicably fallen open as she tried to make sense of this absurd situation.

He performed a low bow, his waving hand indicating the tandem bicycle he was holding, then he gave the bell several more rings. What on earth was he up to? There was only one way to find out.

She pushed up the sash window and leant out. This had to be some new form of teasing he had devised for his own entertainment, a way to ridicule her, or remind her that he once again thought of her as nothing more than his best friend's little sister. Although it did seem rather a lot of trouble to go to just to play some sort of prank. And, at the moment, the only person looking ridiculous was the check-suited man standing on the pavement and attracting the attention of several curious passers-by.

'What are you up to? Why are you here?' she called down.

'I've taken up this new activity.' He gestured with his hand towards the bicycle. 'And, as you can also see,

I've adopted some suitable clothing to go with my new hobby.'

'Well, you look…' She stopped, unsure how to describe how he looked.

'I hope you were about to say "rational" rather than "preposterous". I'd be somewhat shocked if you were going to tease me for my clothing.'

She bit her top lip to prevent herself from doing exactly that.

'I'll have you know that men have been dressing for generations in clothing that prevented them from enjoying sports such as cycling,' he said. 'And I am on a one-man crusade to put an end to it. Hence the attire.' He pulled back his shoulders, placed his feet at right angles, and adopted a supercilious pose, his expression mock-serious.

Daisy covered her mouth to stop herself from laughing. She had objected strenuously when people made fun of her attire. She could hardly now make fun of him. But he did look rather foolish.

'Also,' he continued, 'as you can see, this is a bicycle built for two.'

She nodded.

'And I'm only one person.'

She nodded again.

'So, I need someone else, preferably an intelligent, independent woman who can teach me to ride this infernal thing properly.' He looked down at the bicycle then back up at Daisy. 'And I believe there is only one woman in the world capable of teaching me anything.'

Still fighting to stifle her laughter, she pointed to herself.

'Indeed. You are that woman.'

She hesitated, a small part of her still wondering whether this was some sort of elaborate joke.

'Will you teach me, Daisy?' he asked in a softer tone.

She stared down at him. He did not look as if he was making fun of her. Dressed in that bizarre clothing, it would be difficult for him to make her seem any more ridiculous than he looked.

'Please, Daisy,' he repeated.

'Oh, all right,' she said, but remained where she was, leaning out of the window.

'Then, shall we?' he invited, indicating the bicycle.

She pulled down the sash window, and as quickly as she could ran down the stairs and out of the front door before she had a chance to think this through too carefully and change her mind.

'Madam, your carriage awaits,' he said with a low bow and sweeping hand gesture towards the bicycle.

Daisy took her position beside the back seat of the tandem

'Uh-uh-uh...' he admonished, taking hold of her hands and placing them on the front handlebars. 'You are my teacher, Daisy. You should be in charge. I will do whatever you want of me.'

'Well, climb on behind me,' she said as she swung her leg over the bar. 'The first thing we have to do is get our balance, and then we need to get into rhythm and move together as one.'

Guy raised his eyebrows in a comical fashion. 'Why, Lady Daisy, what are you suggesting?'

Daisy supressed a giggle as he climbed onto the seat behind her. They moved off down the street. At first, they wobbled and moved so slowly it was difficult to maintain their balance, but soon they got into a rhythm, their legs pumping up and down in perfect harmony.

Daisy tried to ignore the body behind her radiating heat and causing her own temperature to rise higher than the level of exercise should evoke. After all, she was merely giving him a lesson on how to ride a bicycle—although why Guy should suddenly be interested in such a sport, she had no idea. But he certainly was a fast learner and they soon started to pick up speed as they pedalled faster and faster.

They both laughed as they raced along, the wind blowing through their hair, the houses whizzing past. They enjoyed the exhilaration of travelling at such a fast pace and under their own muscle power.

'We've got the rhythm and we've got balance,' he whispered in her ear. 'We're moving together as one. I believe we're made for each other.'

Daisy couldn't stop herself from smiling. It was thrilling to ride so fast, much faster than she could do on her own, and it was lovely to share an activity she enjoyed so much with Guy.

'But there is something I need to tell you,' he continued. 'Can we please stop at that park up ahead?'

Daisy directed the bicycle towards the small grassy area at the end of the street. As they approached, they slowed down then dismounted. Guy wheeled the tandem over to a park bench in front of a small lake and leaned it against the pole of a gas light.

'I didn't buy this tandem because I need a new sport,' he said as they sat down on the wooden bench. 'It was so I could demonstrate to you how much I want to change.' He turned towards her, his eyes beseeching. 'I wanted to let you know that I am determined to change for you.'

'Yes, I can see that you have,' Daisy said, indicating his brightly coloured attire and smiling with uncertainty.

Guy looked down at his clothes and laughed. 'And if nothing demonstrates how committed I am to changing, these clothes will. This—' he indicated his checked trousers and jacket '—is how committed I am to becoming a different man. A man you can respect and admire.'

Daisy laughed out loud, then covered her mouth. 'If it's respect and admiration you're after, I'm not sure if those clothes will do it.'

He joined in her laughter then his face became serious as he took hold of her hands. 'I mean it, Daisy. I want to be a man you can respect and admire. I know you think I am nothing more than a rake.'

She went to speak but he placed one finger lightly on her lips. 'But in that I have already changed. All those women I've had in my life, I now realise they were just an attempt to fill a void, a loneliness that I had never admitted to. That is, not until you came back into my life.'

'Oh,' was all Daisy could think to say, and it came out as a small gasp, hardly a word at all.

'You made me realise how empty my life is. You made me realise what I need to fill that emptiness.'

'Oh, so that's why you bought the bicycle?'

He laughed again. 'No…well, yes.' He released a deep sigh. 'I practised what I was going to say to you over and over again, but it doesn't seem to be coming out right at all. Let me start again.

'Daisy Springfeld, what I'm trying to say is, I want to become a man you can not only respect and admire, but also love.'

He drew in a long breath, as if for strength. 'I love you, Daisy Springfeld. It's as simple as that and as complicated as that. I love you with every fibre of my being. I love everything about you.'

Daisy stared back at him, speechless, but she didn't need to say a word because Guy continued.

'I love your humour, your intelligence, your stubbornness and determination. I love the way you never try to be anyone other than just who you are, and to hell with what people think of you. I even love those rid… those rational bloomers you insist on wearing.'

Daisy swallowed, unsure whether this was real or another one of her fanciful dreams. How many times had she imagined Guy telling her that he loved her? How many times had she dismissed those dreams as absurd longings for something that would never happen? More times than she could remember.

'You have made me realise I don't want my old life,' he said. 'I want a new life. One with you at the centre of it, as my wife.'

'You want to marry me?' she asked, unsure if she had heard correctly.

'Yes. Daisy, will you marry me?'

She blinked a few times to try and bring her whirling thoughts into order. 'You want *me* to be the Duchess of Mandivale? To provide you with the heir that you need to save the estate from Horace?'

He nodded, then shook his head and nodded again. 'I don't care about that. I want you. I don't want you because I need to marry and sire an heir. I just want you in my life, for the rest of my life. If we don't have children, then so be it. I'll make arrangements with my lawyer to ensure the tenants are protected if Horace does get control of the estate. I just want you, only you.'

'So you don't want an heir?'

'It no longer matters.'

'Oh, but I like children,' she said, still struggling to take in his words.

'Then we'll have as many children as you want,' he declared with a devilish smile, causing her already pounding heart to increase its tempo. 'And I promise you, we'll have a lot of fun making all those children.'

Daisy gasped in a breath, fought to ignore her tingling skin and fluttering heart and tried not to get sidetracked by the thought of their wedding night but to focus on what he was really saying. 'So, let me get this right. You are saying you love me and you want to marry me? It's not because I'm convenient and it's not because you need a wife—any wife?'

'That is exactly what I'm saying. And more, so much more. I love you, Daisy.' He looked over at the lake then back at her. 'I know you deserve a better man than me, but I promise I will do everything I can to be the man you deserve, the man I want to be. I will do everything in my power to provide you with a happy home, the home you want, the home you deserve. I will do everything I possibly can, every day of my life, to prove to you that you are loved.'

He released her hand and looked down at his own hands, now clenched tightly together. 'But if you don't want me then I will go away and you'll never have to see me again. I wouldn't want to upset you by fawning over you or making you uncomfortable.'

She bit her bottom lip. He was being so serious, and so should she be, but she couldn't resist the temptation to tease. 'I don't think there's anything wrong with a man fawning over his wife.'

He looked up at her, his brown eyes wide, trying to take in the implication of her words. 'Do you mean...?'

She leant towards him so she could whisper. 'I'm not sure what I mean except, yes, I want to be your wife.'

'Oh, Daisy,' he murmured, then placed his hands on her arms and kissed her. It was merely a light kiss on the lips—after all, they were in a public place—but it held such promise that it left Daisy breathless.

'I can't express how happy I am,' he whispered, his lips a mere tantalising inch from hers. 'And I promise I will do everything I can to ensure you never regret agreeing to be my wife. I will do everything I can to make myself a man worthy of being your husband.'

'Well, don't change too much. I rather like you the way you are.' She sat back on the bench. 'No, that's not true.'

He sat up straighter, his body rigid. 'I will change. Just tell me what you want.'

She took hold of his hands and gave a small laugh. 'I'm sorry, that's not what I meant. I meant, I don't just like you the way you are. I love you the way you are.'

She paused and looked at the small lake as he had done, to give herself time to take in what she had said. It was as if saying those words out loud had removed an enormous weight from her heart, and she wanted to say them again and as often as possible.

She turned back to him and smiled. 'I love you, Guy. I love you with all my heart, and nothing would make me happier than being your wife. I know I've always said I object to the way women lose their rights when they marry, and I still do. But I trust you, and I want to spend my life with you. I want to be the mother of your children.'

Her smile grew wider, mirroring his.

'I'm in love, and I'm so happy I feel like I could float away.' She took hold of his hands and looked into those lovely brown eyes. 'It is the oddest feeling, isn't it, being in love?'

He laughed, clasping her hands to his chest. 'It most certainly is.'

She moved closer to him on the bench. 'Isn't it strange the way your emotions are up and down constantly? One minute you're exhilarated, the next you're in the depths of despair, as if your life has been turned upside down and you no longer know which way is up or down.'

'Exactly. That's exactly how I've been feeling,' he said as he moved closer to her.

'It's a bit like riding down a hill really fast then falling into a ditch!' She laughed.

'Or it's a bit like kissing a beautiful woman you find

alone on a balcony on a moonlit night. That can certainly play havoc with a man's emotions.'

He gently took hold of her chin and lightly kissed her again. 'And I most certainly want to get you alone again as soon as possible, so I can kiss you again. You don't know how much I am longing to make you my wife, to make love to you, to show you with my body just how much I adore you.'

A shiver ran through her as every burning inch of her skin ached for him to do what he promised. Did they really have to wait until they were married? It was so unfair, especially when she wanted him here and now.

She inched towards him. Damn propriety, damn the passing pedestrians. She enjoyed shocking people with her clothing. Now she would give them something to be really horrified by. She placed her hands around Guy's neck and pulled him forward. The moment her parted lips touched his, it was as if she had opened up the floodgates and he could no longer hold back his passion.

'Oh, Daisy, my beautiful Daisy,' he murmured as he wrapped her in his arms, pulled her to him tightly and kissed her back. It was no longer a light kiss, but hard and deep, containing a desperation for her that was exciting, exhilarating and a little bit scary—but in a nice way…a very nice way.

As she sunk into his arms, a burning need for him erupted within her. A small gasp escaped as he ran his tongue lightly along her bottom lip. She moved closer and held him tighter, kissing him harder, loving the taste of him, loving the feel of him, loving him…all of him.

He pulled back from her, cradling her head in both

his hands, and looked into her eyes. 'I need to do this the right way.'

'Well, it certainly felt right to me, but if there is another way to kiss then please show me.'

'I'll be more than happy to kiss you in every way possible, and kiss every inch of that lovely body of yours…but I meant I want to propose properly. It will be the only time in my life I propose to you and I want to be able to tell our children and grandchildren that I did it in a gentlemanly manner.'

'Oh, that. I'd rather be kissed, but I suppose a proper proposal will do for now,' she said with a laugh.

He moved off the bench, lowered himself onto one knee and took her hand in his. 'Lady Daisy, will you make me the happiest of men by agreeing to be my wife?'

'Yes,' she said quickly, wanting him to get back to kissing her.

'If you agree, I promise to be a faithful, loving husband…to cherish you, to respect and honour you…to love you.'

'Good, good,' Daisy said in a rush. 'So, are you going to seal it with a kiss?'

'Daisy, will you be my wife?' he asked again, as if he hadn't believed her first response.

'Yes, yes, yes!' she said, pulling him up off his knees.

Her heart was pounding hard, her body thrumming with anticipation as he gently pulled her to her feet and kissed her again. As she surrendered herself to the intoxicating exhilaration of knowing she was kissing the man she loved, and being kissed by the man who loved her, she knew her happiness was complete.

Epilogue

Two months later the Springfeld family assembled again, this time at the family's Dorset estate, for another wedding.

Guy could hardly believe that his life had changed so much. He could hardly believe that it was possible to feel such euphoria, to be so much in love. He was sure he was walking around with a permanent silly grin on his face, but he didn't care.

When the vicar read out the vows, Guy realised just how appropriate they were for how he was feeling. He would love and honour Daisy for better for worse, richer or poorer, in sickness and in health. And from the moment she had tumbled back into his life he had indeed forsaken all others.

When he responded, 'I will,' he meant it from the bottom of his heart.

Then the vicar read out the vows to Daisy. When she said, 'I will,' and they were pronounced man and wife, Guy could hardly contain himself as a surge of exhilaration rushed through him. While he was sure she meant it with all her heart when she agreed to love and honour, he wasn't quite so convinced that she would actually obey, and nor would he want her to. An obedient Daisy would not be the woman he had fallen in love with.

Kissing his bride, he lifted her up and twirled her around, causing Daisy to laugh with joy and the Springfeld family to break into spontaneous applause.

'Oh, Guy, I'm so happy!' she cried, as he lowered her to her feet.

'You can't possibly be as happy as I am,' he said, taking her hand and leading her out of the church.

'Oh, I think I can. I think I'm probably the happiest person in the world right now.'

Guy laughed again, letting his competitive bride have this win, although he was sure she couldn't possibly be happier than he was right at that moment.

Guy had bought the tandem bicycle as a gesture of his love, but discovered that he actually enjoyed cycling—although he bought some more subdued clothing for the many outings he and Daisy took around the local countryside. After all, those clothes had merely been a symbolic gesture, and they mysteriously disappeared once they were married. Guy suspected they were too rational even for his lovely bride and she had somehow disposed of them.

And cycling held another attraction for him. Their outings usually ended with them finding a discreet place where he could indulge in the other activity he thoroughly enjoyed—making love to his beautiful wife. Showing her with his body how much he adored her, how deep was his love for her.

When Daisy became pregnant with their first child, they were sure it had been conceived after one of their cycling outings, and had been tempted to tell Dr Howard that they had proved him completely wrong.

Guy couldn't be more delighted when their lovely daughter was born. The little girl was a beauty, just like her mother, and just as independent and feisty.

After their third daughter was born, Dr Howard had to concede that perhaps he had been wrong in his assertion that riding bicycles ruined a woman's ability to have children. Although, he then claimed that what it actually did was prevent women from bearing sons.

That was an argument that appealed immensely to Horace, who kept encouraging Daisy to ride her bicycle as often as possible.

When their first son was born, that argument too came to an end, and so did any hope of Horace ever becoming Duke of Mandivale.

Daisy continued to take pleasure in riding past the doctor's surgery and ringing her bell, just to let him know that a woman on a bicycle could do anything when she put her mind to it—even turn a rake into a loving, faithful husband and a devoted father.

* * * * *

If you enjoyed this story
be sure to read the other books in
Eva Shepherd's
Young Victorian Ladies miniseries

Wagering on the Wallflower
Stranded with the Reclusive Earl

And why not check out her other miniseries
Breaking the Marriage Rules?

Beguiling the Duke
Awakening the Duchess
Aspirations of a Lady's Maid
How to Avoid the Marriage Mart